THE
GASCONY
LETTERS

A NOVEL

also by

RICHARD
MASSEY

The Southampton Chronicle

Municipal Tilt

THE GASCONY LETTERS

A NOVEL

RICHARD MASSEY

TIREE
PRESS

an imprint of
OGHMA CREATIVE MEDIA

OGHMA

CREATIVE MEDIA

Tiree Press
An imprint of Oghma Creative Media, Inc.
2401 Beth Lane, Bentonville, Arkansas 72712

Library of Congress Cataloging-in-Publication Data

Names: Massey, Richard, author.
Title: The Southampton Chronicle/Richard Massey | Gregory of Bordeaux #2
Description: First Edition. | Bentonville: Tiree, 2018.
Identifiers: LCCN: 2018942272 | ISBN: 978-1-63373-430-2 (hardcover) |
ISBN: 978-1-63373-431-9 (trade paperback) | ISBN: 978-1-63373-432-6 (eBook)
Subjects: BISAC: FICTION/Historical/Medieval |
FICTION/Historical/Renaissance | FICTION/Action & Adventure
LC record available at: https://lccn.loc.gov/2018942272

Tiree Press trade paperback edition October, 2018

Jacket & Interior Design by Casey W. Cowan
Editing by George "Clay" Mitchell and Dennis Doty

 owe a thanks to the following people: Amy Wilson, Bryan Delagardelle, Byron Jennings, Casey Cowan, George Mitchell, Bob Coleman, and Rodney Webb. I also owe a debt of gratitude to the historians who have taught me all I know about Medieval England and France.

This book is for my mother, Mary Rensalear McClure Massey.

THE
ALDERMAN
OF THE VINTRY

regory stood on the wharf, looking over the brooding swirl of the River Thames. An August cold snap brought drizzle, so he turned the hood up over his head, pulling the furred cloak tight about his lanky bones.

The pier sat empty, but it wasn't supposed to be. This wharf, where so much wealth had been made, had sat empty since the Feast of St. John. Gregory could not figure why. *Where is my olive oil, garlic and wine?* He spit into the dark, cold waters. All along the waterfront, burly porters, singing their songs and grunting in rhythm, unloaded ships from across Christendom. Timber, marble and iron, skins, pepper, cinnamon, saffron, and anise—fed into the fanged maw of London as it swallowed and growled for more. But not Gregory's pier, which sat vacant, abandoned, a scene of unexpected ruin.

He leaned against a piling and watched as the riches of others were made, and in vain, gazed east hoping his ship, fat with casks and taut of sail, would appear on the horizon. And gaze he did until the western skyline blazed with sunset, but nothing he saw made him smile. He glanced at the gold and garnet ring on his left pinky and, with his thumb and index finger, rubbed the silver and sapphire necklace beneath his cloak. He would not be able to afford these much longer. A shadow of rue crossed his face. With a deep sigh and a shake of his head, he left the wharf knowing he would return tomorrow, and his fellow merchants, as they had done this day and before, might very well taunt him. If his ship did not arrive tomorrow or the next, that one day, eventually, it would, and once again he could wag his finger and speak as he pleased.

Gregory shrugged off his sullen mood, deciding instead to celebrate his birthday, so he went to the Purple Pot Tavern, a favored haunt of the merchants and bachelors. All the familiar faces greeted him there, Alan Spicer, the four Williams—William Purchase, William Pepper, William Stokes and William Hawkins—Joan the Widow, and the whole lot of those who knew of Gregory's troubles and who wanted to see him smile. He joined them at a long table. A servant brought him a silver trimmed cup of fresh, spicy ale. He took a sip and tried to maintain his dour expression, but he could not.

"This is good," he said, raising the cup.

"That is because it is a special brew made just for you, Gregory," Joan the Widow said. "You may be disappointed with what is happening out on your pier, but here in the Purple Pot, there is no reason for you to be unhappy."

"And praises to you, Lady Joan, and praises to you all, for if you were not here, I would pass my thirty-third year alone and wanting," he said.

With that, they commenced to drinking, eating, singing, and laughing. As the winds raced through the streets, creeping beneath the door and through the cracks in the shutters, servant boys threw coal on the fire and stoked its embers. The Purple Pot grew warm and inviting. The merriment attracted passersby who stopped in for a special ale and to give their regards. As they left, yet others arrived, so there was always an array of people crowded around the jovial group of originals at the trunk-hewn, candlelit table at the far end of the room. If Gregory knew a visitor well, he asked them to sit for a spell, and had the others make room for them, so all at his table were shoulder to shoulder. Thus passed the night of Gregory's lament, with voices drowning out the drum and lute, and with jokes and japes replacing talk of cargo and taxes.

They asked him, as they had many times before, to tell of his travels. Regale them, he did, with his tales from the chronicle, when he rode across the land, from town to town and through the wastelands and back again, always a step ahead of the men who would have him in the gallows. He plunged deep into his memories, timing his words for theatric effect, using his hands for emphasis and show, and turning his face with comic contortions while impersonating his enemies. Gregory was set to continue, and his audience eager, when the Purple Pot's door flew open and did not close. A chilly gust chased away the warmth as well as the cheer. Gregory stood, and with his cup held in front of him, looked through the shadowy tavern light at the two armed men standing on either side of the entrance.

"Who is it who lets out all the heat we have so dearly made this cold and blustery night?" he asked, and took a tipsy sip of ale. "Close that door or I will ask you to tend the fire."

A third man entered. As he approached the table, Gregory sobered. A Blackfriar, no doubt. A ranking Dominican with a silver cross about his neck. Joan the Widow, all four Williams, and Alan Spicer gave Gregory sharp glances because they knew, as did he, that it was foolish, and even dangerous, to chide a Dominican and his associates. When he reached the table, he gave Gregory a gesture of greeting as false and forced as the one Gregory had given him. For an uncomfortable moment, as a bead of wax dripped down the side of the candle, the man of the cross and the man of the coin adjudged one another without blinking.

"Gregory of Bordeaux?" the Dominican asked.

"Yes."

"I bring you this," he handed him a small scroll of parchment.

Gregory took the scroll from him. "And what message is so important that it takes a Blackfriar to deliver it?"

"From what I hear, you are more than capable of reading it for yourself," the friar said. With a darting stare, he turned and walked away, but his guards did not close the door behind him.

All eyes turned to Gregory as he unrolled and read the parchment. His friends looked on and grew impatient at the look of surprise dawning in his eyes. "Well, what is it?" one of them asked.

He looked up from the parchment and with a grin of unease. "I've been summoned to appear at Westminster."

After his return to London five years before, Gregory turned his chronicle over to the Benedictines at Chertsey Abbey, and from the jumble of his originals, they created an illuminated manuscript of enormous beauty. Thick, heavy, and bound in oxblood leather, its vellum pages bursting with red, green, blue, ochre, and glowing with a sheen of heavenly gold. Page after page the tales were told, the laughter, loss and heroism in the realm, the cities and towns as the seasons of history turned. When, after a year, the Benedictines had finished their work, Gregory went to the abbey to claim the treasure. He then rode to Southampton, and in the great hall of the castle on the coast, bent down on one knee and, with the chronicle held out with both hands, presented it to the earl.

What neither of them had anticipated was that one of the monks at the abbey would secretly make his own text copy of the chronicle and send it out to London, where many copied it and spirited the copies across all of England just in time for the winter reading season. By spring, Gregory of Bordeaux had become known by monks, merchants and nobles from Cornwall to Northumberland, and while many were reviled by what he had written, still many others wanted to do business with him.

Traffic at Gregory's pier quadrupled and soon he became head of a loose yet powerful syndicate trading from the frigid ports of the Baltic to the sultry bay of Seville. While Gregory maintained his focus on wine, all manner of merchandise emerged from the holds of the syndicate ships, and in that way, his wealth kept pace with his name. He found that, as he reached farther afield and tried new goods from new ports, he could also reach deeper into the proven places where he had traded for years. He realized the depth of his influence one cloudy day in mid-October when his ship returned after three months at sea. Outbound with Staffordshire wool, it had sailed to Flanders where the fleeces were exchanged for finished cloaks and sheered furs. The ship then sailed to Bordeaux, where the cloth and furs were traded for one hundred tonnes of sweet Gascon white from Sauternes, three pipes of olive oil from Sicily, and four bolts of vermillion silk from Lucca. On the return journey, the ship again called in Flanders, where they traded the silk for fifteen tonnes of wine reputed to be the best in the world—Burgundy red from the famed vineyards of Cluny. King Edward's cellarer waited at the pier when the ship arrived, and though he held a long list of those who wanted a piece of the cargo, it was the king's man to whom Gregory smiled and said, "My lord, it pleases me to do business with the royal household."

That day Gregory could truly call himself a man of means, and plenty of others viewed it the same way. Skepticism turned to deference, and among the older merchants, who once declined to acknowledge his presence, there now came subtle nods of approval. Gregory tried his best to contain his new-found status and behave with the polished reserve his station required, but he could only sacrifice so much to decorum. Soon, he visited his tailor for a luxuriant cloak of worsted wool, fern green and trimmed at every hem with marten, a hat of burnt sienna, and to the jeweler for his gold and garnet ring. Attired in such finery—a flowing belted robe, and on his feet, custom-tooled poulaines—he kept watch on the wharves knowing others, some allies and some not, kept watch over him.

A week before Christmas, the alderman of the Vintry, Roger Walden, slipped on a patch of ice, gashed his head, and two days later, in a fog of fever and delirium, died in his bed. The loss of Roger hit Gregory hard, for he had been a mentor and a friend, and indeed, for all who knew him, Roger Walden's unexpected death caused grief and dismay. Soon after the psalms and the eulogy, the merchants of the Vintry came to Gregory to say they were nominating him as the new alderman.

"And why would you do that?" he asked. "Surely there are others who could do the job. In fact, if you want me to, I can name them."

"There are other choices, true, but you are the best," one of them said.

"Gregory, since you returned from your travels, you have made all of us wealthy," said another. "You know the Vintry and you love it. We can think of no one who could represent our stakes better than you."

The Vintry, one of many ancient wards in the city of London, got its name because the majority of merchants who did business there were vintners. Each ward had its own alderman who sat on the Council of Aldermen, London's governing body. The aldermen, in turn, elected a mayor, who among a thousand other things, served as liaison between London and the royal court at Westminster. Gregory wasn't sure he wanted to be on the council. He found keeping track of his own matters difficult enough. The thought of presiding over the entire ward, and by way of the council, over the entire city, gave him cause for anxiety, but he could not deny the spasm of excitement at the idea of taking the position. Good for business. Also, a good way to turn his brown hair gray, and crease his brow with lines of stress, processes that were already underway and which he did not wish to hasten.

He served the merchants with a glance of disapproval and shook his head to show he had already declined the offer, but he used this trick, a quick show of his hand, so they would show theirs. Their faces reflected genuine disappointment.

"Is there opposition to my candidacy?" He crossed his arm across his chest.

"Du Chase and his cronies, but he has always hated you and your father. He will never support you for alderman," one of them said. "But it is yours for the taking, if you want it, Master Gregory. We have already made the count, and your backing is beyond anything your rivals can muster."

"Du Chase," Gregory sniffed. "He is the burr I have yet managed to pull from my bottom."

"And he is the least of your worries," said one of his peers. "You should think about us, for if you do not accept our support, you will have insulted the best of your friends and associates."

"If that is a threat, do not waste your time with it," Gregory said. "I accept your nomination."

That is how he came to sit at the head of a long table in the north transept of St. Martin's, once every month, and with the red mantle of office draped over his shoulders, presiding over the trials and troubles of his corrupt, turbulent and beloved Vintry.

regory had always known his allotted share of gossip and small talk. In his dual role as merchant and lawyer, very little went on in the Vintry of which he did not know. But as alderman, he learned even more, so much so that, at first, he grew sick of the cheating and lies, grew disheartened by the revealed sins of the past, and grew morose with the thought that, at some point in the future, he could be as tainted as the ward itself. To be alderman of the Vintry meant finding value in the permanent junk of compromise, to know the very disease of life was incurable, and to accept that the top was the middle, the middle was the bottom, and the bottom was bottomless.

Once he'd swallowed the sorrow of his new position, he looked to the deeds of his predecessor, Roger Walden, and what he had done. He kept the weights and measures true, never sacrificed quality, fed the poor, housed the orphans, and jailed the reprobates. He cleaned the streets, repaired the piers, and maintained the church. It fell to him to honor the elders, court the nobles, placate the king, oppose new taxes, teach the apprentices, and marry them well. He commissioned ever larger ships and sent them farther abroad, finding new markets and trade there, making coin for all the associates to prosper and build the city until no shadow could ever darken its fame. So that is what he strove to do, and despite the strain of that endeavor, Gregory found contentedness in each of his days.

Until, of course, his ships stopped docking at his pier.

An order for a white from Entre-Deux-Mers went unfilled, as did one for a big red from Pessac. Buyers, some of whom had known Gregory for years, looked elsewhere. Though he asked them to keep faith, he could not blame them. London's thirst for Gascon wine grew insatiable, and if it couldn't be obtained in one place, then it would be found in another. He knew wine could be fickle. Sometimes it dripped and sometimes it poured. The French, pirates, a torrential season—any number of calamities could befall a shipment of wine.

He found the missing Spanish marble more alarming. The ship had called at Norwich instead and the payload had been sold to a nobleman in Norfolk. Gregory drafted a complaint for unlawful possession, seeking the selling price and a punitive fee, knowing well he would never see a penny. He learned that his shipment of wine had indeed arrived in England; not in London, but in Chester. Gregory filed another complaint, knowing it would never make it out of the pile. That this happened to him gave cause for grave concern, but then it started happening to others, with ships landing in Bristol, Hastings, Dover, and York—anywhere but the Vintry. So, what was once a running sore of Gregory's personal embarrassment transformed into an emergency for the entire ward, and thus, an emergency for all of London. Gregory called a special meeting to discuss the matter, convinced that, when the conversation had run its course, he, and perhaps rightfully so, would be to blame.

"What are you going to do?" Joan the Widow asked.

"If I knew the answer to that question, dear Joan, we would not be sitting here," Gregory said.

"Well, it is clear this is no accident," William Hawkins said. "I must be honest, Gregory, I cannot bear the thought of losing it all. If this continues, I will be finished."

"The same can be said for all of us," Gregory said. "And with that, I will get to the meat of this thing."

He stood from the table and walked around it with a reassuring hand patting his colleagues on the shoulders as he passed. They turned their heads, following him as he went, and in a show of support, some of them reached out and touched him on the arm or the elbow, just a little gesture to convey that they were with him. A weary smile showed on his face as he came full circle back to his place at the table. He did not sit. With his hands on the spine of his chair, he leaned over and looked around at them, the vintners, grocers, mercers, and drapers. The goldsmiths, fishmongers, chandlers, and skinners. He could keep them, but only if he served them. Gregory guessed this was the pivotal moment in his short tenure as alderman, and if he erred here, he could possibly squander all the credibility his family, the du Monts, had spent decades building. He heeded the advice of his parents, Henri and Herleve, and all they had taught him. He had built a place of privilege rather than poverty here by their prudence, and upon that pillar he would stand.

"I will ask you a question, and I want you to answer freely," he said at last. "Today is not a day for lies and half-truths. I assure you, I will hold no grudge if I hear words that don't please me. Was it a mistake to promote me to alderman?"

The north transept of St. Martin's church went silent, and in the jasmine glow of the stained glass, no words echoed in the ceiling's vaulted reaches. Instead, the merchants exchanged sheepish looks, fidgeted and otherwise avoided eye contact with Gregory.

"Please," he said, with a shrug and a shake. "Around me are some of the boldest people in all of England, and I find it impossible that not one of you can answer my question. Was it a mistake, yes or no? Was my election the reason why our piers now run dry?"

That's when a long, braying laugh bounded through the church, a laugh so loud it sent the blackbirds nesting in the rafters fluttering down the nave. Du Chase pushed his chair back and made ready to stand. Gregory's heart sank.

"Gregory, if there is no one else here who is brave enough to answer your question, then I will do it for them," he said, and made an elegant, sweeping gesture with his hand. "You are blessed with many friends, yet you are cursed with many enemies. It is clear your position in our precious ward has motivated them to exact their revenge. If aimed only at you, Gregory of Bordeaux, I am sure none of us would mind. But now that your reputation is starting to sully ours, I must say that it is time for you to do the right thing and relinquish your aldermanship."

Du Chase flashed a needling smile as those at the table murmured and gasped, wrestling with what he had said. And wrestle they did, because du Chase, as unpopular as he was in the Vintry, held much sway outside of it. His older brother, John du Chase, had become an important grocer, the alderman of Cheapside, a confidant of the mayor of London, and a member of the king's parliament. There was good reason to think du Chase was not just voicing his opinion, but the opinion of a much more powerful interest anchored in the royal halls of Westminster.

With that ominous underpinning, the discussion unfolded, with Gregory seated and silent, content to lean on the wisdom of his peers. The heated talks concluded with a hush of agreement. Joan the Widow, swathed in a dazzling cobalt robe and crowned with a matching veil, rose from her chair. She took hold of the candelabrum and held it out in front of her as she made her way down the length of the table to Gregory. She stood just behind him and to the right, the position of subservience but also the one of honor and authority. She sat the candelabrum down, in front of Gregory, so the light from its flickering flames washed his sullen brow with hope. Putting a hand on his shoulder, she smiled at him.

Though he did not know exactly what she was about to say, he knew it would be in his favor, and coming from her, it would have weight. Quietly acknowledged as one of the top spicers in the city, Joan the Widow enjoyed a reputation for her acts of charity, her business ethics, and her shrewd ability to import the best black pepper in the world. When she spoke, people listened, and when she gave a command, it was obeyed. Now, her hand rested on Gregory's shoulder and the light of her eminence danced in his eyes. In a voice as clear and true as a note plucked on an angel's harp, Joan the Widow spoke.

"It was not a mistake to elect Gregory," she said. "Not at all. He is the best of us, du Chase, and we stand with him. Go tell your brother. I am certain he will understand."

"Here, here," bellowed William Stokes, and the others responded with a rousing, "Here, here."

Du Chase, crestfallen, raised his hand and said, "But I hear the merchants of Bread Street and Cheapside are in an uproar because we are losing them money, and if things do not change soon, they will file a complaint in court and punish us all."

"Then let them do it," William Purchase said. "The best lawyer in London sits among us, and we will turn their writs against them."

"But Gregory has already lost his clout and can do nothing but embarrass us when he goes to Westminster," du Chase said. "And Gregory, can you tell us why you have been summoned to the royal court?"

"No, I cannot," he said, as a steely grin crept over his face. "But when I go there, I will be sure of at least two things."

"What might those be?" du Chase asked.

"That I am alderman of the Vintry, and that no mistake was made," he said, and his peers nodded with concurrence.

AN APPOINTMENT AT WESTMINSTER

On the horizon loomed the soaring splendor of Westminster. Though the royal seat of power, Gregory knew it as the wellspring of right and wrong in the realm. It was a place of justice granted and of justice denied, the birthplace of dreams and the graveyard of reality, a world where both angels and demons lurked in the rafters, and where lies and truths stood as equals. Noble ideas lived in the hall, but so did deceitful plots. When good and evil did battle there, more often than not, the side with the most coins won. Even though he felt things would not go his way today, Gregory couldn't resist a jolt of excitement as he crossed the bridge onto the hallowed grounds of the ancient hold of kingship.

He rode to the stables, surrendered his horse to a groom, and made his way by foot to the great hall. He recognized a few faces in the crowd of merchants and nobles and waved a hand or tilted the brim of his hat in greeting. As it almost always was at Westminster over these last three decades, the king convened his council because he needed its consent to levy more taxes to build his castles and fight his unending wars. Those who had to pay his punitive fee had wearied of the king and his requests, and year by year, as they had grown increasingly restless, the king's popularity had proportionally waned. The alienation between the sovereign and his people may have begun as a subtle difference of opinion, but thirty years in, the divide became entrenched and obvious. The realm was not on the verge of rebellion, but feelings were hurt, trust shattered, and lives upended. So, Gregory was not the only one at Westminster that day with the taste of discontent in his mouth.

He stopped and peered into the dim depths of the hall, where a nobleman in red and black, glittering with jewels, gestured with elegance in addressing old King Edward, who sat on his throne in a posture of regal repose. Gregory could hear, but not understand, what the nobleman said, but in his dramatic gestures, he saw passion and anger. The baron concluded his address on one knee and with his hands out, as if pleading, and his peers, standing thick in the gallery, lifted their fists and cheered. Even here, far from the intimate action on the other end of the hall, Gregory saw it in the king's tired eyes—not the man he used to be, and his grip on the reins not as tight as it had been in the verdant years. In that terrifying instant, Gregory knew the world would soon change. He pondered the bewildering thought of life without the only king he'd known, making the sign of the cross as he did.

He heard his name uttered by an unfamiliar voice. His contemplation shattered, he turned, unnerved, and there stood the Dominican friar who had served the summons on him a fortnight ago at the Purple Pot.

"It is good you have arrived," he said. "Follow me."

As they walked down a corridor, Gregory asked God to watch over him this day, knowing no one else would. Following this man in black—his pace brisk, despite a limp, the cross heavy around his neck, a pubic funk wafting in his wake—he walked into the dank bowels of the hall to an unknown destination. Consternation mounting, Gregory found himself eager to discover what this was all about. Once he stepped through a creaking oaken door, past a hissing sphere of torchlight, and down a short flight of stairs, at last he knew. He halted and swallowed a hard knot of panic. There before him, waited a gaggle of men who could speak for months, and even years, and not find one good thing to say of him. His enemies, those he had trampled beneath the words of his chronicle, those who had not met muster when he had put his quill to work.

There sat Lord Lancaster, portly, with death in his eyes. Friar Nicholas, with his black habit and cross of gold. The Bishop of Lincoln peering from beneath his hood. The former Lord Tutbury, in his low gentry rags. Amongst a host of others who Gregory did not recognize, stood none other than Lord Baldwin of Essex. His face, shattered five years ago, had grown over like moss on a stone. A fixed and misshapen mask of crooked eyes, jutting teeth, and a curving jaw, wet with drool. Next to him, du Chase, and next to him, his brother, John, both smug and triumphant.

Gregory tried to be clever, but the aura of hatred pushed against him with such force he could not rally his wits. Convinced he had arrived at an end of his making, he shook his head. What a fool I have been, to think I could have crossed these men and have gotten away with it. No one uttered a word. They sat and stared, allowing him to consider his doom in the heat and silence of their loathing.

"We are all here, together at Westminster," the Dominican said, rubbing his hands together.

Gregory's heart sank to the depths of the poisoned well when he noticed a manuscript, lit by the flickering light of a candle, sitting on a podium. One of the unauthorized copies of his chronicle? It had to be. Well-thumbed and marked, too, the centerpiece of this vexing appointment. Gregory knew what he had written in his chronicle was damning enough, but with a rogue copy, there was no telling what had been changed, rearranged, added, or otherwise fabricated. Those quibbles didn't mean much to his enemies, he knew, so he braced himself for the onslaught.

The Dominican stood at the podium, and with a raised brow and a theatrical frown, leafed through the chronicle. He glanced up at Gregory, and when their eyes locked, he knew he had met his match. This Dominican, Gregory guessed, probably knew Common Law, Canon Law and even Roman Law. He had probably read all the classics from Greece and Rome, as well as the Bible and the Koran and all manner of heresies in between. He probably knew all the histories of the kings and the saints, the achievements of peace and the atrocities of war. Probably of noble birth and judging by the chisel of his jaw and the strength in his bearing, had probably been a fighting man in his youth. Of the utmost, however, was that he was a Dominican, an order that had made its name burning heretics across the sea down in Languedoc in what was known as the Inquisition. Gregory knew there was nothing he could say or do to get beneath, over or around this man, which is why, he guessed, he was the one hunched over the chronicle with the glance of reckoning in his eyes.

"Master Gregory, these are the people you tried to destroy," he began, gesturing toward the jury of foes. "It is my honor to right your wrongs, and right them I will, with your victims as witness. Before we go any further, I must first admit you are a worthy adversary—alderman of the Vintry, owner of a respected wine shop on Royal Street, and by all accounts, one of London's most prominent merchants. You are also a lawyer of note, both at King's Court and Common Pleas. And how can we forget, you are a chronicler of some renown, and are known for your sharp and clever quill—in Latin, French and English, no doubt. They say you are a fine horseman and that you are so lucky that you have never lost a wager. There are few men with your range of talents, Master Gregory, and fewer still who can match your success and fame. Commendations. In a world of sin and shame, you have managed to prosper."

"Friar, you can spare me the backhanded compliments," Gregory said. "As I'm sure you know, of late my prospects have sagged, and try as I might, I have not figured out why. Ships no longer call at my pier, and these days I have more questions than coins. Alas, not a good exchange when you are alderman of the Vintry. But perhaps today, I will have some answers. I will have answers, won't I? Please tell me I did not dress in my finest and make the trip to Westminster only to remain ignorant as to why I suffer."

"Do not worry, Master Gregory. Today, you will be enlightened."

He plunged into the chronicle, flipping the parchments to places marked with a drip of red wax. With the ease of a man who is comfortable with letters, he made his way through the voluminous text, reading in a grating voice of condemnation as he went. All of it planned and rehearsed, tawdry if not for the complainants involved.

Jabbing the chronicle with his index finger, the Dominican reminded Gregory that Simon Le Clerk, the jester who had written The Swan, the Owl and the Finch, had been hanged on charges of slander, libel, and for inciting a riot pursuant to murder. He reminded Gregory he had written glowingly of him and that he had described Le Clerk as a "great thinker, who with the light of satire, rightly exposed the secrets and hypocrisy hiding in the moldy cellar of the Dominican order." The friar asked Gregory if he remembered what he had written about Le Clerk, to which Gregory said, "Yes. True then, as it is now."

The friar broached the matter of Lord Miles Le Gaunter and his death at Sempringham, and Lord Corby and his tragic end, being kicked in the face by a horse. He reminded Gregory he had been implicated in both cases. In response, Gregory reminded the Dominican that Lord Le Gaunter tried to enforce a claim later proved false, and Corby had been charged posthumously, and proven guilty, in the murder of Margery Alesworth. He also told the friar he had paid the blood tax in both instances and had been absolved.

The Dominican went on to say Gregory had repeated salacious rumors about Eleanor of Brittany, the deceased wife of the Lord of Lancaster, and that his chronicle legitimized the otherwise unsubstantiated whispers that she had ordered the murder of her own nephews for the benefit of her eldest son. The friar said there was no proof Marcus of Burwell Priory was in fact the bastard son of the Bishop of Lincoln, that the chronicle had caused the bishop undue embarrassment and distress, and that his ability to lead a cathedral had been compromised. Gregory responded by pointing at the bishop, saying, "There is your proof. Ask him what games he has played with his loins and make him answer it with honesty."

"The questions are for you, Master Gregory, and none other!" the Dominican said.

The inquest played out, with the Dominican speaking to one part of the story, and Gregory, over the Dominican's harangues and protestations, speaking to the other. Gregory knew he had to counter because a royal scrivener, tucked away in a dark corner, wrote everything down. When the final record came out, it had to show he had defended himself to the bitter end. To recant or to reconcile would be to ensure his demise. But it was not easy to withstand the Dominican's tirade. He badgered Gregory with an assortment of accusations, pointing his finger, shouting, overwhelming Gregory's responses with a dour shaking of his head. Those seated in the antechamber joined in. They spat at Gregory, threatened him with violence, and shot at him with repeated volleys of indignities. This went on for hours, his feet tired, his throat parched, and his esteem tattered. The Dominican, showing no signs of fatigue, exhausted his list of claims and arrived at the reason all of them were there.

"Master Gregory, I have an indictment, and if it is signed by the judge you will be charged with libel, inciting a riot, and, most importantly, murder," he said, as he held the bill above his head, waving it with a hint of menace. "Needless to say, a trial on such charges, even if you won, could destroy you, and if you were to lose, you would have your eyes gouged out, and you would surely swing from the gallows at Smithfield. Stephen of Hastings, who teaches law at Oxford, has already agreed to take the case should you choose to go to court."

"So, what do I have to do to keep the judge from signing the indictment?" Gregory said.

The Dominican smiled and cocked his head. He glanced at the others, gloating with them, and turned back to Gregory.

"You must leave England," he said. "If you do not wish to hang, you must leave, within a fortnight, and be gone for not less than two years. You are being banished."

"This is my punishment for writing a chronicle never even meant for your eyes?"

"No, Gregory, this is for the pain you caused people whom you had no right to offend. You are a merchant, not a lord. You want to be one, but your hands are stained with wine, and lordship is not your lot in this life."

"Tell me, friar, how long was this bamboozlement in the works?"

"Since the moment you returned to London, five years ago," he said. "The irony is the chronicle made you influential, but it also made you vulnerable. To cast a net to catch one codfish is not worth the effort, after all. But sturgeon? A different matter."

"You have had many questions for me today, friar, but I have one for you," Gregory said.

"And what is that?"

"Is two years long enough?"

"Long enough for what?"

"To destroy my fortune and my name."

The Dominican laughed.

"Yes, Master Gregory, it is. Upon your return to London we will give you a cartload of mud and dung, so you can build a hovel on the roadside to Norfolk. You can make your living as a curiosity for passersby. Tell them the story of how you made it to the top of the mountain, only to fall into the depths of the chasm. Silver pennies you would get for that story, and plenty of them, but never enough to buy back your place along the waterfront. If we cannot have your neck in the noose, Master Gregory, we will certainly settle for your riches."

A
SOMERSET
ROSE

he groom took his horse, the manservant, his hat and cloak. He retreated to the long table in his rug-and-tapestry hall, a cup of Malbec at hand and a new lump of coal on the fire. He quaffed down the wine and motioned for another. His spirits lifted when the scent of beef stew came wafting from the detached kitchen. He ate and drank in silence, asking himself the same simple question over and again.

Dear Lord, what was he to do?

Two years, he reasoned, was not too terribly long. He had been gone for three during the chronicle, and his business had not suffered. But things were much different now. His cousin, Jean du Mont, had gone back to Bordeaux so he was not here to manage the family shop. And the business, now three times the size it had been during his travels, was a grinding, perpetual series of decisions and deals, made with, or despite, an assortment of ruthless traders from Seville to Bruges. Not just anyone could do what Gregory did, in the easiest of times. And now that a coalition had promised to destroy him, he knew his apprentices, God bless them, were not equal

to the task. A trial on charges of libel and murder, with the price perhaps being his life, or two years in banishment and the prospect of worldly
comeuppance—neither choice pleased him, he admitted with chagrin, and
cursed the Dominican for his cunning.

He could, perhaps, reach an agreement with the Earl of Southampton
to hand over his interests in trust and take control of them upon his return,
but Gregory did not like that idea. He enjoyed the earl's support and the status it entailed. Indeed, it was the earl, and the chronicle he conceived, who
elevated Gregory to the top echelon of London's fickle merchant society.
He even liked the earl and admired his willingness to do what others of his
station would not, reward merit over title. Still, he just couldn't stomach the
idea of placing his business in the possession of a man of such rank. If the
earl ever got his hands on it, and for some reason he reneged, Gregory could
never get it back. A merchant, even if he owned a thousand ships and a thousand piers and could afford to pay a thousand lawyers, could never overturn
an ancient-blooded earl like Richard Beaufort. No, it could not be the earl.
Someone else must watch over his shares while he was away. He went to the
big chair by the fireplace, the one with the cushions and the bearskin thrown
over it. Sitting down, he took a sip of wine and peered into the whispering
flames. Two years. Two long, inconvenient years.

ord of Gregory's predicament soon spread, and by midday, many
merchants had jammed into his hall. There sat Gregory, in the
middle of the tumult, the bearskin draped over his shoulders, as
his colleagues shouted back and forth as to what should be done. Gregory listened as long as he could, but ended the discussion when he stood, motioned
for silence, and in a loud and certain voice, said, "I am leaving."

His declaration prompted a collective gasp of supportive concern, followed by heartened pledges of loyalty. Until this moment, it had all been
fear, anger and panic, but now a deep sadness crept upon him as he looked

into the familiar faces of his friends and associates. They were sincere in their vows to support him, and it was with great emotion that he clasped their hands, hugged them, or exchanged a kiss on each cheek. Yet, he had misgivings. He did not like the idea of others taking care of his business. He did not want them tainted by his troubles or embroiled in the plots and plans of the Dominican and his host. They had their own problems, and over time, they would not have the energy to shoulder his. He needed someone inside his shares, someone who would fight for them because they were fully vested in the outcome. Friends and colleagues were well and good, but what he really needed was a wife.

Indeed, he had a tall stack of proposed marriage contracts sitting on his desk. They had flooded in over the last year, as his status had grown, and having read them all, he knew he had an array of choices that would be the envy of almost any man. He could marry a fourteen-year-old daughter of a petty nobleman in Surrey and be paid twenty pounds to do so. He could wed a nineteen-year-old widow from Berkshire, gaining title to her manor on the River Loddon and live as a country squire. He had an offer from a grocer in Hastings to marry his fifteen-year-old daughter, and as dowry, receive a royalty on all the flour ground at the father-in-law's mill. There also stood a proposal from an aging spinster, she of the cleft lip, who offered him the fantastic sum of 50 pounds if he would marry her and revive the family's declining salt enterprise in Worcestershire. Some of the overtures were laughable, while others were almost repugnant, but a handful of those offers were attractive enough to have made him consider the prospect of matrimony. He had not done it, and his friends joked that he waited in vain for a princess, a peerless woman who could give him an heir, a sword, a scepter, and a throne. Faced with his present banishment, he would accept much less, but knowing he would one-day return, he could not let expedience trump discretion.

The crowd of well-wishers continued to grow, and as merchants had their moment with Gregory and left the hall, others filed in. A pipe of Malbec was tapped, and in short order, the gathering that began on a somber note, achieved a festive, defiant air. Gregory did his best to keep things positive, and on more than a few occasions, flashed a grin and laughed. Among the usual crowd were old friends with whom Gregory had lost touch. Even a few of his rivals were in attendance and well-behaved. In this crowd, he found mirth despite the cloud hanging over him, and with a brave face, he received those who had come with their blessings.

As he leaned close for an embrace, he saw something on the other side of the crowded, hazy hall that filled his heart with an unforeseen wash of peace and desire. Joan the Widow, or more properly, Joan Costantyn of Devonshire. When their eyes locked, he saw nothing but her glittering beauty. He had known her for a decade as Joan the Widow, so named because her husband, Ralph, had met a tragic death while on the night watch. She had famously declared she would never wed again, even though only seventeen at the time. Gregory knew her as an esteemed pepper merchant and member of the grocer's guild, a sometimes co-investor and a reassuring presence on the squalid waterfront. They were easy associates, and in the company of others, had spent many evenings joking and complaining over candlelight and a tankard of wine in a corner near the fireplace at the Purple Pot Tavern. But he had never seen in her the mature, appealing radiance that now shone, nor found in her a special place to plant and nurture his life. He had always thought she had made of him, much as he had made of her, friends and allies, but nothing more. They shared the same space through happenstance, not intention. Or so he thought until this very moment, when she blossomed like a Somerset rose, yearning for light, her splendid petals bettering the world.

People noticed his rather obvious gaze, and when they turned, craning their necks to see what he saw, the meaning of it became clear. Those standing between them inched back and out of the way as an expectant hush settled upon the half-timbered hall. Gregory doffed his hat of burnt sienna, put out his right heel, and in a downward sweeping motion with hat in hand, looked at her. In a voice of ripe solemnity, he said, "Lady Joan, you are as the morning sun glinting o'er a placid sea."

She curtsied deep, imbuing the gesture with pomp and dignity. With her eyes out-sparkling her rubies, she replied, "Dear Gregory, it hurts me that you must leave, but I will be here upon your return."

So, there they stood, suspended in the golden moment when the truth, unbeknownst through the decade of its making, arrived to confront peril.

He went to her, faster and faster until he enfolded her in his arms, her head buried against his neck. He smelled the lavender oil in her hair, heard her muffled cry, and felt the heaving of her bosom. Gregory looked up from her shoulder, only to notice everyone staring at them with bemusement and awe, for such scenes of affection did not unfold inside the merchant halls of London. The two of them shed their embrace and stood side by side, presenting themselves as to what they were about to become—man and wife, a formidable union of wine and pepper. William Purchase broke the silence when he hoisted his cup and bellowed, "Here, here!" The rest of the merchants followed, sounding a cheer of concurrence so spirited and loud it could be heard in the wards of Queenhithe, Bread Street, Cheapside, and Candlewick—where people looked up and thought to themselves, something big is happening in the Vintry, and Gregory of Bordeaux is surely at its center.

He had a lot to do before the banishment. He owned row houses on Porter Lane and the Red Eagle Tavern near Ludgate. He owned a pier and quarter equity in five ships. He had annual export contracts with grain producers in three counties. He had a loan of 30 pounds out to the goldsmiths, and another loan of 20 pounds out to a fishmonger at Bridge Within. He had agreements with wine traders and grocers at ports all along the coast of France, and a private charter giving him the right to deal directly, and tax free, with the Count of Flanders. Wall hangings and furniture, silver plate and kitchenware, textiles and jewels, his hall and warehouse and the contents within—all of it had to be accounted for and placed under Joan's majority. And so, he returned to Westminster, to Common Pleas, and there built a fortress of deeds, writs, bills and notes, and as he filed his pieces with the clerk, he thought, those who would take it all might perhaps regret giving me a fortnight to sort my affairs. He went to city court, where he knew everyone's name, and did the same thing he had done at Common Pleas. As Gregory handled the business end of the nuptials, and said his farewells to associates across the city, Joan handled the wedding end of the marriage. Letters of invitation were sent out to all the Home Counties and as far away as York and Lichfield. Joan met with the tailor, the jeweler, the haberdasher, and the victualer. She ordered beef, pork, salmon, and fowl, all manner of sweets and savories and hogsheads of wine and ale. A small army of roustabouts she hired to clean the streets of the Vintry, to hang festive banners at all corners, and to chase away the vagrants who lounged about the ward.

The fortnight melted away so quickly that Gregory was almost surprised when his manservant woke him one morning at dawn, gave him a sad smile and said, "Today is your big day, Master Gregory." So, it is, he thought, as he climbed out of bed and headed toward the privy. He took his time with everything he did that day—breaking his fast with a sip of watered wine and a hunk of cheese, soaking in a large wooden tub of warm water while reading psalms from his book of hours, dressing himself in blue worsted wool with every hem trimmed with green silk and marten, and jesting with his grooms as he waited for the bells of St. Martin's to ring. When they did, he walked with head high and measured steps down Royal Street, around a tight corner to St. Martin's Row, and to the church entrance at the north transept. He and his grooms, the four Williams and his two apprentices, walked down the nave to the front door, where stood the parish priest.

"You will be pleased, Master Gregory, by the turnout you have received," he said, and opened the massive main doors.

When Gregory went out to take his place on the steps, what he saw astounded him. Spilling out on either side of Thames Street the cream of the London merchants, three and four deep and twinkling with silver and gemstones. He had seen this many people in one place many times, but he was always part of the crowd, not the object of its attention. So impressed was he, and so humbled by their support, he gave a short bow and made a generous yet subdued gesture with the waving of his hand. Flanking the crowd on the north side of the street he saw a line of armed men in helms and mail. In the pay of the guilds, whose gift to Gregory was a wedding safe and sound. There were hot rumors this affair would be wrecked by his enemies, and he knew a whispering campaign, warning people not to attend, had been mounted and implemented with fervor. So, to see them all here today, was more than just a show of support for him and Joan. Their presence was an obvious reminder that the friars and the nobles need not meddle in the work of those who ruled the waterfront.

On the wind, came the gentle blush of the lute and the pipe, and the scents of musk and rose oil circled in the air. As the crowd turned and looked, Gregory squinted for the first glimpse of his handsome bride. An ember of divine light, emerald and cobalt, she appeared, her brunette hair interwoven with violet wildflowers and sprays of Gypsophila. Accompanied on either side by her satin bridesmaids, Joan was the princess of them all, showing everyone she would be a widow no longer and that Gregory had been wise to choose her. When she reached the church steps, her priest gave her over to Gregory. In reverence, he held out his hand. She took it in hers and joined him at the top of the steps. With her on the left and him on the right, they faced the parish priest. He nodded to show he was ready to bear witness. Gregory turned to Joan and gave his consent.

"I take thee, Joan Costantyn, as my wedded wife, to have and to hold, from this day forward, for better or for worse, for richer or for poorer, in sickness and in health, until death do us part."

With a subtle swoon in her hazel eyes, she replied, "I take thee, Gregory du Mont, as my wedded husband, to have and to hold, from this day forward, for better or for worse, for richer or for poorer, in sickness and in health, until death do us part."

From a small pouch at his belt he pulled out a simple gold ring. He invoked the Holy Trinity as he placed it first on her right thumb, then her index finger and then her third finger, where it remained.

"With this ring I thee wed," he said. "This gold and silver I thee give. With my body I thee worship, and with this dowry I thee endow."

The priest made the sign of the cross and sprinkled them with Holy Water. Gregory and Joan turned to the crowd, presenting themselves as husband and wife. And while there was cause for rejoicing, the mood of the moment remained somber. True enough, this was a powerful union between two of the wealthiest merchants in one of the wealthiest cities in Christendom. But also, a union made under duress, a hasty action, nearly a stunt, arranged within the shadow of banishment and the threat of reprisal. In this throng of supporters, Gregory knew spies took note of names and faces and concocted the tale they would tell their employers. Gregory of Bordeaux has shaken his finger at you yet again, they would say, so what will you do in return?

Holding Joan's hand, he knew he had the strength to face whatever came before him—the test, the problem, the puzzle with the missing piece. Yet still, he was frightened, deep down in the marrow, of what the next two years had in store. God has given me many blessings, but he has also given me much heartache. He squeezed Joan's hand even tighter, breathing in the floral aroma of her perfume. Their hearts beat as one, bells hanging in the same tower, foxgloves blooming in the same field.

A breeze lifted from the polluted River Thames. Ships bobbed at the piers. A cock crowed from a courtyard. A stray dog barked and scampered down the street. Such mundane occurrences happened all the time, and did so even on Gregory's wedding day, when he gave himself to Joan and knew the world had changed.

hey poured into St. Martin's for mass and, after that, the grand feast at Gregory's hall. Jugglers and acrobats, fire eaters, and musicians. Breads, stews, fish, broth, roasted meats, tarts, and pies, and a river of wine kindled talk and naughty laughter. Gregory and Joan partook, but sparingly, as the feast rose in a crescendo of celebration. But Gregory had precious little time, and from the sly, furtive glances he had received from Joan, it was evident their love had gone unattended for long enough. Though he appreciated the presence of all those who had come to celebrate the marriage, he was ready for them to be gone so he and Joan could visit the pleasures of holy matrimony. He had ordered one of his grooms, William Hawkins, to declare the feast over at a predetermined signal. He looked down the table to his right, caught William's eye, and after draining his silver goblet, turned it over and set it down. William responded with a smile, had a servant refill his goblet, then stood and cleared his throat.

"Honorable friends and esteemed associates," he declared, as he held out his drink, "on Gregory's behalf I thank you for your support on this momentous day. Your prayers were heard, and your presence was heartening. By so gathering, you have blessed this union that will surely bear fruit. But a man and a woman do not wed just to watch jugglers all night. And the jokes we're telling? Gregory and Joan have heard them all before. There is an heir to beget before he sails over the sea, and that is private business. You see, this feast is over, and you will not dine in this hall until he has returned. So, speak your farewells and speak them now."

For the next hour Gregory stood at the door of his hall and bid goodbye to people who he might never see again. One by one, as they said their peace and left, the sadness in his heart plunged deeper. He did not want to leave. He cherished his life in London. Even with all the preparations he had made, he had not yet accepted what it meant to uproot his routine and flee. But as the crowd thinned, his circumstance grew more apparent.

People pushed coins into his hands and told him things would be fine. But try as he might, he could not convince himself it would be so. He said his last farewell, to William Stokes, and watched him walk away. When he reached the corner at Dowgate he turned and waved, then walked around the corner and out of view. Gregory stood there for quite some time, at the arched door of his great fire-lit hall, in the cold grip of loneliness. He finally went upstairs to the solar, where Joan awaited. Already under the covers, she watched Gregory strip down to his undergarments.

"Joan, I'm scared," he said, as he hung his robe on a wall peg.

"I know you are, Gregory, and so am I, but please, join me," she said.

As he approached the canopy bed, she pulled back the down blanket and showed herself, long and curvy, dressed in a loose-fitting drape of red felt. Gregory slid in next to her, pulling close under the cover. She kissed him on the neck, gently grabbed his hand and guided it down to her patch. He found her hot treasure and rubbed her there until she was flooded and breathing heavy in his ear.

"You are not scared of this, are you, dear husband?"

"No, my bride," he said. "Of this I have no fear."

DOLPHIN
IS MY
FAVORITE FISH

An urgent knocking at the door. Rising from the sweet slumber of coupling, Gregory leaned on his elbow. "What is it?"

"A messenger was just here, Master Gregory, and he gave me a note that he said you must read," said Thomas, his manservant, speaking loudly on the other side of the door.

Stepping into his undergarments, Gregory made sure the bed canopy was closed, walked barefoot across the cold timber floor to the door, and yanked it open. Thomas shoved the note into his hand and garbled an apology for having woken him at such an hour. Gregory opened the note, sealed with a stamped glob of red wax, and held it under the candelabrum in Thomas' hand.

Do not sail from London or you will not return. The assassin is already hiding in the ship's hold and his dagger has been dipped in poison. Ride to Southampton forthwith, and tell no one of which way you go. Head out through Southwark, and when you arrive at the bridge, tell this to the night watch: Dolphin is my favorite fish. Bring nothing but the clothes on your back. Godspeed.

With a furrowed brow and a pounding heart, Gregory looked at the letter's wax seal. It bore the crest of the Earl of Southampton, a boar's head on a shield. To counterfeit that seal would be to earn your place on the gallows, so Gregory had every reason to believe the warning was real and not the lever of a trap. He looked to his manservant and said, "Go and make ready my stallion, and prepare hard victuals for two days. I leave tonight, Thomas, so wake the groom and do your duty with haste."

"Yes, Master Gregory," he said, and scurried away.

"What has happened?" Joan peered out from behind the canopy with a long look of concern.

"That ship upon which I was to sail—it is no good, Joan," he said, shaking his head. "I must take a different ship from a different port, far from here, if I am ever to see you again."

Joan slipped into her robe and climbed out of bed. She sat in a chair next to the table where he placed items pulled from an iron-bound cedar chest—a worn Book of Hours, a leather pack, a sack of silver, breeches, boots, and a pair of brass spurs. He saw the intrigue growing in her as piece by piece he transformed from a worried husband into a hardened man of the road. He pulled into his black robe and tied it off with a heavy leather belt, where hung his sheathed knife, La Bonne Vie. He whipped his cloak over his shoulders, cinching it with a silver and sapphire brooch. As he looked at Joan with a grim smile, he donned his big black beaver and peacock hat, pulling down the brim until low over his brow. In his kit from the chronicle, he smelled the dust and blood of England, and in a flash of foolhardy pride, felt invincible.

He and Joan gazed at one another in sorrow and silence, and in the dim candlelight shining on their lives, searched for reasons not to cry, but none could be found. They fell into a tight embrace, sharing a terrible tear and a sad kiss. Before he left the room, she handed him a long sash of cobalt wool, part of her wedding attire. He put it around his neck and tucked it in beneath his robe.

"I will return, Joan, and our life together will resume."

"And when you arrive home, my husband, I will be waiting for you—your cellar stacked floor to ceiling with wine, and your heir bouncing happily on my knee."

"That, dear wife, would please me." He turned and walked away.

lack Saddle lurched into a hard gallop and soon thundered through the darkness down Thames Street to London Bridge. Gregory wheeled him to a stop, looked up at the grimy guards in the gatehouse, and with authority, said, "Dolphin is my favorite fish." After a tense moment of anticipation, the portcullis rose. Gregory laid in with his spurs and Black Saddle raced over the bridge, splashing through filth and dreck, past shops and shanties, to the gatehouse on the other end. The guards, their helmets and spear tips orange in the torchlight, glared down at the stranger in black staring up at them.

"Dolphin is my favorite fish," he said, but the portcullis did not move.

Thinking he had been trapped, he looked behind him. But nothing.

"And how much would you be willing to pay for a fine cut of your favorite fish?" asked one of the guards.

Of course.

He pulled two silver groats from his pouch. He held the incentive over his head, making sure the coins shone in the torchlight. With the creak of wood and the clink of chains, the portcullis opened. Gregory dropped the groats, tipped his hat, and in a clatter of hooves, bolted out through Southwark. He was tempted to take one last look over his shoulder at the skyline silhouette of his beloved London. But Gregory knew what it looked like, and he knew, God willing, he'd see it again.

"Ride, you devil horse, ride!" he said, and Black Saddle hurtled through the night.

regory had not seen anything during the many looks over his shoulder, but he knew someone out there tracked him. He could feel it, the creeping fear of being prey. He never stopped in open view, and when he charged through a sleepy village, he would flick a penny to the bewildered bumpkin who had managed to catch his eye. The end of the second day drew near, the sky plump with hazy amber twilight. He noticed gulls banking in the wind, and, in the air, a sharp sniff of salt spray. On the horizon sat the great castle keep of Southampton, its stone glowing beige in the sunset, immovable from its perch above the town. The coast, Gregory thought. Respite.

He wheeled Black Saddle to a halt at Bar Gate, doffed his hat and looked up at the tower guards.

"It is I, Gregory of Bordeaux," he said. "I am here at the behest of your lord, Richard Beaufort, and I beg entrance to this noble city."

The drawbridge came down, and Black Saddle's shoed hooves clicked and clacked as he crossed over it. As the drawbridge closed behind them, Gregory looked over his shoulder, and there on the other side of the ditch, he spied three riders in hoods, shadows hanging over their faces. Gregory knew who they were, or at least who had paid them. Before the rising draw-bridge disrupted the line of sight, Gregory made an ugly face. He ran the fingertips of his right hand outward from his neck across the bottom of his chin. And then he spat.

"Those men are not with me and they are not friends of your lord," Gregory said. "If you know what's best for you, do not let them in."

He had been here once before, so he knew the way. He followed the road around to South Gate and cantered Black Saddle into the bailey. As he dismounted and pulled off his cordovan gloves, a groom led his horse to the stables. A liveried steward ushered him to the great hall nestled against the inner wall, and once through the front door, the steward stepped in front of him, and to the crowd of men inside, said, "My lord, I present to you Greg-ory of Bordeaux." Everyone in the hall stopped, and in the sudden silence of his arrival, Gregory bowed low with genuine deference. He glanced up and made eye contact with the earl, seated at his thick oaken chair at the head of his table. He gestured for Gregory to rise, and with another gesture, servants made a place for him. Meat and bread laid out, wine poured, and steady hands took from him his gloves, hat and cloak.

"So, you have arrived, Bordeaux," the earl said. "Eat and drink, and when you are done, we shall talk."

Gregory obliged. The hall grew loud again with laughing and talking as Gregory devoured his pork pie and cheese, washing it down with a cup of spiced wine. He had finished his apple fritter and was licking his fingers when people started to leave the hall. By the time he had washed his hands and dried them with a linen cloth, only he and the earl remained. Gregory followed him to a set of chairs near the fireplace, where they sat for a while and sipped their wine in silence. He had not seen the earl in three years, ever since he had presented him with the chronicle. Southampton had been to Gascony and back, up to Scotland and out west to Wales in that time. Any of the boyish good looks Gregory remembered from the old days were gone. He had killed many men since they'd first met, and many more had tried to kill him. Politics at court, the constant threat of French raids along the coast, and the demands of a surly and dangerous king, had creased the earl's face with thick lines of age, and made his hair go gray at the temples. Such was the way of lords, and such was the price of their privilege. Gregory felt no sympathy for him. Still, he had a deep fondness for Southampton, and as they sat, with only the fire speaking to the coal, Gregory felt his magnetism, saw in his eyes that Southampton was different, and much smarter, than his noble, belligerent peers. Gregory could neither forget nor ignore all that had come before this moment, but if he could, Southampton would still command his loyalty. He had cleared his hall to sit and talk with a merchant. To Gregory, an honor beyond anything he could've imagined. So, when he finally had the courage to speak, he did so with reverence.

"My lord, it is but for your grace I am here and not poisoned and dead at the bottom of the sea," he said, and took a sip of wine.

"I am glad you received my letter," he replied. "I wrote it with my own hand."

"You have learned your grammar well, my lord, for your message was loud and clear," he said. "But I must know. Why do you risk your reputation supporting me? I'm glad you do. But I have yet to detect your motives, a skill of which I am usually keen."

"My reputation?" he asked, and gave Gregory a crooked stare before nodding at the wall to his left, where hung the many war trophies claimed over the decades by the Beaufort dynasty. "My reputation is secure, Bordeaux. I support you because you are a new man, and I like the idea of looking forward, which is not what most people do. They look back to the comfort of what they know and make hard work of change. But you—you would destroy this world if you could."

"I rather think it will destroy me first, but you are right. A few walls would be torn down, if it were in my power."

"Yet you will not be able to do it, but in the process of trying, you will create something unique and enduring. You already have, and you have an opportunity to do it again. You will not be counting your pennies and pipes of wine for the next two years. Whatever will you do to pass the time?"

"I am not yet sure, my lord, but I surmise you have put some thought into the matter. Why else would I be here?"

The earl rose and stood next to the fire, holding out his palms for extra warmth. He then stoked the coals, and from the look on his face, Gregory knew he grappled with important thoughts.

"Bordeaux," he said at long last, "I want you to work for me while you are in exile. If you do not have a patron, it is doubtful you will live long enough to return home to your wife and your business. As dangerous as England is, it is among the easiest of places to stay alive. Swords are sharp everywhere you go, and if you do not have a supporter, you will surely find out just how sharp they are."

"Your employ has been the source of my greatest achievements, my lord, and I would consider it an honor to work for you again," he said. "What is it you ask of me?"

"It is too much to tell on this small evening, Bordeaux, but my scribe has put it all in writing. I knew you would come to me, and there are things only a man of your cunning can accomplish."

"I hope I can meet your expectations, my lord."

"I would not give you the obligation, if I did not think you could meet it. You are, after all, Gregory of Bordeaux, a man of rare and proven ability."

They bid one another good night, and Gregory found a spell of sleep right there in the hall on a pallet next to the fire. A manservant woke him shortly before dawn and told him the ship was ready. He stretched, yawned, and pissed in a pot. He went down on one knee, made the sign of the cross, and in the feint glow of the embers, read a penitent psalm from his Book of Hours. Collecting his belongings, he went down to the dock where a groom held Black Saddle by a tether. The ship bobbed alongside the pier, the moon bright in the sky, and out in the darkness over the sea, loomed Gregory's uncertain future. The earl and his priest met Gregory at the landing. They gave him a leather satchel, heavy with contents. Gregory pulled the strap over his shoulder, so it hung at his hip. He took hold of the tether and led Black Saddle up the gangplank and onto the ship. He would be on this creaking, groaning vessel for at least two weeks, if all went as planned. Its captain, a leathery sea dog with a ponytail and a thick, drooping mustache, gave a command and a rowboat, its crew bent over the oars, towed the ship out into the current of the River Test, which spilled into the turbulent channel.

"God bless and Godspeed," the earl said, calling to the departing vessel. "You will return to more than you have left."

"If it is God's will, then I shall," he replied.

The current caught the ship. A tremendous, sustained gust of wind tore down from the north to fill the canvas sail. Before Gregory appreciated the import of his departure, the hull was cutting through the cold waters. Spray spewed over the bow. Gregory held onto the rigging with one hand and onto his hat with the other, gazing into the vermillion dawn. He sailed to a place where it rarely snowed in the winter, where it was sultry in the summer, and where each autumn the grapes grew fat and ripe on the vine. Where the sun shone with a magical golden hue upon the long sandy beaches and the blue waters of its coast, and where the noble Pyrenees, their white caps gleaming in the sky, bristled on the southern horizon. To the great city at the bend in the great river, where the fine bells of St. André stirred the heart with their melodic peal. A land still scattered with the bleached bones of the ancient Roman Empire, of rolling green hills and walled bastides. A sumptuous place of goose liver terrine, Armagnac for the soul, charcuterie, pungent cheeses, and the divine red of Malbec. To the land of old Queen Eleanor and the troubadours, the artful outlaws, and the poetic warlords. He went to a place where his blood was in the soil of the centuries, where people knew the names of those who had come before him. A place he remembered from his earliest days and where he would be welcome in his time of trouble. Gregory, after a decade away, went back to Gascony and its splendid capital on the River Garonne. Going back home.

Going back to Bordeaux.

An
Unexpected
Arrest Warrant

rom Southampton the ship, a cog called the *Jonette,* sailed over the channel, stopping at St. Mathieu, Blavet, the Ille de Oléron, and La Rochelle. Hugging the shoreline of France as it cut southward, the *Jonette* passed cliffs and dunes, shanty towns and fish villages, watch towers and lighthouses. The Bay of Biscay, its tides alive with cresting whales and leaping dolphins, glittered silver-blue along the western horizon.

Gregory did not sail to Gascony as a cowering escapee hidden in the hold. He served as the shipmaster, the one who dealt with the inspectors and the toll takers at the ports-of-call all along the littoral. These were not cordial visits, but mandatory acquiesces to legal acts of extortion. Stop at the port and pay your duty, present your bill of lading, and show your letter of safe conduct, or risk being boarded by a ruthless crew that would ruin your commerce.

The *Jonette,* loaded with 70 tonnes of wheat and 30 tonnes of wool, its destination the port at Bordeaux. Simple enough. But Black Saddle, tethered below the deck, a rare and unexpected spoil, and when the inspectors discovered him, their interest in the horse could only be tempered with a smooth payoff straight from Gregory's hand into theirs. If paid willingly, then, so too, should it be accepted. To do otherwise was to court trouble, and of that it was certain. When the *Jonette* sailed into port, it did so with the Earl of Southampton's banner, a green field emblazoned with a gold boar, fluttering from atop the mast. Scowling, and with his arms crossed, Gregory, swathed in carrion black and peering out from beneath the brim of his beaver and peacock hat, stood watch from the after castle. His crewmen, all of them seasoned goons, armed with blades and with helms and mail, seemed eager to climb off their ship to pillage and loot. Indeed, when port officials saw the *Jonette* gliding through the mist, and Gregory caught their eye and gave a baleful nod, they made the sign of the cross and swallowed their portion of dread.

The *Jonette* had stores of hard biscuits, salted cod, dried pork and spiced ale. The crew cast nets and lines for anchovy, seabass and sole. In the hold, an oven and hearth, both of stone, and big cooking pots hung from hooks and chains. They made seafood stew, sopped up the succulent juice with crusts of white bread, and ate their plums and apples down to the pitted cores. Gregory bought a whole hog during one stop, and it roasted on the spit as the *Jonette*'s sail went taut with a southerly wind. Gregory spent almost all his time on deck, his eyes constantly scanning the coast and the surrounding waters for trouble. He slept in the after castle on a straw mattress with a feather quilt and a blanket of waterproofed canvas. When it came time to empty his bowels, he suffered the daily indignity of sitting on a board suspended over the side of the ship. He went down into the hold each day to check on and feed Black Saddle, and when he did, he covered his nose with a scrap of wool. The *Jonette*, nine years old, and the sickening stench of excrement and vomit, of urine and sweat, had seeped into the very bones of the bilge. Crawling with rats and haunted by dysentery, a den of squalor and creeping death, the ship's hold was the hell man had created. Yet, from its dark and slimy depths came the wealth that built cities and beguiled kings, and without the floating troves of cargo, man's higher ambitions would go unrealized.

Over the ocean, the days came and went, and at times, the *Jonette* seemed to be the only ship in the world, while at others, it sailed in a hodgepodge merchant fleet racing towards the riches of the Mediterranean. The Spanish and the Genoese, the Dutch and the Irish, all of them flying their flags, working their hulks and cogs and vying for the best place to throw their anchors. At night, singing and hard banter, and at dawn the mariners shrugged off the slosh and, once again, as terns and gulls circled overhead, did their best to conquer the sea. Gregory had not sailed in years and, in the first few days of the journey, went green with seasickness. But a tonic of pomegranate and chamomile revived him, and by the third day, he was fit enough to exert his authority over the crew. When, at the end of a fortnight, he saw the stone beacon at the entrance to the Gironde estuary, its flame flickering in the twilight, he turned to his crew and said, "Well done, lads."

At Royan, a pilot boarded and guided the *Jonette* down the Gironde to Blaye, and then into the River Garonne to Le Port de la Lune—Bordeaux—spilling out from a sweeping bend in the eternal wine river. The city had grown as dark and plump as the grapes that had brought Bordeaux its wealth. Its walls and towers stood guard while glimpses of stained glass twinkled like many watchful eyes. As old as Caesar, yet young in its wealth, Bordeaux was both wise and exuberant. The gem over which the kings of France and England warred, Bordeaux cared not for them but for the taxes and tolls on the bounty of the vines. Gregory, leaning on the starboard rail, looked up at the city looming over him as the *Jonette* was towed to the quay. He put on his hat, adjusted his belt, and made sure the groom held tight to Black Saddle's tether. He secured the satchel over his shoulder and under his arm and swallowed back a mixture of emotions. The place that had birthed him and that had given him his name accepted him back, but he did not know what she had in store for him. Divided with factions and strife, still bleeding from the war, and her heart jaded by the love of money, Bordeaux did not offer her bosom for solace.

A young clerk on the pier inspected the ship, collected the dockage fee, and checked Gregory's bill of lading. The clerk glanced up and cocked his brow.

"From Southampton, are you?" he asked.

"And in the service of its earl, Richard Beaufort," Gregory said, and gave the clerk an assertive look.

Weary from the voyage, he entered the city at Rouselle, found lodging at a squalid sailor's inn on Rue Maucoudinat near St. Pierre, and slept so soundly his fears and uncertainties were, for a time, forgotten. He awoke the next morning, washed his face and hands from a basin, and combed his tuft of hair. He went downstairs to the tavern, breaking his fast with watered wine and a handful of salted almonds. Sitting at a small, rickety table far from the fireplace, he scratched a note on a piece of parchment. He had a servant boy deliver it to his cousin, Jean du Mont. It didn't take long for the boy to return, excited and impatient, telling Gregory to come immediately to Jean du Mont's residence on the Rue de la Devise. Gregory could not contain his cheer. His cousin had moved to Bordeaux to stabilize the family business, and Gregory hadn't seen him in nearly three years. A confidant and father figure since Gregory's early teens, Jean du Mont, more than anyone, was the man with whom he shared his triumphs and failures. He slung the satchel over his shoulder, put on his hat, grabbed his pack, and followed the boy out the door and down a meandering street around tight corners to his cousin's house. When the door opened, Gregory walked past the butler and into the hall, scanning the room for his cousin. He sat at his great table, his parchments laid out in front of him, a candle burning, his hand near a quill and inkwell. A smile shone in the timeworn lines of his face.

"Ah, Gregory, you have finally returned," he said, as he pushed back his chair and stood. "You are as welcome a sight as the first green of spring."

"Dear cousin, three years has been too long," he said, dropping the satchel and pulling Jean into his arms. "You have grown old counting coins and casks, cousin, yet there is still much counting left to be done."

Jean motioned to a servant, who scurried off to the kitchen and buttery for food and drink. Jean took a long look at Gregory, and said, "Though I am happy to see you, your arrival here is a surprise."

"It is," he said. "So, let us sit and talk and I will tell you why I am here."

They convened at the table. The servant returned with bread, smoked sausage, ramekins of baked cheese, and a flagon of reek wine, wine from Marmande that had sat and matured on the lees, and poured them both a brimming cup. Gregory told his story—the reprisal of his enemies—and as he did, Jean shook his head, frowned, made the sign of the cross, and muttered expletives in support of Gregory's narrative. He felt uncomfortable at the beginning, telling his tale of woe so shortly after his arrival, but as he got into the meat of it, he embraced the delight of once again confiding in Jean.

Gregory sat tall in his chair, effected an expression of indulgent self-worth, and said, "I have wed Joan Costantyn, and if it is God's will, she will soon be heavy with our child."

"You have married Joan?" Jean said, a wise grin showing in his eyes.

"Yes—we married for contracts and coins—"

"—And you married for something else, too," Jean said, and took a sip of wine. "She may have been a widow, but a young widow, and from the time you returned from your travels, I could see it in her—you had grown in her esteem. Your rivals have tried to destroy you, but much good has come of your troubles."

"What is your estimation of Joan?" Gregory said.

"You have made a fine choice," he replied. "Joan is among the best of us."

"It is good to hear you say that, dear cousin. And it is good to be here with you."

"Oh, Gregory, your presence makes me happy," Jean said, and they raised their cups of Marmande.

Jean arranged for Gregory to stay in an apartment on Rue Porte Dijeaux, deep in the city, far from the meddling and claptrap of the waterfront. From the broad solar window on the top floor he had a wonderful view of the sculpted spires of Cathedral St. André, and if he leaned out of the window just a bit and looked to his right, could spy the heights of the grand ruins of the old Roman temple, Les Piliers de Tutelle, looking over the port. Save for the ringing of the bells, a splendid peal that bequeathed dignity to the hours, this was a quiet neighborhood—if there was such a thing in Bordeaux—

where churchmen and the wealthy found respite from the city's obsession with the corrupt, alluring wine trade.

Servants cleaned out the home, trapped the rats, fired the hearth, and lit the kitchen. Porters hauled in a large table and brought it up to the solar. Over the table was draped a Persian rug, its weave alive with a soothing hue of blue and gold with accents of oxblood and pistachio. A geometric bonanza of balance, the carpet filled the room with its aura of exotic tranquility. Added to that, a podium for manuscripts, a chair with cushions upholstered in deer skin, and a brass candelabrum with a dozen holders, enough to fill the room with light even on the darkest of nights.

As was his way, Gregory stood at the center of it all, pointing here and there, deciding one way and then the next, saying right and then wrong, until everything seemed situated to his liking. When seated at the table, he could see the tiled rooftops of the city, and catch the orange and magenta as the sun came and went. On one side, the podium and ink well, and on the other, the candelabrum and space for his parchments. He took a seat, propped his elbows on the table, and rested his chin on his clasped hands. A pair of house sparrows landed on the window sill and went busy with chirping before flittering away. If only so easy. Here I am in Bordeaux, and I cannot fly home.

The satchel given to him by the earl sat on the floor next to the chair. Gregory looked down at it. The contents would change his life, he knew, but as of late, he wearied of change. He grabbed it, put it on the table, untied the knot and undid the buckle. He pulled back the flap, looked inside, reached in and grabbed a package wrapped in waxed leather. He sat it on the table, and as he sighed through his nose, broke the seal. The parchments were so tightly bound they sprung out when Gregory untied the strap, and there before him, like a locust climbing out of its shell, a sheaf of scrolls. Each of them numbered, meant to be read in sequence.

He sequestered himself in that room for a week. As he sat at the table, or paced across the floor, or leaned on the window sill, or stood at the podium, he explored the untamed world that bucked and bristled within the many leaves of parchment. These were the guts of Gascony, the known feuds and the nasty secrets of the old wine duchy. With its cities, castles, and rolling hills planted with vines, Gascony endured as the object of desire by rival lords and kings, and silver and promises flowed as swiftly as its many streams and rivers. From Bayonne to Blaye and from Bordeaux to the Brulhois, men spoke with two tongues, in one instance saying the sky was blue, and if it pleased them with profit, then saying it was green. The ineptitude of the king's seneschal, the bickering of the towns, and the shifting loyalties of the border nobles, made of Gascony a furnace white-hot with turmoil. As Gregory read his way through these parchments, tracing each line of text with an index finger, he took notes of his own, pulling out names and places and condensing them into a list.

He looked up from the parchments and took a sip of Marmande. The sun setting on the city, its stone and tile alight in a pale autumn wash. A bank of leaden clouds hung in the southern sky, and up from the street came the click and clack of a horse and the creaking of the wagon it pulled. Gregory held up the list and read through the names. Not a roster of friends and family, but of rivals and enemies, and of places where dark deeds needed to be done. Southampton's list, and in the fog of foreboding rolling in with that realization, Gregory knew he was obligated as the designee, that this was now his list over which to toil. One name in particular—Alphonse of Bayonne—leapt out at him, written in red on the original parchment. He dug back through the ream and found nothing, but then, as the hair on his arms stood on end, and as the caw of a hungry crow echoed in his soul, he noticed something in the bottom of the satchel he had somehow missed before. A warrant, folded in a square and bearing the great tassel and seal of King Edward. Terrifying, the orb and the scepter, alone and brooding as if it demanded its own space. Gregory took out the warrant, held it close to the candelabrum, and turned it in his hands. On the backside, a cryptic message—Alphonse of Bayonne, felon, reprobate, and resident of the gallows.

Gregory went back to the parchments, tracing through them until he found Alphonse's name. He held Castelnaud, a fortress out in the hinterlands high above a bend in the Dordogne River. One of the easternmost outposts of King Edward's province, the counterweight to Beynac, King Philip the Fair's fortress on the other side of the river. But Alphonse of Bayonne had shirked his duties during the most recent conflict with France and counted his coins as French troops stormed through his territory unchallenged. Treason, a sentence of death—but he had first to be arrested.

With his arms wrapped across his chest and his head tilted in thought, Gregory paced across the room, pondering the circumstances. An arrest warrant? *What am I to do?* He took another sip of Marmande and set the cup on the windowsill.

His work was not in Bordeaux. And since arriving here, he had realized this was no longer his town. His namesake, yes, and God willing, the ongoing source of his trade, but he had no place here, nor did he want it. He remained a Londoner, his blood the River Thames, his flesh the Home Counties. The thought saddened him, giving up one place for another. *But in a life, there are many forks in the road, and of those I have already taken a few,* he mused. Still, Bordeaux had all he needed. A bustling market and a teeming port, a district of haberdasheries and tailors, of cobblers and perfumers, a public lane to laugh and gossip, and a fine cathedral to shed one's sins. Indeed, the city did not disappoint. If anything, her beauty had only grown. But she was not his to admire, and his business—the warrant for Alphonse's arrest—could not be served from his apartment on Rue Porte Dijeaux.

Jean du Mont accompanied him to the stables, where they talked as a groom dressed Black Saddle in his gear.

"Your stay was too short," his cousin said. "You leave just as soon as I got used to having you here."

"Forgive me my haste, dear cousin, but a rattle in my bones tells me I must leave," he said. "I felt it when I first stepped off the boat. Bordeaux does not want me here. Even as I am a hunted man, I also hunt another. My work is out there in Gascony."

"I know you must leave, but upon your return home, please, depart from here so we can see each other again," Jean said.

"That is a promise, dear cousin," he replied.

"Go see your uncles Hugo and Helias. They asked about you last year during Christmas. It would please them if you visited them in La Réole. As you said, even if you serve the Earl of Southampton, you must also serve yourself."

"Yes, and there is much wine to ship back home," he said.

They hugged and kissed on each cheek and looked long into each other's eyes. The groom arrived with Black Saddle. Gregory planted his boot in the stirrup and mounted the splendid courser. He looked down at Jean and smiled.

"I don't know when, but I will knock on your door again."

"I will be waiting," Jean said

UNCLES
HUGO AND HELIAS
OF LA RÈOLE

He rode down the left bank of the River Garonne, through Podensac, Barsac, Preignac, over the bridge at Langon to St. Macaire, and onward to La Réole, the august seat of the du Mont family trust. So named, du Mont, because, according to family lore, Gregory's great-great grandfather, himself named Gregory, had worked the cargo barges along the rivers. One year a flood capsized him, but fisherman plucked him from the churning waters at La Réole. He remained in the town where he had been rescued. The locals there took a liking to the earnest kid, and they called him Gregory of St. Croix du Mont, after the village of his birth. In time the surname shortened to du Mont, and thus the family lineage in this ancient town nestled deep in the bosom of Gascony. Both of Gregory's parents, Henri and Herleve, were also from there, though they had matriculated to Bordeaux early on. Gregory had never been to La Réole, the place where his name had been born. So as the miles passed by, and as those he met along the way told him the town was near, his mood improved.

The farms where he stopped to water his horse, plump and tidy, the people hospitable, and the aromas wafting from the spits and kitchens down-right tantalizing. Shady groves gave way to manicured orchards, golden wheat and green waters jumping with trout. This was the Gascony he had hoped to see, and the one from which he was proud his family had come, a bountiful land, a beautiful land, simple and wise, in control of its ways.

At last the city came into view. Ditches, stout walls and corbeled towers girdled La Réole. The barbican, a stone fist jutting out from the main gate, held the draw bridge in its protective grasp. Murder holes, machicolations, a port-cullis, and turrets completed the foreboding silhouette of *Château des Quat'Sos*. For those on the outside trying to break in, it was a death trap, but on this day a peaceful place. A bell rang at the church of St. Peter. The gate was wide open. Wisps of smoke from benevolent fires feathered into the sunny blue sky, and vineyard rows climbed the hills to the east. Peasants worked the fields, a horse-drawn wagon rolled down the road, and kids played at the water's edge. Black Saddle responded to his master's excitement, lurching into a powerful can-ter, pounding down the road, through the arched barbican, across the bridge, through the gate, and into the bustling town.

He stabled his horse, and with his pack slung over his shoulder, walked to the town hall. Inside a young clerk sat behind a large desk, piled high with stacks and stacks of neatly sorted parchments. He looked up from his work, stabbed his quill into the inkwell, and asked, "Your business, please?"

"I am Gregory du Mont," he said, discreetly, but with enough weight to amply suggest he was no ordinary visitor.

"Du Mont," the clerk said. "A common enough name in these parts."

"By God's grace it is," Gregory said. "And I had hoped to seek audience with those of that name who still live in La Réole."

The clerk laughed.

"That will not be hard to do," he said. "One of the du Monts, Hugo, is on the town council, and you cannot go to market without stepping on the toes of yet more of them."

Gregory, of course, knew that name well. For nigh three decades, Hugo and his older brother Helias had presided over this end of the family business, and through contract and the twice-a-year letters, he had known of them since the time he could remember. He had only come to the town hall to clothe his visit with the mantle of legitimacy, to put himself at the feet of the city's dominion, lest he break a rule of protocol—Hugo's protocol, in particular—of which he was unaware.

"Send a messenger to wherever Hugo may be," Gregory said. "And have the messenger tell him I seek an audience."

A boy in official city garb soon sprinted away, and the clerk hunched back over his document and went to work. Gregory stepped outside, leaned against a column and took a deep breath. The town smelled clean, a welcome rarity, and in the steeps and broad lengths of the Benedictine priory, around which La Réole had grown and prospered, he found an abiding cheer. The market arcade, its arches festooned with a kaleidoscope of textiles, hummed with the chatter of seasoned traders. And if the clerk had told the truth, at least some of those merchants were kin. The thought of it brought a smile to Gregory's face, and for a good long while, he savored the presence of an infrequent visitor—comfort.

The boy returned, a spring in his step and exuberant.

"Master Gregory of London," he said, bowing and holding out his arms. "Hugo and Helias welcome you with full hospitality and request your presence forthwith."

Gregory pulled a half denier from his pouch and handed it to the boy. "Take me to them. But do not run, for you are much faster than I."

The two of them walked through the labyrinth of the city, its narrow streets dark between the tall half-timbered houses, their sheer gabled roofs crowding out the sun. They turned down a damp lane, and then down another, finally arriving at a bright and leafy courtyard. At the far end sat two houses, joined at the hip, and in the simple quality of their construction, they conveyed an undeniable opulence. The front door to one of the houses came open, and household servants filed out, forming lines on either side. Not long thereafter a man appeared at the door, an older man with a balding pate, a silver beard, and a sage twinkle in his eyes. Tall enough, but on balance, pleasantly rotund, dressed in a luxuriant belt and green robe, with accents of silk and fur, of shiny metals and stones, he commanded the court-yard with his easy largesse. A heartening grin didn't so much as show in his face, but emitted from his entirety, a gladsome longing polished by the vicis-situdes of time. Humbled by this gush of familial love, Gregory removed his hat and stood subservient and respectful, as a son stands before his father. Though he had never been to this town, and though he had never seen this man, Gregory had no doubt of his identity. Before him stood his great uncle, Hugo du Mont, the wine prince of La Réole.

"Nephew, we must feed you, for as thin as you are, you must be starving," he said, and laughed.

Though his servants were formally arrayed, a ripple of mirth spread through them, and even Gregory bent and chuckled.

"I will surely accept your offer, Uncle," Gregory said. "But I must warn you. Every time I eat, I become hungry all over again."

They greeted each other in the standard way, a light embrace and a kiss on each check. And then they fell into a real hug, a hearty affair, chest to chest, unabashed in their elation, the two of them burrowing down into the warm den of home.

Hugo placed his hands on Gregory's shoulders and looked him in the eye. "Come inside, nephew. Helias is anxious to see you."

They stepped into the main chamber, an intimate space with a low-slung ceiling, deluxe furnishings, lit in some areas with candles, and in others, by sunrays flooding in through arched windows. Gregory was not sure of the fragrance filling the room, fresh and resplendent, and in it he found serenity. Following Hugo at a respectful distance, he stepped deeper into the room, increasingly awed by the sheer value of the surroundings. Wall hangings and exotic furs, Oriental rugs and statuary, all of it forming a resplendent whole in this stout room of finished stone and timber. Along with Hugo, he stopped in the middle of the room, before the great table, and beheld the man sitting alone at one end. Stooped and silent, yet old and proud, was He-lias, bathed in a shard of light.

"Helias, look who has come to visit." Hugo said. "Young Gregory from London, and by the looks of him, he has grown into a fine man."

Helias raised a hand, and despite a face slackened by malady, and despite the trouble it took for him to do so, he managed a crooked smile.

Gregory bowed low, sweeping his arm in a graceful downward arc.

"Uncle Helias." His voice nearly cracked. "It is an honor to meet you."

Helias held out a feeble hand, and Gregory took it in his. The oldest living member of the family, Helias, more than anyone, was the source of the du Mont ascendency. The big brother, the angry uncle, he was the one who had bent Gregory's father over his knee and spanked his rear when he had done wrong. Helias, the fearless one who had trudged into the hinterlands of Gascony, sealing contracts with unknown vintners, lording over the riverfront each fall and spring, and pressing his claims against all until his will was written into the city charter. And here he rested, not long for the world and just about beaten by it, gazing up at Gregory, one of his finest achievements. Try as he might, Gregory could not withstand the weight of this moment, and he cried. He collected himself soon enough, drying his eyes on the sleeve of his robe.

"Taken by 'the pull' about a year ago," Hugo said. "Perhaps it is best you shed a tear but do so no more. The sight of you will keep him happy until his final day."

At Hugo's insistence, Gregory retired to a private chamber, where he shed his hat and cloak, his boots, robe, and breeches. He bathed in a wooden tub of warm water and reclined in bliss as a servant sopped his neck and face with pig fat and potash and shaved him clean. At Gregory's request, he sheared high up the back of the neck and high up over the ears, and when he was done, the servant applied a hot towel. So pampered, Gregory dressed in a soft green robe and belt, a pair of pointed shoes—poulaines—and a mantle lined with deer fur. He donned a *chaperon*, the *patte* and *cornette* tied together, thus forming a turban-like piece of headgear. So attired and refreshed, he returned to the main chamber, joining Hugo and Helias at the table. A servant poured him a cup of wine, and before he took his first sip, Hugo smiled and said, "This is a *Sainte-Bazeille*, and it sits well on the lees."

Gregory took a drink, smitten by the maturity of the wine. Indeed, it had sat on the lees, but that had only made it better.

"I have not had this before." He held out the cup in a show of approval.

"Because it rarely makes it past Bordeaux," Hugo said. "But that could soon change. We are in talks with the maker, and if all goes well, some of the next vintage will ship to London."

"*C'est bon,*" he said. "This will fetch a high price back home."

"That is the hope," Hugo said. "But we will talk business later. Tell us, what has brought you to Gascony?"

Gregory took another drink of *Sainte-Bazeille*, gave a weary smile, and sighed for effect.

"I was banned from England for two years," he said. "So, I came here to sit out my sentence."

"Banned?"

"Wine is not all I do in London, Uncle Hugo. I am also a chronicler, and it seems my writings scratched the wrong people in the wrong places."

"To the point that they banned you?"

"Yes," he said. "Lords, the church, other merchants. My quill has made me many enemies."

Hugo turned to his brother and said, "What do you think, Helias?"

Old Helias beat his fist against the table as his eyes sparkled mischievous and bright. He could only grunt and drivel, but within the infantile gestures of his ailment, he conveyed his appreciation for what Gregory had said. And that's when he realized this was the story his uncles wanted to hear. Business and wine, contracts and negotiations—compared to Hugo and Helias, Gregory remained yet an apprentice. But neither of them had ridden roughshod through England, and neither of them consorted with earls, or insulted bishops, or had criminals hanged from the gallows. So, he told them of the chronicle, going back to that time of naiveté, when he found himself to be more than what he thought he was, and when he learned the most valuable lesson of all—to sit still is to perish. He spoke of Warren and of Southampton, and of Moonbeam and Black Saddle. He told of Margery and Lord Corby, and of Swinton the Red and his vile tower. As they dined on duck, goat cheese, bread and goose terrine, poached fish, and a dessert of baked plums, they emptied the tankard of Sainte-Bazeille, and emptied another, besides. Daytime turned into night, firelight flooded the room, and just before the besotting had gotten the better of him, Gregory knew he had regaled his uncles with stories only he could tell.

"Nephew, you have lived a fascinating life, and it is good your choices brought you here to us," Hugo said. "Here in La Réole, the du Monts aren't quite what they used to be. There are new families who threaten our position. Yet it is nice to know our blood still runs thick in London."

"And thicker still," Gregory said. "I have recently married, Joan Costantyn is her name, and God willing, I shall soon have an heir. At one time, I thought about quitting the wine trade. I wanted to dissolve my business and try a new endeavor. But worry not, for that was long ago. I have since committed myself to doing what the family has always done, and to do it until the day I die."

"Spoken like a true du Mont!" Hugo poured another cup of wine.

Hugo leaned in with both elbows propped on the table, his face set with a stern expression of query. Gone was the grin, the rolling eyes of merriment, and the easy nods of rapport. All of it replaced by the searching scrutiny of a revered and powerful merchant. The change in mood startled Gregory. He set his cup down, cocked his head with concern, put a finger to his lip, and said, "Uncle Hugo, what is wrong?"

"Oh, nothing is wrong," he said. "But I have guessed you did not come here just to see your uncles. Did you?"

"Whatever do you mean?" he said. "For the sake of clarity, don't hint at it, Uncle Hugo. Say it."

"The contract we had with your father... it dies with you, his heir, does it not?"

"Indeed, by contract my father was entitled to the right of first refusal on all wines exported out of La Réole by the du Mont company, of which you and Helias are the guarantors. And indeed, I inherited that contract as heir. But as you say, the contract dies with me because there is no process for perpetuity."

"I forget you are a lawyer," he said.

"Uncle Hugo, that is not the only reason I am here," he said, in a pleading voice. "But I cannot sit here and lie to you at your own table. I had hoped to at least discuss the contract."

To Gregory's immense relief, his comment broke the spell. Hugo leaned back in his chair and laughed so hard Helias awoke from his slumped and snoring sleep.

"Did you hear that, Helias?" Hugo said. "Our nephew did not really come here to see us. He came to discuss the contract."

Gregory looked at Helias, and to his surprise detected a smile in his misshapen face. Half drunk, overcome with fatigue, and in a new and beguiling place, Gregory felt confused. In one moment he thought he had given offense, yet in another it appeared he had made them happy. He held out his hands, his face contorted with puzzlement, and said, "What have I done?"

"Nephew, when you look at me and Helias, what do you see?" Hugo asked.

Gregory made as if to speak, but Hugo waved him off.

"You see two old men, perhaps wealthy, and perhaps surrounded by comforts, but you see two old men at the end of their time," he said.

"But that is not—"

"—Yes, it is," he said. "Nephew, for years we have waited for you to come. We wanted to see you with our own eyes, and now that you are here, I can say it with all sincerity. You are a prince. A London prince. And if Helias could talk, he would say the same."

"Uncle Hugo, I still do not understand your point."

"The contract you have through your father—we are not concerned with that," he said. "We want to bequeath to you the very permit under which we do business here in La Réole. We want you to have it, and in turn you can assign it to your heir."

Though his modesty was real, the thought of such an asset triggered in him an eruption of fantastic silver dreams. Gregory obtained wine from other places, but La Réole was the wellspring. Tonne after tonne floated by barge up the Garonne from the hinterlands—Auvillar, Layrac, Villefranche-de-Queryan, Caumont, and many more besides. Some of it was deemed better than others, but all of it good, all of it craved by the thirsty hordes back in London. Indeed, to control the permit for the du Mont company was to control one's destiny, and perhaps even the destiny of others.

"Uncle Hugo, I am not sure I can accept such a gift," he said.

"But the decision is not yours to make."

"Surely there are others more deserving."

"Maybe, but only one of them sailed over the sea to take the claim," Hugo said, and put a soft hand on Gregory's shoulder.

Gregory remained in La Réole for a fortnight. During the day he met with his new associates, asking them all about the wine trade along the Garonne. He looked for instant connections, and found them in the watermen, the porters, in the merchants, and at the town hall, as if this role was always meant for him, and now that he was here, all he needed fell into place. Hugo, of course, stood always at his side, and one day, Helias, bent and leaning on a cane, appeared in a show of force at the market square.

In the afternoon he sat at the big table with his uncles, and after eating, would sip wine and pore over all the old bills so he knew from whence the wine came, when it arrived, to where it went, in what quantity, and how tallied and taxed along the way. All the while, Hugo told him stories about the family, stories about people he had never met. But all of it pleased him, strengthened him, and as the two weeks melted away, as he feasted on the bounty of La Réole, and as curious visitors came and went, Gregory found himself anew.

When the day of departure came, a groom arrived in the courtyard leading Black Saddle by a tether. Gregory did not want to leave, yet it thrilled him to see his great stallion rigged in tack and saddle, well fed, rested and eager to run.

"So, that is how you do it?" Hugo asked.

Gregory laughed. "It is not possible without him."

A sudden sadness overcame him, nothing left to say but farewell. He embraced old Helias and kissed him on both cheeks and the forehead. A full head taller than this man, shriveled and shrunken by the forces of life, Gregory looked down at him and smiled.

"The wine will flow as it always has, Uncle Helias," he said, and Helias grunted and growled with assent.

He turned to Hugo.

"You have a distant cousin at the priory of Mont de Marsan," his uncle said. "His name is Maynart, and he is the *infermerer* there. If I should hear of anything you might need to know, I will send a message to him. If you are ever around that way, it might be to your benefit to go there and speak with him."

"Mont de Marsan?" Gregory said, and thought about all his errands and deeds. "Yes, I should be out that way in a year or so... thank you for everything, Uncle Hugo. I will see you again, and we will make good as we have these last two weeks."

The two embraced.

Gregory put his foot in the stirrup, took hold of the pommel, and pulled himself up into the saddle. For the sake of theater, he reared the great Arabian, and then sent him trotting in a wide circle, Black Saddle snorting, whinnying, and tossing his mane. Gregory pulled him to a halt, and with his wicked look of the road, peered back at his uncles, and said, "To La Réole! To the du Mont family name!"

He rode east out of the city, into the verdant Gascon countryside. The River Garonne glittered green in the morning light, and somewhere out there his next stop, Miramont. In due time, Gregory would begin his work for the Earl of Southampton—the book, the debt, and Alphonse of Bayonne—but as the head of the du Mont company, he first had work to do for himself.

THE
WINE PRESS
AT MIRAMONT

regory rode into Miramont on one of those sunny autumn days in Gascony—a trace of chill with the morning fog, the fog giving way to blue skies, the assurance of the harvest heavy in the air, a confidence so complete even the doomsayers found reason for hope. Along the gentle hills rolling out in all directions, appeared endless rows of vines, their leaves flecked with orange and gold, their grapes nearly black with ripeness. The abundant harvest was everywhere, the wheat, gold, the tiny gardens behind each home, green with yield, and the hogs fit for slaughter. Miramont, a town of stone with a wall and a church and a market square lined with arcades, like many other towns dotting the landscape of Gascony, hummed busily with work, hungry for self-importance, and earnest in the making of its name.

What made Miramont special was its deep and bold vintage that not only touched the soul but filled it with harmony. Favored by ecclesiastics, nobles and merchant princes, the wine of Miramont always fetched a high price on the quay at Bordeaux. But due to the war and the arcane deeps of the law, all its wine had been forcibly sold to the French for a decade, so none of it made its way to Bordeaux, to be loaded on the Easter fleet. During the war years, while under writ and decree, a mystique grew up around the wine of Miramont. During its absence from the English market, its value increased. But the war was over, at least for now, and this year, Miramont's wine was once again available for sale. That's why Gregory was there. Uncle Hugo had told him to buy all Miramont's vintage and have it shipped back to La Réole and, eventually, to London, where wife Joan would turn the profit. He knew he would have to compete with other merchants, but as head of the du Mont company, he knew he would be hard to outbid.

The peasants made small wine out of their garden grapes before they had fully ripened. It tasted of dreck and not fit for commerce, but it served its purpose—to prime thirsty gullets in anticipation of the real harvest. The town was drunk and giddy on it by the time Gregory arrived at the tavern, aglow with a fire and crowded with all walks of life, a tumult of music, dance, and laughter. Gregory inched through the gathering and found a spot near the fire. Like everyone else, he quaffed from a brimming cup. The short wine, acid on his tongue, burnt going down, but drinkable nonetheless. The conclusion of a joke arrived with a raucous crescendo, and as the wench filled his cup yet again, Gregory felt the wash of sweet inebriation flowing over him.

A woman in a blue robe, her silver hair interwoven with a tiara of leafy vine stems, stood on a table next to the one where Gregory sat. In one hand she held a cluster of grapes and in the other a pruning sheer. With a simple glance of her wise eyes, looking from one end of the room to the other, the tavern fell silent. With nary a word of introduction, and accompanied by drum, pipe, and lute, she sang. Her voice started in a tempting whisper but grew into a contralto with a chest note so round and determined, yet so light and effortless, that when it rang at full timbre it surpassed the vocals of even the haloed angels. Her arms outstretched in exalted grace, her bosom heaving with an exquisite tremor, the peasants gathered and listened to her tale.

The sun, the moon, the stars at night
We live the vine at harvest time
When birds return to fill the trees
When ships set sail across the sea
The grapes come green to trellis home
Another year of toil and cheer

Falling down her back, her locks
The early years turn golden clear
Pots and pans and fire bright
She cooks and serves the gift of light
She milks the goat and plucks the fowl
Begins the day that never ends

Axe to wood and sweat of brow
The net, the trap he daily sets
Crystal well, stone and thatch
He and hound the hare they catch
Build the boat, man the oars
Life is work, the sharpened knife

Steal away behind the barn
Alone in love the turtle doves
Beget with child, a boy and girl
A ruby dawn across the world
At the hearth and in the fields
A family grown of blood and bone

The prince at war the army called
He sheds a tear and hoists his spear
The battle fought and there he fell
A mournful peal, the village bell

A mother, a daughter, a cheated son
The rain and wind, unyielding pain

The sun, the moon, the stars at night
We live the vine at harvest time
When birds return to fill the trees
When ships set sail across the sea
The grapes come green to trellis home
Another year of toil and cheer

The ballad ended as the butterfly lands on the wildflower, with the delicate flutter of shimmering wings. Gregory wiped a tear from his eye, and with his spirits invigorated by the hopeful melancholy of her song, knew his stay in Miramont would somehow be of consequence.

Seigneur Miramont owned the wine press, a hulking contraption hewn and shaped from an entire oak. A screw gear that took two men to turn and housed in a three-sided stone enclosure with a soaring timber roof. Baskets and vats, barrels and a basin, the wine press stood as the rustic monument of commerce in this little town. As large and imposing as a siege engine, the press creaked to life each autumn, squeezing out the precious juice of life. *Seigneur* Miramont was the fourth *Seigneur* in the family line to hold the rights to the press, legitimized by a charter signed by a lawyer up at the royal court in Paris. And what a charter it was, meticulous in its wording, authoritative with intent, its beige parchment adorned with a seal and blue tassel. He sat near the press during harvest time, high and proud in his cushioned chair carved with eagles and hounds. He watched the peasants and townsmen arrive with their grapes, make their must, and leave with their wine, the charter rolled and ever in his hand.

For the privilege of using his press, the locals gave *Seigneur* Miramont a portion of their yield—and by law harvested his domain for free—so no one ever produced as much as he and, of course, no one ever matched his profit. Those who actually worked the fields laughed behind his back and said, "It is funny how he who does the least somehow claims the most. We know how to stoop and work in the sun, but perhaps we should learn how to sit and do nothing in the shade." *Seigneur* Miramont knew they chided him, and it bothered him, but he did not let on. His charter, and the security it engendered, had never been challenged. And this year, the winds had blown as happy gossip, the sun had shone with the mercy of God, and the rains had come as tears of compassion, blessing the vineyards with plump and plenty. Indeed, *Seigneur* Miramont sat high and tall in his chair, watching the juice bleed out into bulging hooped casks.

Seigneur Miramont did not sit alone. Men-at-arms with blades and cross-bows flanked him, and a clerk, smug and seated at a desk with his quill and parchments, recorded every transaction. The men who operated the press, *Seigneur* Miramont's men, knew exactly when to crush the grapes and how to apply just the right amount of pressure so the juice came out full and flavorful, but not overly sharp with tannins. Since he owned all the barrels, marked with his insignia—a cross and a cask—the reputation for quality was his. His men and machines produced a prestigious label, and though he did none of the work, he was known as a master maker.

But this fall, a strange tension pulled at *Seigneur* Miramont's otherwise routine annual rite. Gregory had heard all about it the night before at the tavern. When the woman had finished her soulful singing, and after Gregory had bought everyone a round of small wine, the locals treated Gregory to a hot helping of village hearsay. Gilbert le Blanc, they told him, was a local winegrower who had run afoul of Miramont's authority. Years ago, he had built his own winepress with the hopes of making his own vintage—and cutting Miramont out of the tally. But before the wine was made, Miramont confirmed his jurisdiction, obtained a restraining order, seized le Blanc's press, and had it destroyed. He had also levied a penalty in which le Blanc was forbidden from using Miramont's press for a full four years, a sentence that had reduced le Blanc to poverty. But, the locals said to Gregory, le Blanc had managed to survive, doing this and that to keep a roof over his head, shoes on his feet, and food in his belly. And now, four years later and at the end of a great season, he had three large carts piled high with baskets of grapes. Even with a full house, the roof still leaked, so to speak, the locals told Gregory, with one of them saying, in a cryptic sotto voce, "There will be trouble on the morrow."

Gregory sat on the rim of the town well, watching the villagers come with their grapes and leave with their must. Were it not for Miramont's greedy gaze and his cadre of armed retainers, Gregory thought, this would have been a pleasant day. But wine is too valuable for innocence, and besides, I am not here for pleasantries.

Le Blanc, amiable throughout the day as he waited in line, at last found himself at the front of the queue. Gregory stood up, straightened his robe, and moved a few steps closer.

"*Seigneur* Miramont," le Blanc said, and bowed. "'Tis a year given to us by God, for all of us will count our casks and coin this time."

Seigneur Miramont looked at his clerk. They shared a nasty, deviant little grin. The clerk turned in his seat to a podium behind him, where sat a stack of parchments underneath a small iron weight. He lifted the weight, thumbed through the parchments, and with an exaggerated and sarcastic gesture of relief, pulled a parchment from the pile. At the sight of the parchment, and of the clerk's chiding eyes as he set it on the desk, le Blanc stopped, his shoulders slumped, his hope seeming to vanish in a bleak cloud of doubt.

"Gilbert," the clerk said, "you are right in that this will be a most favorable vintage. Our dear priest was diligent in his prayers, and it seems all of us have been rewarded for his earnest work at the chapel. But here in my hand I have the bill, written and witnessed four years ago, that outlines the terms of your punishment for defying *Seigneur* Miramont. And according to the terms, you are not to use the wine press until the day after the Feast of St. Michael. As you know, that is not until the twelfth day of November. But here you stand, in October, ready to press your yield."

"But four years has gone," le Blanc said, his voice pleading for sympathy. *"Seigneur* Miramont assured me that in the fourth year, the agreement was null and void."

"I told you no such thing," Miramont said, leaning forward in his chair, gripping the arms with his bony hands. "You rebelled against me years ago. Do you rebel against me now?"

"No, *Seigneur,"* he said. "But I met the terms of my punishment, and now it is time to make my wine."

"No," Miramont said. "You were not to use the press until after the feast of St. Michael!"

"But my grapes would have withered on the vine by then," he said.

"Then you should have waited until next year, Gilbert," the clerk said. "In your haste to make a triumphant return, it seems you have arrived early to an ambush of your own making."

"So, you will not let me use the press?" he asked. "What if I give you double the normal fee?"

"I am in no need of an enhanced fee," Miramont said. "I am here to enforce the terms of our agreement and will be content to do that and only that."

Le Blanc looked around at the villagers who had gathered to watch the confrontation. None of them looked back at him. Indeed, they stared at their feet or over their shoulders, or up into the blue autumn sky, anything but to empathize with the target of *Seigneur* Miramont's ire. Le Blanc shook his head, and as he searched the crowd for support, angry embarrassment showed in his face. Gregory was sure le Blanc had seen this moment in his head many times yet had never identified himself as the fool. But here he was, trying in vain to find encouragement in the blank faces of the villagers as Miramont and his clerk, both jolly and snide, watched from their seats of power.

Gregory pitied le Blanc, who in his patience had not been patient enough, and who had trusted a man's word even when his letters said otherwise. Gregory knew he should say nothing and that this confrontation, between a cheap local lord and a reckless townsman, should be allowed to play out with him speaking nary a word. But holding his tongue was not Gregory's way, and, he reasoned, he had a stake in the outcome of this squabble. In his satchel he had a bill of sale. Here to purchase the entirety of Miramont's vintage, and once the bill was signed, and once the wine had been taken by barge down the River Dropt to the Garonne and into Bordeaux, many livres would flow into Miramont's hands. He took a long look at le Blanc, who even in his distress showed the rugged cut of an honest man. His big feet and breeches, his apron and cap and thick calloused hands—he himself a vine grown strong in this turbulent land. And as he stood there, alone and imperiled and ignored by those he thought would rally around him, he exuded a goodness Gregory could not forsake.

"*Bonjour, Seigneur* Miramont," Gregory doffed his hat and bowed. "Please excuse me for interrupting at such an inconvenient time, for I know how important it is to meet the terms of a contract. But I have a contract of my own, and perhaps we can negotiate an agreement that will be to your liking."

Miramont turned in his chair and glanced at Gregory, the lord old and thin, his face a landscape defined by a long nose inflamed with rosacea, high knobby cheeks speckled with age spots, and a pointed chin adorned with a scar and a mole. His green eyes were remarkable, ponds in need of rain, his brows coming together in a bristling caterpillar of reeds. Difficult to tell if he were closer to life or to death, but a full set of teeth he had, and with those teeth he summoned a frown of frightening vigor. Draped in a mauve robe and glittering with old ornaments of turned silver set with stones and crowned by the rich folds of his feathered chaperon, no doubt a lord with much to flaunt as he sat in his country throne. His clerk, as young and handsome as the lord was timeworn and hideous, rose from his chair, quill in one hand, and with the other, gestured in Gregory's direction.

"Who is it who bothers my lord when he is meting out justice?" he asked, in the haughty tone of a man trying both to impress and to intimidate.

To Gregory, the clerk appeared nothing more than a prig, a man he had seen and scolded countless times on the waterfront back in London. He relinquished no poise as he looked at the clerk, then at the scowling men-at-arms, and then at Miramont himself, and said, "I am Gregory du Mont, a wine merchant of Bordeaux and La Réole, and I am trying to fill a ship bound for the Easter market at London. I was told the wine of Miramont was the best, and I am anxious to conclude a sale. But you must know—I am here to buy all your wine, not some of it."

The clerk made as if to speak, but Miramont silenced him with a stare. Cocking his eye at Gregory, he said, "And what do you mean by all of it?"

"*Seigneur* Miramont, I did not come all the way from Bordeaux only to buy a portion of the vintage," he said. "I will make you an offer, and at a premium, but only if you include the yield produced by Gilbert le Blanc. If you relent in your punishment of him, it would be to the benefit of all."

With his old arms propped on his knees, Lord Miramont leaned forward in his chair, collecting his strength, and voiced his displeasure with a cough and a sigh, as he pushed himself up and stood. Hunchbacked, gimp-legged and with a hand deformed by arthritis, time had left a contorted rod of a man. But he wore the ring and robe of lordship, so as he rose, the villagers bowed—but not Gregory. Instead, he donned his hat, crossed his arms over his chest, and remained square and motionless as the afternoon breeze kissed the back of his shaven neck. He and Gregory traded gazes as the throng of townsfolk, peeking up even as they cowered, murmured and gasped. The old lord put a hand on his clerk's shoulder for balance, and once settled, cleared his throat.

"It matters not if you have come here from Bordeaux or La Réole," he said. "No merchant can tell me what I will or will not sell, and no one can question my justice here in Miramont."

The clerk flashed a smile and, with an emphatic show of agreement, nodded his head. Miramont, energized by the enthusiastic support of his subordinate, continued.

"You are not the only buyer able to make an offer on this wine, a fact of which I am sure you are aware," he said. "So why is it you are so bold in a place where you are a stranger and where you have no authority?"

"Why would I buy four parts of five when I can buy all five, and why would you sell on those very terms?" Gregory said. "It is not your authority I challenge, *Seigneur* Miramont, but I do hope you and your clerk can grasp the logic of numbers. The goal of punishment is to exact your fee. That has been done with Gilbert le Blanc. Perhaps it is time to do good business."

The clerk whispered into Lord Miramont's ear, and he responded with a slow nod. The clerk put one foot forward, and with a hand on his hip, cocked out an elbow to effect a stance of readiness and aggression, a show of taking charge of the market, the vintage, and the fate of this town. Young and smooth of skin, a dark brunet in the peak of youthful shine, that fleeting twilight before the morrow's dawn of age and time, his eyes burned beneath the crimson swath of his turbaned chaperon, and he was made tall and full by the sustenance of his lord's support. He tilted his head and gave the grin of a man who knows he is about to win.

"You say you have a bill of sale," he said to Gregory. "Can I see it?"

Gregory pulled it out of his satchel and handed it to a pageboy, who scurried back to the clerk and handed it to him. The clerk opened it and read it in silence. When he was done, he looked up from the parchment and shook his head.

"This is no good," he said, and ceremoniously threw it to the ground. "We do not do business with the du Monts, and if you are of that family, then my condolences."

He walked over to the three wagon loads of grapes brought to the market by Gilbert le Blanc, and plucked one of them from the stem. He bit into it. A moment later he made a sour face and spit it out. He looked at le Blanc, back at his lord, then to Gregory, and then to the growing crowd of townspeople.

"These grapes have already gone to vinegar," he said. "They are not fit for Lord Miramont's press."

He motioned to the men-at-arms.

"Burn them," he said, pointing at the wagonloads of grapes. "Right here for all to see. Burn them so everyone will know bad grapes grown by a dishonorable debtor are not allowed here at *Seigneur* Miramont's press."

One of the men-at-arms walked away and soon returned with two buckets of pitch. They tilted over the wagons, pulled all the grapes out onto the ground, doused them with the fuel and lit the pile with a torch.

The mountain of grapes, fine cot from old vines tended by the hands of a master, engulfed in flames. The townspeople groaned as the perishing fruit spit and sizzled in the fire, and le Blanc, his future roiling away in a plume of smoke, appeared crazed and on the verge of a stroke. Through the warped and bending haze of the heat, Gregory saw the heaving of his chest, the hurt in his eyes, and the devil playing chance in his mind. Gregory had seen this wild swell of rage before and its levy of needless carnage. He did not want to see it again.

"Gilbert, no!" Gregory yelled. "No!"

Pulling his knife, le Blanc paid him no heed. Holding it high over his head, he lunged at the clerk before the men-at-arms could stop him. The clerk, his eyes wide and bright, a shriek bursting from his throat, tried to turn and duck. But the knife plunged hilt-deep into his throat, and like wine spilt from a dropped cup, his blood sprayed out of him. He fell to the ground, limp and lifeless, as le Blanc stood above in a shadow of irreconcilable regret. He dropped the knife, fell to his knees, put his face into his hands, and wept. *Seigneur* Miramont, stumbling backward and with his arthritic hand over his heart, coughed violently but managed to point at le Blanc and say, "Arrest this man!"

The men-at-arms crowded around le Blanc and beat him to the ground. With his feet dragging behind him, they took him to a cellar and locked the door. *Seigneur* Miramont looked at Gregory and then down at the grisly heap that was the slain clerk's corpse. With great effort and difficulty, the old lord knelt beside the clerk. He whispered a prayer and stroked his fine brunet hair. He kissed his fingertips and placed them on the clerk's forehead, and as he did, he shook and choked with emotion. After a long while of silence, Miramont collected himself, rose up, and with the help of his page, climbed into his horse-drawn litter. The men-at-arms loaded the clerk in the back of one of the grape wagons and climbed in themselves, and all of them rode out through the northern gate and up the rutted road to Miramont's manor on the hill.

Gilbert le Blanc was hanged the next day when the bells rang the hour of None. Granted absolution, he kissed his wife and daughter goodbye, and in front of a somber crowd of family, friends and rivals, was hoisted up at the market square. Out of choice and circumstance, Gregory stood alone and watched. He did not want to speak with anyone, and they did not want to speak with him, a man who reeked with the stink of not one death but two. Gregory did not blame the townsfolk for their unease. I am like the crow, black and foreboding and always arriving in time for the kill.

A western breeze billowed through the market. The rope creaked as le Blanc swung to and fro. The crowd dissipated, and people returned to their routines. The smithy went loud with hammer and anvil, merchants manned their stalls, and tanners went back to their hides. The barrel maker fitted hoops and staves, and the wheelwright shaped an axle. At the press, the winemakers squeezed the juice into great oaken barrels, one peasant after the next making good on their fee. Gregory had come to Miramont to buy *all* the wine, not some of it. Instead he would leave with a portion of guilt no coin could assuage. How foolish was he to think he would have his way? And how wrong was he to have even tried?

He made the sign of the cross and headed toward the stables.

Time to leave Miramont and never return.

he priest watched the courier ride away, a cloud of dust in his wake. He leaned into the window, looking across the rocky chasm to the path on the other side. A box, the old battered wooden box sat mounted on a post, a letter inside. Rare it was, these days, a delivery to Castlenaud, home to Alphonse of Bayonne, the fallen favorite now on King Edward's black list. From his high perch in the gatehouse, the priest peered across the valley below, noting peasants working in the fields. A plume of lazy smoke rose from the village. A waterwheel turned at the mill.

"Lower the gate," the priest said, dashing down the spiral staircase to the stone landing.

The crossbowmen, their weapons cocked, levelled, and loaded with armor-piercing bolts, stood in position, covering all directions. The gate fell open. The priest walked across it. Making the sign of the cross with one hand and plucking the letter from the box with the other, he returned over the drawbridge, which closed behind him. Holding the rolled parchment above his head, he ran across the courtyard and into the tower saying, "A letter, my lord, a letter!"

They crowded around the table, Alphonse and his men, in the stone-vaulted kitchen where the day's spiced game simmered in a pot. Sick of chess, dice and cards, bored by their own voices, poisoned by tedium. A ripple of excitement moved them, these miscreants confined to this bleak castle on a high rocky shelf. A letter from outside, they received a visit from someone new. In the old days, before the war and before the fall from grace, the minstrels and the acrobats, the thespians and the magicians, came in droves. But all that went away after Alphonse had sided with the French, earning his place at the gallows. So, this letter, a rolled parchment tied off with a scrap of gut, stirred in them their moribund appetite for entertainment.

"Read it." Alphonse took a sip of spoiled ale.

The priest unrolled the parchment, spread it out on the table, tracing the lines with his index finger.

Greetings, Lord Alphonse.

I am Gregory of London, a wine merchant, searching for a fine vintage to ship back to my cellars for the Easter market. Indeed, I found it in Miramont. Alas, my offer refused. Wine, the blood of Christ, but so, too, it is the blood of man. I will be in Gascony for many more months, searching for what has thus far eluded me. Perhaps my journey will lead me to Castlenaud, which, from what I hear, is in need of mirth and merriment. I will bring wine, the best I can find, and you can tell me of how you earned the wrath of our dear king.

The priest, sensing an insult, glanced up from the parchment, sheepish as he looked into the yellowed eyes of Alphonse. He saw the wheels turning. Alphonse had wanted something special but had received something mundane. He took another sip of ale and set the cup down.

"What is his name again?" Alphonse asked, his voice disinterested.

"Gregory, my lord," the priest replied. "Gregory of London."

THE
PHILOSOPHERS
OF ISSIGEAC

regory rode through the gate at the village of Issigeac. He stabled his horse, walked to the market at St. Felicien, and after tasting several wines and inspecting the swine, bought a pipe of *Bergerac* and the fattest pig in the pen. He had them delivered to the great house of an important man whose name he did not know, and then took a room on the third floor of the leaning, half-timbered *Auberge de Bonheur*. He napped through the morning, rose at Sext, and freshened himself at the wash basin. Before heading out into the village, he read a psalm from his Book of Hours and made the sign of the cross.

The street bustled with many people headed in the same direction. As the bells rang, and a pack of boys sprinted by, he hoped to arrive on time. An overflow crowd jammed the front entrance to the great home—of honeyed stone, two stories tall, broad windowed with open shutters, and a sheer roof pierced by a chimney—a few even pushed and shoved. Gregory shook his head and sighed. He knew he would never get past this crowd, so he kept walking, turning down narrow lanes, ducking into alleys, following pathways between courtyards and stone fences until he arrived at the home's outdoor kitchen. There, the servants dressed the pork with a rub of dried spices, fired the ovens, and had already decanted the pipe of Bergerac. His arrival surprised them.

One of them used his apron to wipe pig's blood from his knife. "Who goes there?"

"The man who so graciously provided this banquet with pork and wine," Gregory said. "Now put down that knife and show me into the hall."

The cook did as he was told, Gregory soon inching and weaving his way through the crowd, touching a shoulder and begging pardon, making way for those who looked important, and skirting around clusters of men deep in conversation. When one man rose from his seat at the end of a crowded table, Gregory quickly took his place. A servant boy brought him a cup of wine. The faint sound of music accompanied the din of discussion. Gregory drained his cup and beckoned for more.

He had more important business back south in Marmande, where he hoped to complete the first of Southampton's tasks. But Gregory was early, so he detoured to Issigeac, as many others had, to attend the memorial banquet for the late Félix of Dijon. His title came from the fact he had made his name in the ducal court there. But Félix hailed from right here in Issigeac, born in a leaning half-timbered house just off *La Grande Rue*, and baptized at St. Felicien. Starting out as an itinerate scribe in the old Goliard tradition, Félix remained in Dijon for years, under the protection of the powerful Duke of Burgundy, and launched repeated harangues against the successive kings of France. "You who are so hungry for land should try looking under your nails, where you will find plenty of dirt over which to rule." He even lampooned the greatest thinkers of the day, Siger of Brabant, Albertus Magnus, and Thomas Aquinas. *Faith and reason, one truth or two, they say, but the point of it all is not to discover God's grace, but to see whose piss makes the biggest splash.* So sharp was his quill and so round were his diatribes that he had enemies and supporters in every corner. Even those who disagreed with him showed respect because he argued without fear or compromise. To those of his ilk, part of the fraternity, and for those with lesser hearts and lesser minds, a beast to be feared. *A man who has not the courage to be original is a man who does not believe in his own ideas, and a man who hides behind the thinking of others is a man who does not deserve to be found.*

Under the weight of disillusionment, Félix tried to retire and live a life of mundane solitude in some town or another, but people always sought him out so wherever he lived, a small school grew up around him. He taught the sons of lords, merchants, and craftsmen, the progeny of practical men who did not like the meddlesome and heavy-handed ways of the church. His last stop had been here in his hometown of Issigeac, where he waited out the petty war between the English and the French, and lived his days in obscurity, surrounded by a small cadre of students. Now dead, his corpse in the ground, and all that remained was a vast trove of documents, from the lowest of schoolboy poems jotted down on scraps of parchment, to important theological treatises bound in handsome volumes.

Gregory had read his share of Plato, Aristotle, and Euclid, but only with the goal of refining his mind, not of unearthing the deepest secrets of God's universe. The same could not be said of many of the men in this room. They had devoted their lives to the pursuit of knowledge and enlightenment and reveled in discussion and debate. They called themselves philosophers, and if not for the dignity of their pursuits, they would perhaps be known as paupers. Rare was the time when they had two deniers to call their own, and among their many loves, the mistresses of debt and destitution. They embraced their poverty as a mark of honor, and in their threadbare robes and timeworn shoes, held their heads high with arrogance. So sat Gregory, who in his Merino wool, beaver skin, and cordovan boots, and who with his necklace, bracelet, ring, and brooch, was conspicuously over-dressed. On a few occasions, a philosopher would look at Gregory and sneer, carrying on with his conversation without offering even the slightest nicety. Gregory didn't mind the disdain. He was comfortable knowing it was he who had purchased all the wine these philosophers now imbibed, and that it was he who had procured the hog now roasting on the spit. Enjoy, you sophists and pedants, for it is the merchant who has made you happy this day.

Content and comfortable, a cup of Bergerac in his hand, he said nothing. Rather, he fixed a blank expression and peered out from beneath the brim of his hat, making sure to avoid eye contact, to remain silent and not to fidget, and to otherwise melt into the boisterous throng. The philosophers spoke French or Latin, and in an array of fine and coarse accents from across Christendom. Though self-important in tone and melodic with pretension, the banter of these philosophers was the chorus of the intellect, the refrain of discovery, and Gregory was pleased by the rising crescendo of this cosmopolitan host.

Félix had been on his sickbed for months, and it was known upon seeing the last of those he'd loved, he would surrender to the angel of death. What was also known was that his library was worth a fortune, filled with the collective wisdom of mankind, and in the darkest depths of the stockpile, perhaps a bit of heresy. The great irony was that a man of such letters had not taken the simple step of writing a will. While life as a scholar and satirist had brought him notoriety and fame, it had not brought him riches. Long the list of those he owed, and his manuscripts would be easy to use as de facto collateral for any unpaid debts. From the bits and pieces he'd gleaned through eavesdropping, Gregory knew that chief among Félix's creditors was his old employer, Robert, the Duke of Burgundy. Therefore, Gregory was not surprised when deep into this banquet, as the candles flickered in the trays and after the tide of wine had already crested, a man in the silk and fur of the court entered the hall. He took a cup of wine, leaned against the wall and casually watched as one of the philosophers stood at a podium and orated. Gregory peered at him through the long shadows. He saw touches of silver and gold, and in this man's eyes he detected a wrought and seasoned wit, and the conceit of a man whose assurance is complete. Indeed, pinned to his chaperon the feathers of gold and blue, livery of the utmost rank, the badge of Duke Robert. The orator grimaced and stopped reading, the minstrel put down his bagpipes, and the hall went silent as the philosophers realized the newest man among them was not one of their own and was also their superior.

He walked to the head of the hall. The philosophers opened and formed a circle around him. A smarmy smile came to his face, and he said, "Please, do not halt the festivities for my sake."

The priest who had presided over the banquet, Father Aimery of the church of St. Jacques in nearby Bergerac, stepped into the circle of onlookers. He held out his arms in a gesture of conciliation, and in a voice of strained welcome, said, "Master Reinald, what is it that brings you here?"

"Like the rest of you, I heard Félix had passed," he said. "I wanted to pay my respects to a thinker as exalted as he. As you know, I was once a student of his, and he taught me much about the ways of the world."

"It is true," said Father Aimery. "But it has been many years since you were his pupil, and it is a long way from Dijon."

"I know," he said. "I have traveled for three weeks, and between there and here, I have slept in sties and hovels, and have eaten many crusts of stale bread. But my business is urgent, and hardships are to be expected."

"So, tell us, Master Reinald, what is so urgent that you would trade the comforts of Dijon for the rigors of travel?" asked Father Aimery.

Master Reinald looked into the eyes of many of those standing around him, reeling them in with his charisma, affirming his clout. He raised his voice and spoke to everyone in the hall.

"Lord Robert, the Duke of Burgundy, is laying claim to the entirety of Félix's works," he said, and held up a document. "This is a writ of seizure approved by both the King of France and the Seneschal of Gascony. As the creditor-in-chief, the duke has a priority lien on any and all of Félix's chattel."

The hall went loud with murmuring and protestations, and some booed and hissed, but Father Aimery motioned for silence. When the hall fell quiet, he held out his hand and said, "May I see this writ of seizure?"

Master Reinald, with a sour sniff, handed it to him. As Father Aimery read the writ, Gregory worked his way to the front of the crowd. Father Aimery looked up from the document and said, "You value Félix's debt at two hundred livres? I am no master of the exchange, but that is surely an inflated figure."

Master Reinald smiled. *"Deux cent!"*

"But it says here," Father Aimery said, pointing to a passage in the writ, "that the debt may be redeemed by a third party before the manuscripts are seized. So, if my church wanted to buy Félix's work, and keep his legacy here where it belongs, this writ says that is a legal option."

"Yes," Reinald said. "But I'm afraid the duke's men rode out from Dijon more than a fortnight ago and are expected here tomorrow morning."

"But that is not fair. You have not given ample notice."

"The duke is not concerned with your notions of fairness," said Reinald. "If you are truly an interested buyer, then you will do what is necessary to effect the purchase. Otherwise, rest assured that Felix's writings will go to a good place. Dijon, as you know, is a shining center of education."

The hall went foul with protestations and invective, and one philosopher, drunk beyond restraint, jumped up on a table, pulled the sleeve of his robe up to his elbow, pointed his finger at Reinald, and yelled, "Tell the Duke of Burgundy he can wipe his ass with the manuscripts, for the duke is so low, and his aspirations so crass, he is at his best only when he squats to empty his bowels!"

Another philosopher leapt up onto the table, put his arm over his colleague's shoulder, and shouted, "The duke's mind is as sharp as a rounded stone, and his ideas are as bright as a moonless night. Let him have the manuscripts, so at last he can feed something other than his face!"

The circle around Reinald tightened, and a few philosophers jostled him. Father Aimery, with exaggerated gestures and desperate calls for calm, stymied the hostilities. Once in control of the crowd, he looked all about him, searching for an answer in the faces of his cohorts. Not finding one, his expression deflated with despair.

"What shall we do, Father Aimery?" a philosopher said. "Even if there is treasure in the crypt, there is no way we can get to Bergerac and back before the Duke's men arrive."

"I know, I know. We walk, or we ride nags, and that is not enough."

Gregory took a sip of wine, and to imply he had an important thing to say, cleared his throat in a suggestive manner.

The priest recognized the gesture. "Yes?"

He peered into the eyes of Reinald, and then into those of Father Aimery. A new depth of silence enveloped the room, and Gregory felt expectant stares training on him from all corners of the hall. They had ignored him all afternoon, yet now they could not wait to hear what he would say.

"I have a horse that can outride the duke's men," he said.

Craning their necks, standing on their toes and peering over shoulders, the crowd of philosophers, like a great bellows at an eternal forge, sucked in a gulping gasp, and emitted it with a collective, putrid exhale of breath and anxiety. Reinald waited for the upheaval to subside, and then gave the dismissive laugh of a man who is sure he's heard an empty boast.

He leaned, propping one hand against one of the hall's oaken support beams, and with the other, gestured toward Gregory. "No one can outride the duke's men."

"You do not know that for sure," Gregory said. "My horse is the fastest in all England, with thirty-two wins and only one loss, and even then, in a race undoubtedly rigged."

"Surely you exaggerate," said the priest.

"I do not, I assure you. But even if I do, you have nothing to lose by taking a chance on me."

"But I can hear it in your voice. You are half drunk."

"Indeed, but that has never stopped me before," he said. "And besides, my horse has not been drinking."

Gregory read the expression—not convinced.

"Kitchen boy!" Gregory called, and he came hither. "Go to the stables and fetch my stallion. He is a chestnut courser, as long as a barge and as lithe as a swan. You cannot miss him. And bring his tack and saddle, too."

The boy dashed off to the stables, and as Gregory made his way out of the house, the throng of philosophers, some giddy, some dour, all of them loud with excitement and doubt, followed him into the street. Flanked by Father Aimery and Master Reinald, Gregory waited for the kitchen boy to arrive with his horse. When he appeared around the corner leading Black Saddle by a tether, and lugging the gear over his shoulder, the doting began.

"That is the finest horse I have ever seen," gushed Father Aimery, as many behind him whooped and cheered. "I fashioned you a fabulist, but perhaps I misjudged you."

A groom arrived and dressed Black Saddle in his accoutrements—the Persian rug padding, riding tackle of Spanish leather and Dutch brass works, riveted red ankle boots, and a face guard of boiled, tooled leather adorned with a short iron spike. His croup and thighs gleaming, his chestnut coat a luxuriant sheath, Black Saddle tossed his head as the groom fastened the girth around his barrel. As the stallion's splendor took shape, so too did Reinald's vexation.

He looked askance at Gregory, and then to Black Saddle. "For all his finery, I doubt he is equal to your boast. He is a prince of a horse, I must admit, but I have seen many in my time, and his best years have already been lived."

"Then you do not know horses as well as you think. Your writ is flawed and now you will pay. Perhaps next time you will think twice before leaving a loophole." Gregory turned to Father Aimery. "Tell me where it is I go and what I do once I arrive there, and I will be on my way."

The older man's face turned sour and it creased with the apologia that proceeds a particularly uncomfortable question. He bent into an anxious and pleading bow, opened his arms and held out his hands. "I do not know you. I cannot possibly entrust this to you, but is it possible one of my deacons takes your horse?"

"Only one man rides Black Saddle. I understand your trepidation. You think I will get my hands on the exchange and never return."

"—Yes, I do," he said.

"Would it ease your mind if I left an item with you, an item so valuable I must return?"

"But what can you possibly possess, other than your horse, that is worth what you would go to retrieve?"

Gregory turned so his back faced Reinald. He reached into his chest pocket and pulled out the arrest warrant. Father Aimery's eyes lit up with fear at the sight of the document bearing the royal seal—King Edward holding the orb and scepter, crowned and seated on his throne. To reinforce the import of what Father Aimery beheld, Gregory turned up his face and narrowed his gaze.

"Perhaps I can leave this as surety," Gregory said, and made as if to hand the warrant to Father Aimery. But instead of taking it, he pulled his hands back, gave Gregory a quick look over, and taking pains to be discreet, said, "That will not be necessary."

He rode through the night, with Black Saddle walking and trotting, exerting himself but leaving his puissance undisturbed. "Getting there will be easy, my boy," Gregory said, "but the telling will be in the return." The thrill of the departure, and the buoyant spirit of the wine, had dripped away, only to be replaced by the bump and drudgery of the road. He skirted nameless villages, cresting hills and dipping through valleys, under an onyx night with a million eyes, and a taunting crescent moon. The hours passed, the world turned, and the pitch gave way to the creeping scarlet of dawn. On the northern horizon loomed the silhouettes of the city walls and the bell tower at St. Jacques. A cluster of ships bobbed at the quay, a stone bridge arched over the glittering Dordogne, and a sweeping grid of vineyards lined the hills. Bergerac, the plump berry Gregory had come to pick.

Out of the town came a militant host, a lieutenant and his suite of armed retainers. Flecked with blue and gold, grit and steel, their mounts a stampede of power and pedigree, these were the duke's men. On the final leg of their exhausting journey, and seemingly convinced of their success, they poured out of Bergerac with little urgency. Gregory did a headcount, fifteen, and all of them soon to be fools. He passed them as he headed toward town, and though he did not look upon them long, look upon them he did. Hard men, mature in their dourness, bristling with weapons and etched with the sharp lines of cruelty. Trusted killers who cherished their trade, and unyielding in their support of the duke, hell would happen if someone snatched their bounty. Gregory swallowed a lump of doubt and made the sign of the cross. "Dear Black Saddle, we cannot afford to lose this race," he said, as the prancing stallion clattered over the bridge.

He rode through the tangled city center, still yawning from its slumber, to the chapter house at St. Jacques, a brutish church in the old style. He dismounted, wrapped the reins around the hitching post, and knocked on the door. It soon opened, an anxious face peering out at him. With one hand Gregory doffed his hat, and with the other, he held out the letter Father Aimery had scrawled last evening. Gregory showed confidence, but he was anything but. The letter had been written in private, and bound with the signet of St. Jacques, so he did not know its contents.

"I have an urgent message from Father Aimery," he said to the holy man sizing him up with an inhospitable stare. "Are you Deacon Marcel?"

"Yes," he said, and yanked the letter from Gregory's hand. He cracked the seal, opened the missive, and leaned against the doorsill as he read it. Gregory watched as his lips moved in silence, his eyes widened with disbelief, and his brow twisted with intrigue. Finished with the letter, he looked at Gregory and shook his head.

"I did not expect this when I awoke this morning," he said. "But tell me this, from which city did you travel?"

"Issigeac," he said.

"And who has left this trove of documents for our benefit?"

"Félix of Dijon."

"And who has come to take them away?"

"Master Reinald of Burgundy."

"And how much does he want for the documents, if Félix's debts are to be redeemed?"

"Two hundred livres."

"And what is your name?"

"Gregory of London," he said.

"Now," Deacon Marcel said. "Show me your—other letter."

Gregory pulled out the arrest warrant, King Edward's royal seal and tassel in full view. Once Deacon Marcel appeared satisfied with the display, Gregory slid it back into the breast pocket of his robe. Before going back into the chapter house and closing the door behind him, the deacon gave Gregory a hard look, adjudging him, weighing him, and searching for a signal he would not honor the arrangement. Gregory donned his hat and peered back at him from beneath the weathered brim.

"Collect what I need while I water my horse," Gregory said. "For I am ready to ride."

Black Saddle slaked his thirst at a public trough, and Gregory trotted him back to the chapter house door. Deacon Marcel emerged with a small leather pouch and handed it to him.

He tucked it into his boot. "Deacon Marcel, it has been a pleasure."

He pulled on the reins, worked a spur, and Black Saddle, seemingly aware of the stakes and eager to catch his prey, sprinted down the city streets, over the cobbled bridge, and out across the field, a billowing cloud in his wake. He settled into a smooth canter, reeling in the road, devouring the miles, his hooves clapping out an assertive cadence. Topping a ridge, Gregory saw the duke's men up ahead, and while they did not dally, neither did they push their steeds. Talking amongst themselves and jesting through the morn, they gave no heed to the equine comet hurtling in from behind them. Black Saddle descended the hill and burst over the flatland, his sinew taut, his full stretch the easy effort of a champion. When he arrived within earshot of the duke's men, the commotion of his work alarmed them. They glanced over their shoulders, exchanged looks of bewilderment, and wheeled their horses to a halt.

As he closed on the stalled retinue, Gregory veered Black Saddle out from the road. With a whip of the switch and a kick of the hoof, they blew past the duke's men in a black-and-chestnut blur of stupefying speed.

Making their pass, a spray of turf and stone arcing through the air, Gregory glimpsed the leader of this host. When their eyes met, he smirked. Turning his attention to the road, Gregory laid willow to Black Saddle's rump and said, "Ride, you devil horse, ride!" As Black Saddle veered back onto the road, pocking it with the fury of his gallop, someone called, *"Catch them! Do not let them escape!"*

But they had no say in the matter. Rider after rider made his run, and each of them failed, not coming to within five lengths of Black Saddle's tail. At last the walls of Issigeac appeared on the horizon, the sun high in the sky. Just as soon as they barreled through the gate, it closed behind them. Winding down from his run, the great stallion, lathered in sweat and snorting, trotted in a wide circle and stopped. The throng of philosophers crowded around him, and Black Saddle, his eyes shining from behind the spiked facemask, basked in their adulation.

Gregory dug into his boot, pulled out the pouch and tossed it to Father Aimery. "Just make sure you leave a little token for me."

"You will be justly recompensed."

Gregory searched the crowd, and after looking into many faces, found Master Reinald. Scowling and petulant, he stood by himself, trying to ignore the harangues heaped upon him by a cluster of young philosophers.

"You have made an enemy this day," he said, wagging his finger.

"Oh, I have made enemies before, Master Reinald, so do not think of yourself as unique."

A tower guard walked out onto the battlements, cupped his hand over his eyes and gazed into the distance. The peasants had finished their work for the day. The fields sat empty. Fishermen collected their nets. The blacksmith locked up his shop. Hearth fires twinkled from the stone-and-thatch homes as a lonely sunset cracked across the sky. In this ordinary moment of life, the guard noticed something of interest. He turned and called.

"Priest, a rider approaches."

The priest hitched up his habit and climbed the spiral stairs from the hall to the door leading out to the battlements. As the guard had said, a rider neared the path and switchback up to Castlenaud, a Benedictine in a cloak and habit, his tonsure overgrown.

"Who goes there?" the priest asked.

"Only a messenger," he said, pulling a rolled parchment from his belt.

He rode up to the battered wooden box and dropped the letter inside.

"From where did it come?" the priest asked.

"I know not, but only where it goes. May God have grace on your soul, brother, and on that of your lord."

He turned his horse and rode back down the path, pushing his mount into a gallop once he reached the valley. Through the village and down the road, the priest watched him leave, wishing he could leave with him. A foolish notion, thought the priest, but one that had crossed his mind many times.

"Open the gate," he said.

He retrieved the letter, and as the drawbridge closed behind him, made the long climb to the hall saying, "Lord Alphonse, another letter!"

They convened at the long table, a table that had not seen feast or frolic since the sentence of treason. Half drunk on bitter wine, ensnared in a predictable mood of despondency, Alphonse cheered at the arrival of the letter and its promise of good tidings, of a pardon or reprieve. A beleaguered smile, like a flame at the end of a dying wick, guttered in Alphonse's scarred and stubbly face.

"Read us this letter," he said.

The priest unrolled the parchment, held it with both hands, and paced around the table.

Greetings, Lord Alphonse.

It is I, Gregory of London, and I write once again to tell you of my doings. It should please you that I have seen my circumstances change. While I failed to accomplish my goal in Miramont, the same cannot be said of the results at Issigeac. I will save the details for later, when at last we speak in person. But I should tell you I raced against a full retinue of mounted men in the service of Duke Robert of Burgundy. As you must know, his horses are among the fastest in Christendom, and that besting them is no trifle. If there is one thing you must know about me, it is that I love the horse race. Betting on them, riding in them, and otherwise tasting the fruits of victory. Perhaps I am this way because in England I have always won. Yet even here in Gascony, my horse, Black Saddle, has proved superior to all his competitors. Perhaps it is a conceit, but I feel I must let you know—no matter your horse, mine is better.

Alphonse looked around the table at his men and all of them laughed. They knew their lord had an astounding horse, a devil horse that had never been matched in chase or in battle. Alphonse had ridden him for years, but even he did not know from whence the courser had come. A spoil of war from long ago, a treasure reined from the fire. It seemed he never ate or slept, but when it came time to sprint or to charge, or to kick or to trample, he was ever ready and eager. Many elaborate names had been proposed, but none of them stuck. Instead, Alphonse opted for simplicity. He called his horse the Blue Stallion.

Rigged, a Wager in Marmande

Gregory rode south to Tonneins and lodged at an inn. He trudged up three flights. Once inside his room he dropped his bags on the floor and threw his big black hat on the bed. He scratched the back of his neck, ran a hand through his hair and winced when a stab of pain shot through his road-rattled ankle. He laid on the bed, locked his hands behind his head and tried to sleep, but the adrenaline of travel and a mind loud with thought allowed him no rest.

He rose, paced across the narrow room, and opened the shutters of the only window, high up between the triangular peak of the gables. He leaned on the sill with both elbows and gazed out into the gold and salmon sky. The majestic River Garonne, gurgled in the twilight, winding through the handsome countryside while cranes stalked its banks. The leaves made wet and motley smears around the trees from which they had fallen, naked limbs beckoning winter from its sleep. On the horizon, a magnificent flock of migrating swallows turned through the sky, bending and coiling, the flock speeding back on itself in a sweeping eddy, shattering into a million falling shards, then gathering again into a billowing whirl. Gregory wished he were one of those swallows, his throat filled with song, free and flying and surrounded by his kind. But he knew he was no swallow. Alone at every turn and always the stranger, he was the black cat with the nasty hex, hunter and hunted and almost always up to no good.

The sun sank beneath the land, a single red ribbon the only proof the day had ever shone. As the world fell into darkness, an unnerving chill crept into the room. Gregory pulled the cloak tight about his shoulders, but he found no succor. The hand of loneliness, its fingers sharp and icy, clutched at him with a steady grip. He thought of his life. Years of travail had brought him here—to this dank room on a dreary autumn night, in a ramshackle town, in a land not his own.

What a waste.

He dug into his pouch and retrieved the rubies Father Aimery had given to him two days ago in Issigeac, after an epic run from Black Saddle and Félix's trove of writings in the right hands. Father Aimery had been good to his word, too, giving Gregory much more than he had expected—three rubies.

Two for the road and one for the woman he loved.

He turned them in his palm, marveled at their enchanting light, and took some measure of comfort.

Refreshed by a good night's sleep and a series of pleasing dreams, Gregory rode out from Tonneins at dawn. With the River Garonne glistening on his left and the road opening before him, he coaxed Black Saddle into a terrific burst before bringing him down to a trot. He went to Marmande, where the pennons would fly and where the trumpets would call, and where hope would live and die. Two men—Bernard de Fumel and Pierre d'Agen—had competing claims on a fiefdom, but only one could hold it. Writs, words, promises, and coins had not been enough, so it would be settled the Gascon way, with arms on a sanctioned field with the high and low bearing witness. At stake sat castle Bonaguil, high on a rocky spur in the eastern wilds of the Agenais, and its associated charters and privileges. After much haggling and ill will, the two sides agreed they would meet at Marmande, even though the castle lay many miles to the east, and duel *à outrance*—to the utmost for the right to hold the fiefdom.

Gregory arrived a week before the tournament. He paid a few extra deniers and secured a room at the Blue River Inn, where he had an excellent view of the eastern gate and the port.

Each afternoon, once he had completed his writing, he went downstairs to the inn's tavern and ate cabbage and pork, or fish with roasted garlic, or stuffed duck with onions, and drank bright local wine with the other travelers in town for the duel.

"Who do you think will win?" someone would ask, and Gregory, wary of saying too much to someone he did not know, would simply grin and say, "Ask me when the duel is done." Each day more and more people arrived, and as the inns filled and the extra rooms, empty cellars, and barn lofts were rented out and occupied, Marmande, decades ago the scene of a horrific massacre, grew boisterous and rowdy.

Both of the dueling lords came from old, known families, and for them to cross swords meant people had to take sides. Though they tried, the town officials, or *jurats*, could not control the behavior of the strangers who poured into their town. They destroyed a tavern during a brawl. A fire broke out at the market, and Marmande awoke one morning to find a man gutted, gelded, and dead in the town square. But all of it to be expected, and as long as the silver continued to flow, and as long as all manner of goods were bartered, Marmande turned a complicit eye to the debauchery, embracing its moment at the center of Gascon society.

The day Gregory had waited for finally arrived—Bernard de Fumel and his flotilla of barges pulled up to the quay. Gregory made his way to the riverfront, along with dozens of others, and watched as Fumel and his householders stretched, found their land legs, greeted the town's jurats, and headed toward the city hall. Gregory did not follow them. Rather he stayed to watch what happened with Fumel's barges. He kept a cold face, but inside he smiled. What he had been told was true. Homeless, landless, and fearful his goods would be plundered if they were not with him, Fumel travelled with a large baggage train of booty he'd accumulated during his adventures in the Orient. There it sat, stacked, crated, covered with canvas tarps, and sitting on barges bobbing at the quay. Under the watchful eyes of a jurat and a gaggle of men-at-arms, stevedores unloaded the freight and hauled it to a large warehouse alongside the town wall.

On his way back to the inn, Gregory stopped at the market and bought a sash of canary colored wool. Before retiring to his room, he sat in the tavern and ate a trencher of smoked beef in broth and a plum baked in honey, elbow to elbow with other men who slurped their wine, smacked their lips, and licked their fingers in gluttony. As they tore at their bread and meat, they jested, boasted, chided, and laughed. The conversations were coarse and jovial, but Gregory, aside from a polite chortle or a curl of his brow, did not join their banter.

The day of the duel began with a yawning saffron dawn. Honking geese in a ragged arrow flew southward over Marmande. People's breath came in bursts of fog as the overnight embers were stoked to life. The cocks crowed, the dogs stretched and sniffed, and the acorn-fattened hogs wallowed in their ordure. Gregory bent over the water basin and washed the sleep from his eyes. He knelt, read a psalm from his Book of Hours, and made the sign of the cross. He broke his fast with a hunk of soft goat cheese he pulled from his pack and took a sip of spiced and watered wine. Opening the shutters, he looked out the window as the church bells rang Prime. Boys and teens ran this way and that, and veiled women, some with buckets on their hips and some with babes in their arms, congregated near the well. The town bloomed with colorful sprays of pine, and spices and incense burned at all four corners of the wall.

Townsmen had already built the timber cordon within which the duel would unfold, right in the town square, and people busied themselves claiming places along the railing. Nobles, ecclesiastics, merchants, freemen, and peasants—all of them cavorted, and some of them sang. As time idled by, they segregated into two distinct camps, one flecked with the blue of Lord d'Agen, and the other with the yellow of Lord Fumel. Shouts and wagers flew between them as a slow-moving, jolly crescendo. But Gregory knew this festive bravado could very well end in a riot, so he stayed in his room as the belligerence swelled. He reached into his satchel and pulled out a parchment, one of the ones given to him by Southampton before he'd left England. He had read it a few times before, back in Bordeaux, but now that the killing hour neared, he thought it wise to read it one more time.

Lord Fumel had been disinherited even before the French war, when already the heir but not yet even a teen and replaced—for reasons still unknown—with the obscure d'Agen line. With only a few sous to his name, Fumel headed east with a caravan only to become a mercenary. He had made his way to Constantinople and, early on, earned his way fighting the enemies of the Byzantines—up in the mountains, out over the plains, over the sea and back again. But he went deeper still into the untold peril of the Orient where, it was believed, he'd found his pot of gold. He returned to Christendom and did much dirty work in the trade wars between Venice and Genoa. In Italy was where his story became immediate, and from where he made it clear he would return to reclaim his inheritance, by treasure and force if needed, from the usurper Lord d'Agen. Castle Bonaguil, an austere fortress on a remote outcrop, offered meager revenue from its estate, but a lordship nonetheless, and if there was one thing that could be said of a Gascon noble, it was that he cherished the soil that had first dirtied his feet. Though Fumel emerged as a source of fascination in his own right, he kept in his baggage train a trophy more exotic than even he.

A book written by a Venetian merchant who had lived many years in China at the court of the great Mongol ruler of half the world, Kublai Khan. Upon his return to Christendom, the merchant joined the Venetian war against the Genoese. Captured and imprisoned, he dictated the stories of China to a fellow inmate, who recorded them with ink and parchment. The story, copied again and again, appeared in merchant halls, monasteries and castles up and down the Italian peninsula. All who read it were awestruck by the sumptuous account of how enormous and fantastical the world really was—the Silk Road and the seas, mountains, deserts, and endless stands of trees—palaces the size of cities and sprawling kingdoms ripe and verdant with untold riches, and a people capable of astounding feats of ingenuity. This book cracked open the hard nut of imagination, giving birth to a profound yearning to see beyond the known, to peer into the depths of darkness only to find light.

A copy of the book was now in Marmande, supposedly tucked away inside Lord Fumel's baggage train as a spoil of war. The book would not be difficult to recognize. The size of a man's torso, bound in gem-encrusted leather, and illuminated with paint and gold leaf. But if identifying the manuscript would be easy, getting to it would prove much more arduous. The baggage train remained under constant guard, and even within Lord Fumel's hoard, Gregory felt certain it was under lock and key. But a lock can be opened, the lid of a great trunk can be lifted, and a book can be pilfered if one is able to think on his feet.

Done reading the parchment, Gregory rose from his seat on the edge of the bed and tucked the parchment back in his pack. The herald trumpets called. A roar echoed through the streets. The murder of crows perched on the ridge of a church roof rose in an excited circle of flight. The death match between Lord Fumel and Lord d'Agen seemed about to begin, and from the third-floor window of the inn, Gregory had a clear view of the proceedings.

Lord Fumel left a Christian and returned a man of Jesus, or so it was claimed. But, as Gregory saw with his own eyes, he had absorbed the exotic accoutrements of the Turks he had fought. His helm with the pig-snout visor was crowned with maroon and gold brocade, and from a pearl and silver pendant sprang a clutch of chartreuse parrot feathers. From his shoulders hung a crimson cape lined with the spotted fur of a hyena, and on his surcoat, patterned with black and jonquil chevrons, the markings of the hornet. His face, clean shaven and lined with tenacity, bore the certitude of a man who knew no fear. Girded with a sword in a bejeweled scabbard and sitting high and square on top of his black charger, Bernard de Fumel, in polished mail and plate, appeared as a glittering star fallen to the earth. Arrayed on either side of him were his people, family, friends, and men-at-arms, all of them martial and motionless as the flags above them snapped and curled.

Facing him, Pierre d'Agen, a standard-issue esquire, raw and unrefined, who, in comparison to the resplendent flower of his opponent, a low and bothersome weed. Attired in his faded blue garb of yesteryear, he looked as he was, an impoverished lord who could barely maintain his kit. But there bubbled a crude promise of ability about him, and in his vaulted jaw, shovel nose and foundry eyes, the unyielding, juvenile pluck of courage. As with Fumel, d'Agen was accompanied by his supporters, a hodgepodge of dour householders, vicious in their threadbare destitution and reckless with patrician self-regard.

Attired in a ceremonious hood and cloak, the town crier stood between the two camps, and from a parchment role, read aloud the ancestries of the combatants, the genesis and course of the dispute, the guidelines of the duel, and the consequences of the result. When the crier finished, both Fumel and d'Agen would be given an opportunity to speak as they pleased and to speak at length, because for one of them, or perhaps even both, those would be the last words they would ever utter. The formalities could take hours, maybe even all day, thus suspending Marmande in a trance of anticipation. So, as the town crier authorized the scene with his eloquent and copious legalese, Gregory made his move.

He stopped off at the stables. He gave the groom a denier, instructed him to ready Black Saddle and take him to the barn, and promised him more coins at the end. Adrenaline drove him as he cut through a narrow lane between a tidy row of homes, and down another lined with small courtyards and gardens. He came out at an open space in front of the barn where Lord Fumel's booty was stashed. Just as Gregory hoped, the barn's large double doors, hewn from sturdy planks of oak and bound with thick iron hinges, were closed but not locked and in chains. He took a deep breath and sighed through his nose as he walked the final steps to the soaring, slate-shingled barn. He approached the hatch next to the hulking cargo doors and, with his right hand balled into a fist, knocked loud and urgent, relaying no hint of secrecy. As he awaited a response, he thought of his words and hoped they had worked, for on the day Fumel arrived, Gregory had written an anonymous letter and had it sent to the Bailiff of Marmande.

> It has come to my attention that on the day of the duel, and as it is in progress, thieves will attempt to steal a book, an extraordinary book written by a Venetian merchant, from Lord Bernard de Fumel's baggage train. This is a true account, as I heard it with my own ears the night before Lord Fumel arrived. Drunkards they were, and it was their boasts that betrayed them. Men of the devil, I say, and possessed of his cunning. The only way to catch a thief is to catch him red-handed, and then and only then will the full extent of the syndicate's plot become known.

Gregory heard the fanciful drone of the crier coming from the town square and could sense the growing zeal of the throng. Accompanied by a roar emboldened by the latest vintage, another staccato burst blew out of the trumpets. Still no answer at the door, so Gregory knocked again, louder and with more urgency. He took a few steps back, and just as he did, the hatch flew open and out stepped two armed guards, the Bailiff of Marmande, and a man in a cloak and chaperon who Gregory assumed was Fumel's Page. Their suspicion lay heavy upon him, and when their eyes met his, Gregory said to himself, *Dear God, please let me have this day.*

The Bailiff put a hand on his knife and scowled. "What is your business, here?"

The guards positioned themselves on either side of Gregory.

"My apologies." He gave a slight and perfunctory bow. "I know you would rather be at the duel than to be here listening to my commotion."

The Bailiff pursed his lips and rolled his eyes to show that, indeed, he was an unwelcome burden. "I asked you, who are you and what is your business here?"

"Did you receive a letter two days ago?"

"I receive letters every day. Can you be more specific?"

"A short note—it was about a book, thieves, and a syndicate."

The Bailiff's eyes lit up, and so, too, did those of Fumel's Page. They glanced sideways at one another, and then back at Gregory. He saw the knit of curiosity in their brows, and could see impatience gnawing at them, like a rat on a bone. They were expectant, almost desperate to hear what he was about to say, and to learn of the mysterious letter that had arrived on the cold breeze of surprise. Gregory took his time, and instead of elaborating, he studied the two men confronting him, their clothes wrinkled and strewn with pieces of hay, their chins dark with stubble and their breath foul with morning stink. Bloodshot with irritation, half-drunk from the night before and likely being teased by cranky bowels, these two would be hazardous and short for trifles, but otherwise ripe for the ruse.

"Out with it," said the Page. "What do you know about that letter?"

"Everything," Gregory said. "I am the one who wrote it."

"So, have you come to tell us something we need to know?"

"Indeed, I have, and alas, it is not good news," Gregory said. "I stayed at the same inn as the thieves, and this morning I overheard them, in the room next to mine. They have already stolen the book and left town. As I'm sure you know, the market in rare manuscripts is quite competitive in Paris. My guess is they are halfway to Bergerac by now, and in a fortnight, will be hawking the manuscript in the Île de la Cité."

"But that is impossible." The Page voice was thick with smug assurance. "We have been here waiting in ambush for two days, and nothing. That book is where we left it, in the bottom of a trunk bound with a lock for which I have the key."

"Are you sure?" Gregory asked, and with squinted eyes and a flexed brow, challenged the Page's confidence. From his pouch he pulled out the biggest of the rubies given to him by Father Aimery. He turned it in his fingers and held it up to the light, so it shone with the entirety of its bewitching splendor. Convinced Lord Fumel's Page was mesmerized by the sudden daydreams a jewel of that size could conjure, Gregory flashed a sporting look and said, "Page, I bet you this ruby the book is gone."

"And if you are right, what do I owe you?"

"I'll make it easy on you," he said. "Two deniers."

Without taking his eyes off Gregory, the Page said, "Gervaise, Arnaud, bring me the chest."

They disappeared into the barn and soon returned, lugging a huge wooden chest between them. They set it down with a thud at the Page's feet. He smirked, pulled a ring of iron keys from his belt, and as they clinked and clanked, he crouched down, slid one of them into the lock, and gave it a hard turn. The lock creaked open and the clerk pulled up the lid. From where Gregory stood, he could not see into the trunk, but reading the delight on the Page's face, he knew, as he had always known, that the book lay inside. The Page reached into the trunk and, with a giggle of triumph, looked over the lid, taunting Gregory with a childish smile. He pulled out the book and held it high over his head. The manuscript just as Gregory had been told, big and sumptuous and bound in leather with twinkling stones. It possessed the heft of importance, the promise of enlightenment, and even Gregory, who had seen and read many manuscripts, put a hand to his mouth and gasped.

"You should learn not to listen to the drunks at the tavern, as their tongues are often laced with lies," the Page said. "Now pay me and be on your way, or I will have you hauled before the jurats and questioned."

With a twirl of his fingers, Gregory positioned the ruby in the nook between his thumb and index finger, and flicked it high into the air. But instead of aiming at the Page, he aimed at the Bailiff. His eyes grew wide and bright as it arced through the air in his direction. He reached out and snatched it, and when he did, a nasty look of greed washed over his face. With a sour expression, the Page turned to the Bailiff and said, "Are you going to give that to me? I won the wager, not you."

"Give you what?" the Bailiff said, in an imperious tone. "I am a sworn official of Marmande, but you are the lowly Page of a lord who at this time is landless and homeless, and is perhaps even a heretic. You have no authority to ask anything of me."

The Bailiff turned to walk away, and as he did, the Page, red with fury and his lips moist with spittle, cocked the book over his shoulder with both hands and swung it with all his might across the Bailiff's head. He fell to the ground with a groan. As the Bailiff tried to collect himself, the Page jumped on top of him. But the Bailiff recovered, and the two of them went rolling across the ground, punching, swinging, kicking, clawing, biting, and cursing as they fought over the ruby.

As the bloody tussle continued, the young groom arrived, leading Black Saddle by a tether. Gregory looked at the men-at-arms who just stood there, awed by what was happening. He knelt down, picked up the book, couched it under his arm and walked toward his horse. He put the book in a pack, grabbed the pommel, and pulled himself up onto his steed. Ever ready to run, Black Saddle whinnied and flinched to show he was game. Gregory looked down with disdain at the Bailiff and the Page, both winded and panting and resting on hands and knees. Through the mess of hair hanging in front of his eyes, the Page glanced up at Gregory, spit out a glob of blood and said, "Damn you!"

"Cheer up, my boy," Gregory said. "You still have the duel and we all know who will win. Lord Fumel is a man and Lord d'Agen is a boy, and in Gascony, a son is never better than his father."

Gregory slapped the reins and worked a spur, and Black Saddle galloped full tilt down La Grande Rue and out through the east gate. He looked over his shoulder, Marmande sinking below the horizon. He heard the faint call of trumpets and the hungry response of the crowd. He'd paid a ruby for a book. A good deal—and Southampton would be happy.

nother letter arrived. This one delivered on a dark and rainy day as lightning danced in the sky. The rider came and went in haste, but the priest recognized him. One of the couriers from Agen, a regular who worked this corner of the world. Feeling lazy this day, the priest sent a servant boy over the drawbridge to fetch the missive, snatching it from his hand as soon as he returned.

He knew Alphonse was in the tower, humping a milkmaid from the village. But one of the priest's secret pleasures was to needle his lord with annoyances, even if doing so courted danger. So, he stood at the base of the tower, cupped his hands around his mouth to amplify his voice, and called, "My lord, another letter!"

He waited, and eventually the shutters opened. Alphonse looked out the window, frowned and said, "Priest, it can wait."

"Can it?" the priest said, holding up the letter. "Perhaps it is what you have waited for. If so, why delay?"

Alphonse stretched and scratched his bare chest. "Come up."

The priest climbed the spiral stairwell to the fourth floor of the tower. He entered the room, dimly lit and heavy with carnal stink. Alphonse, wearing nothing but breeches, sat at the end of the ornate canopy bed. The milkmaid, the covers pulled up to her chin, turned away. The priest sat on a stool and opened the rolled parchment.

In Marmande I found a manuscript that so delighted me I simply had to have it. Imagine my discontent when I learned it was in the possession of another. I had not the means to buy it, nor did I have the strength to take it by force. So, I took it by guile, instead, as I am not bound by the restrictions of the courtier's life. That is a trait we have in common, our disdain for empty conventions. Where we differ is my treachery is reserved for an inferior, or even a peer, whereas you are foolish enough to try and cheat our dear king. That is why I am yet free and why you have been sentenced to the gallows.

The priest looked up from the letter, excited by what he would see—Alphonse smoldering with the glowing embers of agitation.

Alphonse stood and walked over to the window. "Is this from Gregory?"

The priest, quick to peeve his lord, in a singing voice said, "Gregory of London. It could be from no other."

Hands pressed against the window sill and hunched, Alphonse looked over his shoulder, his face in rugged profile.

"If ever I catch him, I will send him to the silver mines of Bohemia, where he will live in a hole for the rest of his life," he said.

"Indeed, my lord," the priest said, knowing that Alphonse had done just that—to innocents and to enemies—many times in the past.

A
WINTER RIDE
WITH KUBLAI KHAN

Slow rain dripped from the sagging brim of his beaver and peacock hat. He shivered, squinting, peering out into the distance. Beyond the city of Pau, on the back end of a desolate valley, rose a wall of mountains, stoic blue sentinels in the gloomy haze, the upturned, jagged end of the world. Steep and remote, its high passes lined with narrow switchbacks and snowy peaks, this the land of sheep and shepherds, of cirques, gorges, and cascades, was the home of the magnificent bearded vultures gliding on the winds of time, and of the stout villages peopled by those who had lived there since beyond memory. Battered by gales and scorched by the sun, frozen in winter and lush in spring, these mountains reached so high into the heavens they were first to receive God's blessings and punishments.

Deep and scattered within the vast stone hinterland, arches and bell towers, built by those who were perhaps closer to salvation than the rest, but, as of yet, not quite there. Ancient, stood these mountains, already old and noble when man was just beginning to find his way, the keepers of secrets that would never be told, and the guardians of wisdom that would never be learned. But to climb into the elevations and reaches, and to move among the granite cliffs and chasms, was to imbue one's soul with a zest too pure for the city and too rare for the hills. Stretching for hundreds of miles from the Bay of Biscay to the Mediterranean Sea, their slopes bristled with pine and their inclines teemed with nimble Ibex.

From Gregory's vantage point at Pau, he observed this august range, a billowing belt of silhouettes brooding along the southern skyline. He knew it would be cold, and probably lonely, and that he would grow weary of the whispering wind, the slanting snow, and the nagging voice in his head. Yet the sight of the mountains filled him with hope, and when he took a deep breath, his blood ran hot with vigor. The corner of his mouth bent into a smile as he absorbed the immensity of what was before him.

At last. The Pyrenees.

He reached down and patted Black Saddle on the neck. The horse tired after eight days of relentless travel out of Marmande. They swam across the River Adour, arriving early for high mass at the abbey at St. Sever. He managed a narrow escape near the bridge at Orthez, and another at the crossroads north of Cézéracq. It became a race against the sun throughout. He needed new shoes, a stable with fresh hay, a bag of oats, and a good brush to brighten his soiled mane and coat. Gregory leaned into the stallion's ear and said, "Stay with me, dear Black Saddle. Soon you will rest, and you will like the air up there."

He arrived at Leschun, a village with one main road lined with a jumble of tidy, mortared homes, and anchored by an ancient church with carved arches and a fortified pepper-pot tower. Nestled in a plateau bounded by an eruption of stupendous horns, Leschun looked down at the world in one direction, and up at it in the other. Powdered with early morning snow, its chimneys exhaling smoke, and with the tantalizing scents of burning wood and baking bread, Leschun sat silent in the December chill.

Hunkered down beneath his hat, and with his fur-lined cloak pulled tight about him, Gregory trotted his horse down the main street toward the church. He looked neither to his left nor his right, so as to avoid curious village eyes, but with Black Saddle's hooves clopping across the cobbles, and being the shadowy stranger who'd arrived unannounced, Gregory knew they were upon him nonetheless. He circled the church, a mishmash of construction with competing patterns of stonework, an adjoining cemetery and chapter house, a rectory and barn. He dismounted, tethered Black Saddle to a post, and with his boots crunching out footprints in the virgin snow, approached the door.

He knocked. The door soon creaked open, letting out a shard of firelight. The elderly parish priest stood there looking at him with a face radiant with challenge, his tonsure overgrown, his chin stubbly, and his vestments lax. He looked Gregory up and down, but did not display the yokel's rude wonderment that usually greeted him. He opened the door a bit wider and said, "Come in, *monsieur*. The outdoors is no place to linger when winter is at hand."

Gregory entered. In short order his hat and cloak hung on a peg, his bags piled on the floor, his hands held out toward the fire, and Black Saddle on to the stables. A gush of anxiety dissipated with a sigh, and with a surprise flicker of emotion, his heart welled with peace. For the first time since leaving La Réole, he felt safe. He turned to the priest and gave a smile.

"It is hospitable to let your guest warm his bones before asking questions," Gregory said. "Your accommodation is genuine."

"Hospitality is God's work," the priest said. "And there is always a bed available for a tired traveler."

They made small talk as household servants prepared Gregory a dish—smoked chicken with black pepper, fresh river trout, a hardboiled egg, a piece of white bread with butter, and a goblet of watered Jurançon wine. He abandoned all pretense of refinement as he dug into the meal. He had eaten nothing but hard, unleavened biscuits and salted goat jerky for three days, so the yeast and the yoke and the thigh of fowl, not to mention the trickle of white wine, soothed his gut and settled his nerves. As he pulled a piece of chicken from the bone, sopped bread in the butter, and sipped at his wine, he looked around. The rectory was sparsely furnished and rustic, but the fireplace as tall as he, the rafters sturdy, and Gregory sensed an eternal goodness nurtured through centuries of fellowship and respite. A church that actually serves God and its people—how refreshing. He swallowed a morsel and reached for more. Finished eating, he washed his hands in a bowl, dried them with a linen cloth, and returned to the fire. The priest had left the room, so Gregory could eat in peace, but he returned, and both he and Gregory took a seat on a pair of old stools on either side of the fireplace.

"So, what brings you to Leschun?" the priest said.

"I was told I would be safe here, and as you know, you cannot say that of many places in Gascony," he said, and leaned in so his elbows rested on his knees. "They are still recovering from the war up there, and there is not enough to go around."

A weary expression came across the priest's face, his response a knowing nod. Gregory grabbed the iron and worked the fire. The embers crackled as he lifted one piece of wood and pulled another one forward so the flame flickered beneath a piece of fuel that had yet to catch. He leaned the iron back against the wall and glanced over at the priest. He did not want to lie to this man, nor did he want to tell the truth. But to get from Leschun what he had come for, he must first offer the golden ingot of trust.

"I am a merchant from London, but due to my place of origin they call me Gregory of Bordeaux," he said. "I am the head of a trade syndicate, and my bills of lading are on ships sailing from Seville to Lübeck. In their holds are wine, wool, grain, and every sumptuous luxury you could imagine. My wealth has brought me much status, but it has also brought me much despair. For me, wealth is not the only source of my troubles. You see, I am also a chronicler, and my words have inflamed hatred in my peers and my betters. I was banished from London, under pain of ruin, and even death, forced into exile for two years. So here I am, in need of shelter."

The priest contemplated what he heard, gazing into the fire. He scratched at his chin, glanced up toward the rafters, as if searching for a thought that had escaped him, and as resolution settled in his old benevolent face, he appeared to have arrived at where he had begun.

"We usually receive pilgrims on their way to Santiago de Compostela," he said. "But in you, I see we have a man at odds with the world in which he lives."

"Indeed, but it is also a world I cherish," Gregory said. "I have friends and trusted associates, and I married—not just for contracts, but also for love."

"It is good you speak of love, for in God's eyes, love is the only thing that counts," the priest said. "But tell me, Gregory of Bordeaux, is there anything else I need to know? Is there a truth you must admit before your residence here begins?"

The priest looked into Gregory's eyes, and though he was not confrontational, the sheer force of his certitude demanded that Gregory respond. Like an old alchemist trying to remember the recipe for a magic elixir, Gregory tried to find what the priest wanted to know. Down into the depths of his past he peered, but no confession was there. Gregory shrugged to betray confusion, and perhaps even to invite acceptance of his silence, but the priest would not relent. He refused to let Gregory get something for nothing, and as the test of minds unfolded, he felt himself on the verge of being overwhelmed. In the priest, Gregory saw all the seasons at once, the moon at waning, waxing, and full, and the sun at dawn, day and dusk. Challenging him on such a full front, the priest pushed Gregory back on himself, not into the misty chasm of years ago, but into the realm of his recent travails. With nowhere to go, Gregory realized he had met his match in this priest and that the hardened old Basque would have his day. And once he admitted defeat, he knew what he had to say.

"I am in possession of contraband," he said. "It is a book, and I stole it— but only from a man who himself had stolen it. In due time, it will be returned to its rightful owner. Priest, is that what you wanted to hear?"

"Yes," he said, and a gentle smile crept over his face. "Secrets do not sleep well in the rectory at Leschun."

Gregory donated a sous to the church, and was not surprised the priest, Father Guillaume, gave Gregory full run of the upper solar of the rectory. The laundress washed the Persian rug Gregory used as a saddle pad, and he laid it across the table where he worked. Soon, surrounded by his documents and scrivener's kit—inkwell and ink, goose-feather quill, lead pencil, ruler, pumice stone, and erasing knife—and with light from the candelabrum, Gregory fashioned a proper den for scholarly toil.

At last, he pulled out the book, and for the first time since it had been in his possession, beheld what he'd won in the rigged wager at Marmande. Named *De Mirabilibus Mundi*, the book was an edifice of the mind, its parchments sewn and bound between pieces of beveled beech dressed in tooled, burgundy leather with brass corner pieces and latch plates embossed with silver stars. Adorned with a brass centerpiece in the shape of a lotus flower encrusted with rubies and emeralds, the book was as much a showpiece as a source of learning. He undid the clasps, opened the tome, and as the gold leafing shown with a heavenly luster, Gregory breathed in the scent he so cherished—a rich mix of ink and stretched skin. The text was written in an exquisite hand of Latin, and in the margins fantastical scenes with animalia, exotica, and mundane portraits of daily life in a land of towering mountains, congested ports, and crowded market places. The dazzling color of the paint and the robust skill in the art shocked Gregory, and as he slowly turned the pages with the moistened tip of an index finger, scanning words and images, he smiled and shook his head in amazement.

Gregory looked up at Father Guillaume, who stood on the other side of the table, and said to him, "We are in for an eventful winter."

And so, it began, the arduous days of sharpening quills, dipping them in ink and copying the book page after page, of working until his fingers ached and his elbow grew stiff, of standing up to stretch and to stave off the fatigue of his work, of looking out the window at the sunset kindling the mountaintops, only to sit down and start again. So engrossed was he that Christmas came and went with a kneel and a prayer, a salty pork gelatin for repast, and a half bucket of wine.

Part of his payment for private use of the solar was that Father Guillaume would make a copy of the book for the church's manuscript collection. Gregory and the priest quickly fell into a routine. Gregory would finish a page and begin another, and Father Guillaume would copy the page Gregory had just completed. The work became consuming, and Father Guillaume ceded all but his most important duties to one of his deacons, so he could concentrate on transcribing his edition of the book. Gregory liked being in close quarters with the priest. Father Guillaume, older, wiser, and having studied at Bologna when young, knew Latin much better than Gregory. But it wasn't all work. Sometimes they put their quills down, sat downstairs near the fire, drank Jurançon wine and talked of the adventures in this book by the Venetian merchant named Marco Polo.

"Can any of this be true?" Gregory said.

"His stories seem impossible, but at the same time he is authoritative," said Father Guillaume. "And we must remember, there is a big world out there, and not all of God's creatures are the same."

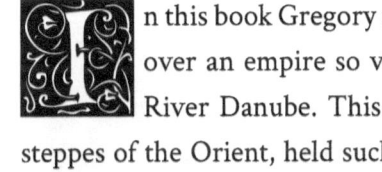n this book Gregory met Kublai Khan, the Great Khan, who ruled over an empire so vast it stretched from the Sea of Chin to the River Danube. This Khan, a Mongol from the frigid, northern steppes of the Orient, held such sway over his wealth and armies, Gregory figured he was the better of even the greatest of the Roman Caesars. A couple of years ago Gregory heard the Great Khan had died, and his empire declined, but still, Gregory shuddered at the thought that, in his own lifetime, a man as omnipotent as the Khan had lived.

Gregory took a drink of Jurançon. Outside the rectory door, the wind howled and the snow lay in great drifts throughout the sleeping town of Leschun. A wall hanging rustled as a draft snuck in through a window, and the candle flames bent and danced in the trays. He sat in a chair with his feet, tucked inside thick woolen socks, propped on a stool close to the fireplace. The book sat open in his lap. Across from him Father Guillaume, in a similar state of repose, read over a copied page.

"Listen to this," Gregory said. "The Great Khan had four wives who sat as his legitimate consorts, and the chief of them bore his successors. But

Kublai also had a stable of concubines in waiting to satisfy the imperial appetite. Most of these maidens came from the Ungrat tribe, a Mongol clan known for the comeliness of their women. Each year as tribute, and in exchange for royal favor, the Ungrat sent one hundred of their best maidens to be groomed for the Khan's private chamber. Given to elder women who took them to bed and slept with them to determine if they had good morning breath, did not snore, and were sound of body and limb. Those deemed worthy were presented to the Khan, and served him in turns, six at a time for three days, and at the end of three days, another six throughout the year. Father Guillaume, what do you make of this?"

"A perpetual churn of sin and servitude, and most certainly a bonanza of fornication," he said.

"This Marco Polo claims the Great Khan had twenty-two sons by his wives, twenty-five by his concubines, and an untold number of daughters," Gregory said. "Indeed, the Khan commanded a great army, and with his tireless loins, sired one as well."

"Perhaps his lust is distinguished by the magnitude of his spawn, but this Great Khan is no different than the lords who live here in Christendom," he said. "They go hunting and whoring, and that is their lot in life."

"I agree," Gregory said. "Let me tell you about the first King Henry. The young runt of King William's litter. He stole the crown from his brother, sat on the throne for thirty years and, as much a lecher as a king, is said to have fathered twenty-seven children—twenty-four of them bastards from a succession of mistresses."

"Oh, I am familiar with the first King Henry," he said. "And as I recall, God was not pleased with his proclivities and punished his realm with rebellion. I am a priest, and a long time ago I gave myself over to a life of chastity and service. But what about you? Is there a Great Khan deep inside of you, and do you secretly wish you could bed as many maidens as old King Henry?"

Gregory laughed. He took a sip of Jurançon. A sweet memory from his wedding day came to mind.

"No," he said. "The Great Khan can have his concubines and the king can have his whores. I have a wife, Joan Costantyn is her name, and the peak of my ambition is that she and my heir are waiting for me when I return to London."

eschun was covered so deep in snow it seemed as if the town were dead. True, the church bell rung the hours all day, so at least someone was up and at their task. But when Gregory looked out the window and down into the street below, he saw no foot prints, heard no voices, and in the stillness of it all, missed his life back in London. He longed for fresh apples in the fall, warm bread spread thick with butter, clothes worn for the first time after a wash, and his rose garden in full bloom. Two apprentices, a manservant, a groom, the cook, the scullion, and the laundress—he boasted a proper, tidy household in his whitewashed, stone, and timber hall near the Thames. He could count the days until his return, but what a waste of time. He scolded himself for letting out all the heat, and closed the shutter. He stretched one more time, returned to his table, and opened the book to the place he had marked with a slip of wool. He dipped the quill into the ink well and made ready to transcribe, but heard footsteps coming up the stairs. He looked up from the book and saw Father Guillaume.

"I am glad you are here," Gregory said. "I was lonely and nostalgic and about to fall into the trap of self-pity."

"Two children were born this day, Gregory," he said. "I baptized them before the devil got their souls."

"So, there is life in Leschun?"

Father Guillaume smiled.

"God has seen fit to bless us with much of it this day."

Father Guillaume set a flagon of wine and two cups on the table, and filled them before taking a seat. With the palm of his hand, Gregory gestured at several parchments.

"I have been at it all day, so I have a good lead on you," he said.

"But my quill is quicker than yours," quipped Father Guillaume, "and I will catch up to you soon enough."

At opposite ends of the table, the two of them hunched over their work, the only sound between them the scratch of quills upon the calfskins. Hours dripped away, and with the dark of night came a storm of bitter winter wind. A servant boy came to them with heated stones wrapped in leather, which they put beneath their feet, and when the cold crept into their bones, they draped thick fleeces over their shoulders. When, finally, the bell rang at Compline, Gregory gave in to his fatigue and set his quill in a tray. He refilled his cup and took a long drink. The Jurançon hit home. The aching ebbed, and the pleasure flowed.

"Father Guillaume," Gregory said, "Marco Polo says he has been to the seven kingdoms of Persia, Tabriz, and the port at Hormuz. He says he has crossed the steppes and the plateaus of Great Turkey, and it took him a month to cross what he calls the Taklamaken Desert. This I can believe. But he describes cities of silk, chalcedony and rhubarb, and palaces of gold and silver. Can this be so, or does he tell lies? I have been to the great cities of Paris and Bruges, but never have I seen the likes of what he describes."

"But he is not talking about Paris and Bruges," Father Guillaume said. "He is talking about a legion of merchants doing business in Cambaluc, and one hundred thousand tartars charging south to do battle with the Song. We drink wine made from grapes, but they drink wine made from rice. What we see and do here is not what you would see and do there."

"Perhaps you are right," he said. "But I am skeptical. He says the River Caramoran is afloat with fifteen thousand ships, but in all my years in London—and I have seen the Christmas wine fleets—never have I counted so many sails."

"And what about the great canal and the cities of Coiganju, Paukin, and Cayu?" Father Guillaume asked. "Their commerce is sugar, pearls, porcelain and indigo, ginger, cinnamon, fruit, and turquoise. If they are lies Marco Polo tells, still they are a delight."

Gregory took another drink of wine and looked long and hard at the big book in front of him. From the teeming ports and prosperous cities, the Great Khan took his toll to pay for his diversions and his armies, but still the people had plenty. His sorcerers, clever in their diabolical arts, steered the clouds and storms away from the Great Khan's summer palace at Xanadu as long as the Khan was in residence there. When he drank the milk from his fantastic white mares, the music played, and his subjects went silent and bowed. Near the sea in the heart of the empire stood Kinsay, known as The City of Heaven. Within its one hundred miles of compass were twelve thousand bridges of stone, lush gardens, and the handsome homes of the merchants who made profit there. So many goods passed through its markets the quantity was beyond the estimation of even the keenest mind. Its streets were paved with stone, and its people enjoyed the comforts of its three thousand hot baths. Out on West Lake, lined with mansions and abbeys, friends and family glided along the water on pleasure cruises, and within the city, covered carriages rumbled through the streets. Kinsay, so fair the Great Khan spared its charms when he and his Mongol host came to conquer. Beyond his empire, east across the water, the gold mountain of Chipangu, which the Great Khan tried to plunder. But his ships were blown asunder by a violent wind, and the surviving Mongol horde was slaughtered by the islands' courageous *Samurai*. Even the sun, giving and glorious as it is, always must set.

Father Guillaume saw the wry smile in Gregory. "What is it, my friend?"

"This Marco Polo." Gregory hoisted his cup. "He tells the truth."

he snow came in flurries and torrents, the winds were an endless refrain by a choir of insane and livid angels, and the sky, gray with vengeance, had banished the sun and the stars for having dared to have shone in other seasons. Gregory hoped winter's grip on the Pyrenees would loosen so he could shed the heavy fleeces and furs that burdened him, but he came to accept that his wants had been ignored. A Bordelaise by blood and a Londoner by choice, he expected to be broiled in July and to be chilled in January. But this coercive freeze, this commandment from on high that mankind should be shivering and miserable, was more than Gregory wanted to endure. What, at first, he saw as an open and inviting rectory had become small, and the solar where he worked and slept had become even smaller, the walls falling in on him, the food beginning to spoil, and the Jurançon, so sweet a month ago, now going sour. Hibernation does not suit me. His spirits rallied when he looked over at Marco Polo's book. More than half-way through the manuscript, and soon, he would have his own copy. If this is the reward for spending winter in this mountain hermitage, then it is a handsome reward indeed. He breathed a sigh of resignation and returned to his seat at the table. He lit a piece of frankincense. Its aroma soothed him. He dipped the quill in the inkwell and went back to transcribing.

When the Great Khan went fowling with his gyrfalcons, he lounged in a great timber pavilion, lined inside with textiles and sheets of beaten gold, and draped outside with the skins of leopards and lions. Carried on the backs of four elephants, this canopied pavilion, with its carpets and curtains and bed of silk, sable and cushions, was the better of any hall in all of Christendom. When at the hunt in spring, seeking out his hare, stag, buck, and roe, no man within a twenty-day ride of the Great Khan could employ his hawks and hounds, it being a capital crime to take game while Kublai gave chase. A horde of courtiers followed him wherever he went—nobles and magistrates, merchants and magicians, astrologers and sorcerers, and concubines and their keepers. In the thousands they were, slaves to his largesse, living in a city of tents, and moving in a throng as he travelled from the hunt back to his palace at Cambaluc.

The Great Khan did not plunder Cathay, but governed it. He swathed himself in the garb of those he had dethroned, and took their ways as his own. He made enemies of his kin, the nomads of the steppe, who accused him of betraying the old ways. But his power was such that they could do little more than complain, and in the face of their disappointment, he abandoned the behavior of a warlord and made of himself a king. He built roads and granaries and apprised himself of all doings with a corps of couriers who crisscrossed the empire at all hours of everyday. He issued paper money stamped with a vermillion seal, and for himself kept the gold and silver. Through force of arms he maintained the great corridors from east to west along which the silk and spices flowed, and his writ, too, at the tip of a poisoned arrow, ran from the Sea of Chin to the edge of Christendom.

Gregory was not surprised at being fascinated by the Great Khan and his sprawling empire of riches. What he hadn't expected, was that this book would challenge his appreciation for his own world. All Gregory's life, Edward had been king, and many times Gregory bowed low and dutifully as Edward and his court made procession through London. As a recognized citizen of the city, Gregory paid taxes into the franchise as an official member of King Edward's realm. He loved the king. He served the king. And if any man should rise in rebellion against the king, then he would be Gregory's enemy. But reading about the Great Khan, Gregory now had a point of comparison, and when made, he could not deny that King Edward seemed a very small man. It was all Edward could do to keep London under his control. Even with his amercements and tolls, he remained always destitute and begging his nobles for money. He owed debts to merchants from Kent to Carlisle, and rumors were that he had defaulted on his obligations to his bankers in Lucca. So poor, King Edward, that in the eighteenth year of his reign, he expelled all the Jews from England, repeating what he had done in Gascony a few years earlier, with all outstanding debts owed to them turned over to the crown. Popular moves, Gregory knew, but desperate ones as well. Edward could not sustain an army in Flanders or in Gascony, and even after years of travail and the imposition of his hated war taxes, had yet to subdue the upstart clans in the misty mountains of Scotland. If Edward is a little king of a little island, then that is a little opinion I should keep to myself.

Finished for the day, he went downstairs to the hall and ate with Father Guillaume. As they dined on white bread, goat cheese, roasted saffron chicken, smoked pork, and a dessert of dried dates, they made small talk. But when the meal was done, and they sat by the fireplace with cups and a surprise flagon of Malbec, the conversation turned to *De Mirabilibus Mundi*.

"I read a curious passage today," Gregory said. "There are Christians, Muslims, Buddhists, and Jews at the Great Khan's court. And he allows them to worship as they please. I ask you, would any Christian prince be so tolerant?"

Father Guillaume crossed his arms over his chest and tilted back his head, as if in deep thought. Gregory read his eyes and knew the priest had a debate within himself, and that one side or the other would have to win before he said anything. Gregory set his cup on the floor and leaned in with his elbows on his knees. When the priest spoke, Gregory wanted to hear each and every word, and with the sharp attentiveness of his posture, tried to convey to Father Guillaume that silence would not be a suitable answer. Father Guillaume, wrestling with discomfort and uncertainty, glanced at Gregory with pleading eyes, a wordless request he drop the question and continue. But Gregory shook his head, and as he always did when serious and looking for a point, held up an index finger and set his jaw.

"Tell me, Father Guillaume, is there a Christian prince who would be so tolerant as the great Kublai Khan?" he asked.

"Our lords value obedience over tolerance," he said. "It is no secret, many of them have failed to embrace the Christian virtues of love, mercy, and acceptance."

"But it is more than that," Gregory said. "The church, and the lords who support it, only accept one view. Think about the Cathar heresy, not far from here and not too long ago. The Cathars were massacred at Béziers and burned at the stake at Montségur. Their only crime was the Pope did not like the way they worshipped. Why is it so?"

A baleful shadow showed in Father Guillaume's eyes, and he shrugged his shoulders in a show of confessional embarrassment.

"Land and treasure," he said.

"Coming from a man who has taken his holy orders, I know that is a lot for you to admit," Gregory said. "And, of course, you are right."

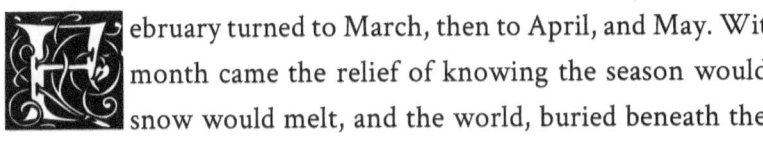ebruary turned to March, then to April, and May. With the new month came the relief of knowing the season would turn, the snow would melt, and the world, buried beneath the blizzard's frigid waste since before Christmas, would emerge anew. The shepherds and their herds would return from the valley, the mountains would go green, and the orchids and asphodels would open their petals and pray to their god, the sun. The chirping of the thrushes, and the sounds of the towns at last back at their work, would please the hearts of men and women cooped too long around their dreary hearths. For Gregory, it meant he would soon be on Black Saddle, back out on the road and orchestrating his final campaigns in Gascony. The thought of galloping across the fields and passing through the gates of cities and castles, and of the danger awaiting him in the vineyards and hills of the low country, made Gregory want to mount up and ride at that very moment. But he looked over at the book, *De Mirabilibus Mundi*, and knew work still needed to be done, still isolation to be endured, and that he was not done looking at the same walls that each day crowded against his sanity. He leaned back in his chair, threw his feet up on the table, locked his hands behind his head, and in a cranky voice, said to himself, I am dripping away in this rectory, and this book is not worth my time.

Yet in the cracks in the window's shutter, Gregory saw an enchanting glow. He went to the window and pulled open the shutter. The sun was setting in the west, but it was throwing light back east across the mountains. It set them ablaze with a purple and gold so deep and bright, it was as if the peaks were molten. The air, cold and crisp, was not as bitter as before, and in the street below, the village kids played tag. A dog barked. Singing came from the tavern. Young lovers, hand in hand, stood on the steps of the church and gazed into each other's eyes. Perhaps I have grown cantankerous, but God has blessed me with these months in Leschun. He went back to the table, but before he sat, he lit every candle and every chunk of Frankincense. As the candle light filled every corner of the room, and as the fragrant smoke curled through the air, the solar seemed much larger than it had just moments ago. He returned to his work, reading and copying and turning the page, and as he did, he hummed an old London song, *Saying Farewell is Never Easy*, again and again.

The next morning, he was glad to see Father Guillaume appear at the entrance of the solar. Looking a bit tired but content, the priest appeared ready to plunge back into the tedious task of duplicating a book as challenging as *De Mirabilibus Mundi*.

"I have fortified myself for the final push," Gregory said. "I will soon be finished with my work, but there is yet plenty for you." He turned and gestured to the stack of parchments he had finished in the last few days, then to the few remaining pages in the bound manuscript.

Father Guillaume pursed his lips, nodded his head, and said, "You have been busy while I was away. Pardon me for my absence, but even in a place as small as Leschun, there is much to be done, and I cannot trust everything to the care of my deacons."

"You owe me no apologies, father, but you do owe me your curiosity," he said. "Please, sit with me, for I came across one of Marco Polo's tales you should like to hear."

The priest, energized by Gregory's enthusiasm, took his seat, propped his heels on a foot stool, and with his eyes wide and inviting, said, "Tell me what it is that has pleased you so."

Gregory thumbed through the pile of parchments, pulled out the few on which the story appeared, cleared his throat, held the parchments out in front of him and read.

> *Princess Aiyurug is the daughter of Prince Caidu of Samarkand. With her jet hair and onyx eyes, and a headdress dripping with rare and dazzling gems, she was a field abloom with mountain iris, a distant flume sparkling in the sun, or a band of stars blinking in the cloudless Turkish night. Renowned for her beauty, she is as famous for her prowess in the field, as in battle, she is the equal of any man. Long and shapely and of pleasing proportions, almost a giantess, when she pulled her sword, readied her shield, and*

bellowed her battle cry, many a knight did shudder. And while her parents were proud of their beautiful daughter, she also caused them much conster-nation. They wanted her to marry, you see, but Aiyurug was stubborn and would submit to no man. Finally she agreed to be wed, but only to one who could best her in a feat of arms. She sent her challenge to all corners of the empire—win my hand in combat or in defeat give me one hundred horses.

Gregory lowered the parchments and peered over the top of them to see the look on Father Guillaume's face. Rapt, and with an expression of faux puzzlement, as if to ask Gregory why he had stopped, urged him to continue.

They came from near and far, the high and low, the foul and fair, and soon Aiyurug had a great herd of mares and stallions. Then arrived a val-iant prince, handsome, revered and so sure of his ability he wagered not one hundred horses, but one thousand. He and Aiyurug met in the great palace at Samarkand, and before the court and its fawning masses, she wrestled this prince, and through great exertion, grappled him to the floor. Full of shame and humbled, the knight left, and Aiyurug, her breast heaving, stood victori-ous. Her father, Prince Caidu, was disappointed. He reckoned the prince a good man who would have made a good husband for his daughter. But at last he conceded to her will, and from then onward, she went with him on campaign, mounted on a fine war horse, a bow across her back, and draped in mail.

"Well? Is there any woman in all of Christendom to rival her?"

"It would seem she has no rival in all the world," Father Guillaume said. "But let me ask you a question. You have spoken a few times of your wife, Joan. Where does she stand in comparison to Princess Aiyurug?"

As Gregory thought about his response, he set the parchments on the table, poured himself a cup of watered Jurançon, and with one shoulder, leaned against the wall. He took a sip, cradled the cup in both hands, and surrendered to a big, soulful smile.

"She is no warrior princess and she is certainly no giantess," he began. "The top of her head barely reaches to my chin, and as discreet and decorous as she is, she is a mistress of social graces, not of war. But she is a patrician by blood and by trade, and she is comfortable in her privilege. She is reserved, even in private, and is always careful to ration her sentiments. On the rare public occasion when she does smile, I assure you, she can heal the soul of a sinner, and when she has had enough of stupidity and speaks her mind, the pigheaded scurry away. She is prim, Father Guillaume, but she is also splendid. I have seen her with a tiara of silver and roses, an embroidered silk veil, and a necklace of gold and amethyst. But when she is in her fur and robes and at the fullest extent of her station, she still can't be outdone by her finery. She herself shines as sapphire, and when she enters the hall, the music is sweeter, and the light is brighter. She is a pepper magnate, and knows her business well. I gave her my rights before I left and trust that when I return my house will be intact."

"So, your Joan is exceptional all the way around," Father Guillaume said.

"In my eyes, indeed," he said. "This Princess Aiyurug is good for fanciful daydreams, but believe me, I prefer my Lady Joan."

It was a scene he had witnessed before and one he appreciated—everyone in the village coming out to watch him leave. He hadn't spent any time among them. Instead, he had cloistered himself in the rectory, hunched over his parchments, reading and writing and talking to none but Father Guillaume. But surely the servant boy or one of the deacons had spread word of a stranger in the church, that he had a great book, and that he and Father Guillaume had spent much time pouring over its contents. So, the villagers, these simple, rough-hewn mountain folk, with their squat thighs and broad shoulders, had come out to see the scribe before he left. Gregory didn't know enough about this place or its people to be saddened by his departure, but he couldn't help but think a piece of him would always remain here. With that thought came a pang because he knew he would never return. He climbed on his horse, and as soon as he did, Black Saddle, fat and rested and eager to run, snorted and flinched, and with violent hoof work, pranced in a wide circle. Gregory pulled in the reins. He doffed his beaver skin hat and held it over his heart.

"God bless Leschun," he said. "May it never again endure a winter like the one it endured this year."

Gregory donned his hat and tugged the brim down low over his brow. He looked long and deep into Father Guillaume's eyes.

"We rode with the Great Kublai Khan, did we not?"

"And ride with him still and forever," Father Guillaume said.

Gregory and Black Saddle pulled in behind the guide for the long, dangerous descent down the switchbacks. He took a deep breath of uplifting mountain air. He looked over his shoulder, prepared to give one last wave, but Leschun was already out of view.

The priest took a long look at the men gathered in the hall. Crowded around Alphonse, who sat on a battered wooden chair, his false throne. The loyal men, the holdovers from the culled herd, those who had not been swayed by the bounty on their lord's head. The rest of them had been routed out and hung from the castle wall, nine of them left dangling for the carrion birds. A gruesome time when the plot had been discovered and quashed, treachery upended by a sustained act of cruelty. Now, there remained this handful of men, louts and crooks in helmets and mail, clinging to their allegiance.

The priest knew them well. Were it not for the dignity of his holy orders, and if not for the privilege of literacy, he would have been gutted along with the rest of them. Even Alphonse could not kill a man of the cloth, giving the priest his place among these rogues, a higher place to which they could not climb—or so the priest hoped. And it was with a poisonous drip of doubt that he stepped up on a chair, unrolled the parchment, and read the latest of Gregory's letters.

I have been in the mountains breathing the fresh air. It is an act of freedom to feel the wind tearing down from the cliffs, to watch the sun set across the peaks, and to taste the virgin snow. These simple pleasures are denied to you because you have been condemned. You are stuck in your rat-infested castle, smelling the stink of your sinful crotch, shitting in the same hole as your lice-ridden men, and eating pot after pot of pauper's gruel. You should think of the mountain air and what you did to deprive yourself of it.

The priest looked up from the parchment, spying, as he knew he would, the chagrin in Alphonse's eyes.

"Gregory taunts you, my lord," he said.

"And do you find it amusing?"

"I do. But I am sure you do not."

Alphonse creased into a familiar, drooping sneer of displeasure. His men did the same. "When I catch this Gregory, what should his penalty be?"

The priest smiled, because he knew the answer. "A red-hot poker, my lord, up his ass. One of your favorites."

"That seems a heavy price for breathing the mountain air."

"Perhaps, but he is a braggart, and braggarts should be humbled."

Alphonse pulled out his knife, and with its point, started carving the dirt from beneath his fingernails. Nail after nail he went, starting from his pinky and working across to his thumb. Thinking, the priest knew, about the merits of the poker. Pretending to be calm when in fact a storm of vengeance swirled within. He switched to his other hand, scraping out gunk and grime, clipping and filing, grooming his war-torn hands. Finished, he stabbed the knife into the arm of the chair.

"A red-hot poker," he said, nodding his head.

THE
NIGHT WATCH
OF BAYONNE

regory travelled to Oleron, St. Palais, La Bastide de Clarens, and then Bayonne, the city of whalers and fishermen, of shipyards and sailors. It was a city of salt and dye, of wharves and tax rolls, the pugnacious port at the very bottom of King Edward's world.

The promise of summer filled the air, and when Gregory took a deep breath, he smelled the brine of the sea. He stabled his horse and found a room at the Green Dolphin inn. He ate fresh mackerel, soft cheese, olives, and white bread smeared with garlic and butter. Sitting at a candlelit table in a dark corner of the crowded tavern, he sipped on *Nérac* and counted his blessings. The mountains had been good to him. He had a manuscript in his pack, fresh wind in his lungs, and, if the empty faces all about him were any indication, no one in pursuit. But his comfort did not last long. He still had many months left in Gascony, and if the first leg of the exile had been one of danger, it was nothing but a preamble to the story about to unfold. There remained the ship, the debt, the hostage, and the arrest warrant, all left to be done. He took another sip of *Nérac*, but found little solace.

Part two of the ordeal, the one that would surely kill him, began tonight.

But it would not be without its enjoyments. You see, he waited for his dear friend, Warren, who would ride with him deep into Gascony's forbidden precincts, on a fleet horse with mail and helm, and a blade of thirsty steel. Warren was a lord, no doubt, yet hungry for a higher title, a thinker and a fighter, hand-picked years ago, who had lived up to his promise. Gregory grew anxious as one candle burned-down and another was lit. He drained the dregs from his cup and filled it again. And so, the evening passed, hand to cup and cup to mouth, past the ringing of the curfew bell, outlasting the locals who left for their homes, and remaining with only those who lodged there. About to call this an empty day and retire to his room, he caught a second wind and ordered another flagon. He slid a coin across the table. The taverner took it without saying a word, and Gregory lit another chunk of Frankincense.

Though the second round of *Nérac* was as good as the first, he knew it would make him pay on the morrow. So, he drank it deep and swallowed without flinching. If I am sick when I awake, at least let me be happy before I go to sleep. The tide of wine rose and fell, and Gregory felt himself drifting out to the straits and into a much deeper pool of reflection. He needed sleep, he told himself, but instead he poured another drink.

His patience, at last, was rewarded when a man appeared in the doorway. He filled the threshold, not with a pompous chest and pretentious air, but with the weight and patina of heroics. He carried a bundle of gear slung over his shoulder, a sun swept brow and fine garb weathered by the tumult of the sea. Gregory looked into his eyes and saw the smile of an old friend. He stood up and walked out from behind the table. He stepped forward and met him halfway across the floor. Within feet of each other, both of them stopped. Warren dropped his kit and held out his arms, and Gregory stepped into them without hesitation. They clasped each other by the shoulders and exchanged long looks of admiration. The world they had shared back during the chronicle sprung to life. A crash of noise, flashes of light and darkness, the scents of cities and battle filling the room. They conjured an intimacy that would never be lost to time, that would never fall victim to neglect. This reunion, big and abrupt and outlandish in its show of emotion, boiled over with the laughter of love and relief that can only be shared by old friends meeting at the end of long roads.

"Master Gregory," he said.

"Warren, my boy," and they hugged again.

Seated at the table and looking through the candlelight at his former page, Gregory felt old. A slave to his commerce, mired in urban squabbles, and ever fretful over his business and dealings, he knew part of himself had already become that crotchety burger he had mocked not long ago. And it was not as if Warren hadn't aged. In the mournful deep of his blue eyes, it was clear he had. But with wind burnt cheeks, bright blond hair, and the hard lines of war and adventure, he still pulsed with the gush of youth. So strong the beat of Warren's heart, Gregory felt it in his own chest, and as the cadence thumped, and the sound of the drum grew ever louder, Gregory sensed himself anew.

"It has been too long."

"Our lives get in the way of our friendships, I'm afraid," Warren said. "It is only six days by horse between Lichfield and London, but it may as well be the known world. I can never break away from my duties for a visit to my old friend."

"And London life keeps me busy," Gregory said. "Until I came here, I had scarcely gone beyond the city walls since the days of the chronicle."

"I know the circumstances are not of your choosing, and I know you left much behind, but it must feel good to be back on the hoof. Tonight, you have lost your edge because you have had too much to drink. But you look strong, Master Gregory. You have honed your guile while in Gascony, I can tell."

He chuckled and tapped his middle and index fingers on the side of his cup. "It is true I have exercised my wits, but also true I grew tired and rested in the mountains. Somewhere out there, men are looking for me, and I do not know for how much longer I can stay a step ahead."

"Now that I am here there will not be much running," Warren tilted his head into a cocksure glare. "I have my orders from Southampton, and one of them is to get you back to London alive."

"And you think you can do that?" Gregory asked, and smiled over the brim of his cup.

"And more." Laughing, he drained his share of Nérac.

So the night went, drinking and talking, sharing gossip and whispers, with frequent brays of laughter and the sweet effusion of reminiscence. They relived the danger and discovery of the chronicle, exchanging memories, suspended in time's lustrous amber, of their now heralded gallop across the realm. Not surprisingly, their conversation turned to the horses, and that's when Warren appeared sad.

"Master Gregory, I do not have Moonbeam anymore," he said. "She died a year ago. She caught the cough and was gone soon thereafter, not long before you sailed for Gascony."

Gregory's eyes moistened when he heard the news, but his love for her overpowered the grief of her passing. Her grit in the north—the star of Durham—the decider at Corby, the old Spanish mare had bitten, kicked, and trampled anyone who had gotten in her way, and was big-hearted enough to serve two masters. A once-in-a-generation horse, Moonbeam held top place in the pages of the chronicle. And Gregory knew she lived on through her progeny, a foal she had begotten with his horse, Black Saddle, three years ago when they had made good on their promise to put the horses together at a small stable in the village of Tatenhill.

"So, if Moonbeam is no longer with us, what do you now ride?" Gregory said, a hopeful note in the question.

Warren gave a gap-toothed grin. "The new filly. *The* filly. She will be as mean as Moonbeam and as fast as Black Saddle—in due time."

"Is that possible?" Gregory asked.

"I named her Lady Tatenhill, after where she was conceived, and during our journey, we will find out what she can do. And how is Black Saddle?"

"Perhaps a bit too old," Gregory said. "This is his last ride, but there is fire left in him still, and I should think he will want to teach a thing or two to his daughter."

Warren raised his cup. "Indeed."

n the privacy of the narrow room they shared at the inn, Gregory and Warren plotted the upcoming escapades. Sitting at a rickety table on rickety stools, and drinking from a hogshead of ale, they colluded with hushed tones and knowing glances, and built the scaffolding of their plan. Sink the ship—absolve the debt—free the princess—arrest the outlaw—and return to riches and fame in England.

"Easy enough." Gregory stretched his arms and shoulders.

Warren took his cup of ale and stepped over to the window, leaned on the sill and looked out over the city. He halfway glanced over his shoulder and beckoned Gregory to join him. So, the two of them stood there, elbow to elbow gazing at Bayonne's timbered stories and stone arches, its clutter of rooftops and the imposing Cathédrale Sainte-Marie, to the shipyard and the quay, with its bobbing hulks and cogs. Their long journey began there on the waterfront, among the masts, cargo and warehouses, inside the maritime slum of broken hope and silver dreams, Southampton's second task.

"There." Warren pointed to a cog with a little blue banner hanging from the stern castle.

"And how do you know?"

A sinister little crook showed in his smile. "I sailed over on that ship—I hung the banner—so that is how I know. The ship does not belong to Alphonse of Bayonne, but to a consortium of merchants sympathetic to his plight."

"Ah," Gregory said. "Now I am beginning to understand."

"Two years ago, these merchants sold Southampton ten tonnes of spoiled Easter wine, and it was only then he learned of Alphonse and his transgressions against the king. This is revenge, but it serves a bigger purpose than revenge."

"If Southampton wrecks Alphonse, then he gains favor with the king."

"And if we are the ones who do the work, then we gain favor with Southampton," Warren said. "If the ship's cargo is sold, then a portion of the profit will find its way to Alphonse, who needs the coin to pay his men, stock his larder, and maintain his network of bribes. But if this ship sinks, he is weakened, and perhaps makes it easier for us to arrest him."

Warren turned to Gregory with a rotten smile, and in it Gregory saw the compromise of adulthood, the hypocrisy of lordship, and the erosion of idealism. But it suited him, the ease of maturity, and as Gregory looked into his chiseled face, he was glad Warren was fully grown.

"Do you have a stomach for mischief?"

"That is more than mischief," Gregory replied. "Were we to be caught, we could be hanged for destruction of property."

"Then we will not let ourselves be caught."

"I think I liked the old days of the chronicle," Gregory said. "We were— innocent back then."

"And I have fond memories of those times, too, Master Gregory, but we have not been innocent for many years. We are roarers now, miscreants in service to our lord. Embrace your role and help me sink that ship."

They snuck out of the inn long after the ringing of the curfew bell, when the streets were dark and draped in shadow. Enveloped in hooded black cloaks, their faces covered with grotesque masks—ears, horns and fangs, and long pointed noses, relics from a forgotten mystery play—they slunk like demons down crooked streets, slid through alleys slick with rot and offal, and as they crouched and tiptoed peering around every corner, they reached the great quay. Hiding behind the corner of the custom's house, they waited for the night watch, half of them drunk and drinking from skins of wine, to pass them by. They sprinted down the quay and up to the ship, its deck vacant of captain and crew. They climbed aboard and plunged down into the hold, the reeking orifice of trade, greed's dank cavern infested with hungry rats. Stacked high with grain, fleeces, lead and coal, the bounty in the belly of this cog of such value it could either make a man or destroy him. Gregory pulled the mask up over his head and did a flash count of the quantity of goods and the money to be made. Knowing its fate, and indeed, of the ship in which it sat, he shook his head and sighed.

"I don't want to do this," Gregory said. "There is too much cargo to simply destroy. There has to be another way."

"Perhaps there is, but we are not doing it this night. This is the way it has to be, Master Gregory, for we are not making all the rules on this journey."

From beneath his cloak Warren pulled a sledgehammer and a long iron bar, which he handed to Gregory. Resigned to the necessity of this dark duty, Gregory squatted down, and using both hands, snugged the tip of the iron bar into a seam between the planking. He held it in place, leaning his head away and closing his eyes as Warren cocked the sledgehammer over his shoulder. A jarring jolt of energy ripped through his hands and arms when Warren struck the head of the bar. He recoiled and struck it again, and did it one more time. The seam split with a shriek. The bar powered through. Water rushed through the opening. Gregory and Warren climbed on top of the bar, standing on it and rocking downward until the hull ruptured. Water spewed in.

As the flood ran over his boots, Gregory felt the excitement of crime, the rush of destruction. "We have sunk a ship!"

"And let us leave before we sink ourselves!"

They climbed up to the deck, leapt to the quay, and even as they fled, the ship listed starboard.

Squinting through the eyeholes of their wicked masks, they ducked and slithered back to the inn undetected. With his knife, Warren jimmied the front door. They stepped inside. Warren closed and locked the door behind them. Gregory looked to the stairs leading up to their room, and for a fleeting moment felt the elation of having gotten away with it. But out of the corner of his eye, a sight made him stop and tremble. The taverner was sitting on top of a table with his feet on a bench, and next to him, his wife. The people who, for the last five days, had cooked his food, served his wine, and who had emptied the piss pot in the corner of his room. They had laundered his robes and cleaned his boots, told him the best place for a haircut and a shave, and had changed the hay in his mattress upon his first request. He liked the taverner and his salty wife, who just the evening before had led the guests in a rousing rendition of *Jolie Gabrielle de la Mer*. A memorable night of laughter and song, and Gregory wished he were in that moment again.

He removed the mask, painted red and black, and set it on the table next to him. Warren did the same. Gregory put a hand to Warren's shoulder, and with the slightest push backward, intimated to him he was not the arbiter of this encounter. Gregory held out a hand in a gesture of peace, and showed regret in his face.

"You broke curfew, Gregory," the taverner said. "I did not think you were the kind of man who played games beneath the devil's moon."

"There are times when I must," Gregory said.

"If wrongdoing is discovered tonight or on the morrow, I will have to bear witness," he said. "You have been a good guest, but it is I who must live here."

From the inn, the shouts and alarms unintelligible, but a great cacophony sounded from the port. The footsteps of many running men, the spit and glow of their torches, and the ringing of their hand bells signaled a calamity. The taverner's eyes grew narrow and accusatory, and his wife, pushing herself off the table so she stood, revealed a meat hook held cleverly in her hand.

"It seems as if the wrongdoing has already been found," Gregory said. "But I must say, it sounds worse than it is."

"And what is it?" the taverner said.

"We have sunk a ship," he said. "Not just any ship, but a ship controlled by an enemy of our king. We sunk it because we are in the king's service."

"You? The King? Why should I believe you?"

"Because I tell the truth, but at this very moment, even if I lied, it would be to your benefit to indulge me."

Warren took the masks to the fireplace. He hoisted up the ember log with the poker and tucked the masks deep within the bed of coals. They quickly caught fire. As the flames consumed the evidence, Gregory and the taverner looked at each other, both of them searching for a hint as to which direction it would go. The taverner or his wife at any moment could sound the hue and cry, or Warren could lunge across the room and do his handiwork. Gregory couldn't allow either of those things to happen. Instead, he hoped to settle this situation as he'd settled many before. He would offer an enticement.

He recollected everything he had seen, done and heard since arriving in Bayonne, and the Green Dolphin inn five days ago. He sifted through those recent memories with the real urgency of a man who cannot afford to offer the wrong answer. A crafty grin sparked in his eyes and he conveyed to the taverner an exaggerated expression of conclusion.

"The other night I overheard you talking to your friend," he said. "You told him you wanted to open another inn, but you could not afford to buy another permit."

The taverner and his wife glanced at one another for assurance, and then the taverner turned back to Gregory. "Continue."

"I can solve the problem tonight, but you must keep my secret."

"How?"

"In my room I have a very rare and expensive book," he said. "Its cover is encrusted with precious stones. Perhaps your silence is worth a few of them? As you well know, if I am arrested by the night watch, all my chattel will be seized and turned over to the bailiff. In that case, there are no emeralds, and no permit, for you."

"Show me this book," the taverner said.

Just as Gregory made as if to head upstairs and fetch *De Mirabilibus Mundi*, there came a frightful pounding on the inn's front door. When the taverner did not immediately respond, there came a second knock, this one so forceful and so pregnant with violent intent, it seemed as if the door would spring from its hinges. Gregory and the taverner shared a dour moment of reckoning, and in the tiny fraction of time before chaos entered, he did his best to show confidence, to tell the taverner in one furtive glance that indeed, a handful of gemstones awaited him.

"Open up, innkeeper!"

He opened the door. The watchmen, all nine of them, stormed in. Molten with the righteous zeal of the mob, a porcupine of spear points, blades and torches, the death squad spilled through the room and occupied it.

Their leader, a bleached bone of a man with an axe and a kit of leather and steel, stood in the taverner's face and scowled. "A ship has been sunk. A witness said there were two of them, and they wore masks. We heard they came this way. Did you see anything?"

Like the breaking of dawn, the answer came slow. As Gregory waited to hear what the taverner had to say, he wrestled with the troll of fear. Here stood the rodent men of Bayonne, renowned for their cruelty and valor, easy to offend and impossible to placate. They had found what they looked for but did not know it just yet. But when and if they did, Gregory knew what they would do—drag he and Warren off to the gaol, beat them to within a breath of their lives, and say to them, "Men of England should not come to Bayonne to commit crimes!" They would confiscate the horses, the coin, the rubies, the manuscripts—everything. And if they didn't haul them off to the gallows, they would assess an absurd fine. Much more than a legal entanglement, an arrest meant catastrophe.

"I have seen nothing, my lord," the taverner said. "I awoke to the hue and cry and here we are."

The watchmen turned to Gregory and pointed. "And who is he?"

"A guest," the taverner's wife said. "He has been here all week. He came down from his room to ask us about the uproar."

"And what is your name?"

"Gregory du Mont," he said. *Je suis un marchand de London*, and I am on my way to Cahors, where I hope to negotiate a shipment of Easter wine for my employer, Richard Beaufort, the Earl of Southampton."

"And you? Who are you?"

"I am Lord Warren of Tutbury." He spoke his title with grave dignity. "And I hold three manors in Staffordshire."

"In Bayonne, we do not care so much for lords," the watchman said, and spit. "More to our liking is the catching of crooks and criminals. Innkeeper, you say you saw nothing?"

"Indeed, my lord."

"Are you sure?" He grabbed the taverner by the hair and yanked him in until the two were nose to nose. "Look at me and tell me what you saw!"

"Nothing, my lord," he said. "I saw nothing."

The watchman took the head end of his axe and rammed it into the taverner's gut. Doubling over, the watchman slammed him against the table. As two of his men held the taverner down, the watchman looked at Gregory and said, "I do not believe this man, but I must take him at his word."

He looked back down at the taverner, pressing the axe blade to his face. "Tell me innkeeper, what did you see?"

"I tell you, watchman, nothing."

The watchmen worked his axe across the taverner's right pinky and lopped it off. As the taverner howled in pain, clutching the wound, falling to the floor and writhing, the watchman held up the pinky and then tossed it into the fire, his way of telling Gregory and Warren that perhaps he knew the masks were in there burning.

"It is a long way to Cahors," he said. "Perhaps you should get an early start in the morning."

The watchmen, turning over tables and chairs, and breaking jars and crockery as they went, filed out of the inn. The taverner, staunching the wound with the hem of his robe, huddled on the floor with his wife. She looked up at Gregory and said, "We do not want some of the gemstones from your precious book. We want *all* of them."

He exchanged an astonished look with Warren. "They are yours."

Alphonse sat in the garderobe, relieving, as he had done daily for a fortnight, a testy set of bowels. The priest sat just outside the chamber, listening to his lord's travails—the gas and spray, the grunts and groans, the agony of sick innards. As he waited, one leg crossed over the other while sitting on a stool, the priest opened the letter and read it to himself.

Dear God. If the infection did not fell Lord Alphonse, perhaps this would.

He considered destroying it. A flame flickered in the fireplace on the other side of the room. Shove it in beneath the bottom ember and be done with it. But the priest did not hide secrets from his master and, besides, he wanted to witness his reaction. He knew it would be terrible, a molten tirade, a shouted pact with the devil, the crazed fuming of a man holding a bad set of dice.

"Lord Alphonse, it appears we have another letter from that scoundrel, Gregory of London."

At last he emerged from the garderobe, his face gaunt, eyes bloodshot, enveloped in a vile fever cloud. He put on a robe and sat at the table near the fireplace. "This ailment is killing me. God's curse, no doubt."

"My lord, you have been sick before, and it has never killed you," the priest gestured with the letter. "But perhaps God does curse you—with Gregory."

He sat at the table with Alphonse who, fatigued by his ordeal in the garderobe, did not consent or protest. Eager to entertain himself, the priest began.

I had the misfortune of visiting your namesake city of Bayonne. Too ugly to be Bordeaux. Too small to be London. A polluted side street in Paris, overrun with men swollen by the hollow pride in their town. But they know how to build ships, the better for them to sail away and never return, to find the remainder of their life in a better place. It is what you tried to do, but you failed, as you have only managed to lock yourself in a prison of your own making. Still, more suitable than Bayonne, where I was asked to leave and eagerly obliged. But before I rode out of town—another trick added to my list—I went to the port and found an old leaking cog. I sent it sinking down to the bottom of the river, a fine calamity on a moonless night. If you guessed this was your ship, and that its cargo is lost, then you would be right.

Alphonse stood, grabbed the table at both ends and hurled it across the room. He smashed his stool against the wall and bellowed with rage. The priest put a hand to his mouth and gasped when he noticed a trickle of effluvium running down Alphonse's leg.

The priest understood his lord's disappointment. The ship was his last tie to the outside world, a relic of the days when he had the good graces of the king. The ship called at Bayonne twice a year, and after its cargo was converted into silver, a rider would arrive at Castlenaud with a small chest full of coin. He needed the money to induce the locals and to buy from them the meats and cheeses, the bread and the wine, and the fuel and the fodder needed for his household. Without the ship and the revenue, he only had two choices—dig into the treasure hoard he surely kept hidden somewhere inside the castle, or raid into a land teeming with people who despised him, and who would benefit handsomely if they were to capture or kill him.

As he oftentimes did, Alphonse went to the window, pulled open the shutters and looked out from his room in the uppermost reaches of the tower. Before he had let the French stab through this land, all that could be seen from here was under his control. The priest had peered through this window many times, so he knew what Alphonse looked at, and he knew the regrets that chided him. The priest shook his head and sighed through his nose. Alphonse—in his silhouette the priest saw the angled cut of his shoulders, the long splay of his frame, and the slight tilt of his head. Once a gallant man with a wife and an heir, a young and loyal brother, and a network of allies from here to Bordeaux, and even south through the Agenais, the Brulhois, Armagnac, and Bearn. He was a rising noble with a cutting smile, ever ready with a song, happy on the hunt and feasting in his hall. And then King Edward and King Philip went to war, and Alphonse made his catastrophic, baffling, bewildering, and inconceivably foolish deal with the French. For a large sack of silver and the promise of a second estate, he let them plunge deep into the king's counties, torching and looting as they went—the exact kind of intrusion, *La Chevauchée*, Alphonse's presence at Castlenaud was supposed to prevent. And it was a short war, too. Peace returned, back to where it all began. But not until Alphonse had lost it all. The priest re-rolled the letter and tied it off with its piece of gut.

"Lord Alphonse, I have never asked you this, but perhaps now is the time," the priest said. "When you made your agreement with the French, did you truly think they would win, or was all of it a grand emprise gone terribly awry?"

Still looking out the window, Alphonse turned his head in profile. The sun shone on his sunken cheeks, exposing the difference between the beauty of yesteryear and the homeliness of today.

"Je ne sais pas," he said. "And it is the doubt that drives me mad. Priest, what are your thoughts on the matter?

"Oh, if you do not know, then I do not know," he said, in a tone that clearly suggested that he did, that his opinion was formed and immovable. But the priest could not openly call his lord a buffoon, so he sufficed that his innuendo had been enough.

"When I am well, we will pillage Goursac," Alphonse said. "It has been a while, and they are due for a visit."

"Reprisal for Gregory, my lord?"

"The blood of Goursac will be on his hands," he said. "And he owes me for a ship, a debt I will collect."

A
COAT OF MAIL
AT HOSSEGOR

They arrived at the sand-swept whaling village of Hossegor just before Vespers, a place of ships, ropes, nets, and harpoons, a bleached enclave of baleen nestled behind the tawny dunes. They rented a vacant fisherman's cabin stinking of oil and scales, but a private hovel with a detached kitchen and cesspit. A hired hand unharnessed and fed the horses, built a fire, and prepared a meal. When the succulent aroma of roasting mackerel wafted through the air, and he had hoisted a cup of wine, Gregory knew this place would do. He and Warren feasted on oysters and mussels, anchovies and prawns, and for dessert, pear fritters and honey.

They drifted into the easy banter of friends, talking a lot, but in fact saying little. They rehashed the other night—the taverner, the watchman, the burning masks, the severed finger and the sunken ship. It seemed as if the conversation would remain that way, one detail after another, a laugh and a shudder, the refrain of a harrowing tale. But a solemn look overcame Warren, enough to convince Gregory something else, something much more important than reliving a recent adventure, was at hand.

Sure enough, Warren dug into his pack and pulled out a folded piece of parchment. In a soft voice he said, "Master Gregory, you must read this."

Gregory took the parchment, unfolded it, and with both hands, held it in front of him. He took a deep breath. It was a letter from home.

My dearest Gregory,

I hope this letter finds you healthy and happy and that your journey through Gascony is blessed not only with God's grace, but with your native wit and luck. It has not yet been a year, but it feels like ten. I did not know how much I would miss you when you left, but now that time has shown its ugly side, I can say with all my heart I am wounded by your absence and contemptuous of those who took you from me. Perhaps I owe them a gesture of goodwill, for they are the same ones who brought us together. But seeing as how they made it so, I suspect I will never offer them a word of thanks.

I pine for you, Gregory, and each day I think of our wedding and how proudly you stood on the steps at St. Martin's. When Ralph died, I told myself I would never remarry, but looking back, I see you had always been there, never too close, but never too far. And now that you are the sun in my day and the stars in my night, I should never again relinquish your hand and lose you to danger.

Forsooth, du Chase and his faction have grown ever bolder. They filed a writ of seizure and asked the court to confiscate a recent shipment of pepper, saffron, and fifteen tonnes of vin de Cîteaux. They argue that, since you are in exile, you, and by extension, I, do not have the right and privilege of the city franchise. I had the writ quashed, but they have vowed to file more grievances against my imports and exports. I fear they will try to board our ships when next they arrive at the port. I am prepared to hire men to guard our cargo, for we cannot allow our goods to be thrown overboard.

Du Chase has also made a formal plea before the mayor and the town council to have you removed from the board of aldermen. I have filed for a continuance, asking that the case not be heard until you return, and I have filed a counterclaim, for harassment, with the hopes I can keep du Chase at arm's length. Your friends at the courts have been of great assistance, and you should know your closest allies here in London remain steadfast in your defense.

My dearest Gregory, my honorable husband and my dutiful lord, you have sired twins, a boy and a girl, and they were born a fortnight before the Feast of St. John. They were baptized at St. Martin's. Both of them have their father's eyes. I have named them Gregory and Herleve, after you and your mother, so you can begin building your noble legacy.

My beloved Gregory, my dear man who must grapple with the envy of his inferiors, I beseech you to return at the earliest opportunity once your obligation has been fulfilled. London needs you. Your family needs you. Make haste, great lord, and may your ship glide swiftly over the sea.

Your true and loving wife,
Joan du Mont Costantyn of Devonshire

The letter seemed a lonely voice and a lonely song, the mistress of despair performing way down yonder in the rocky shoals of regret. Twins—a devoted wife—a noble legacy. Gregory wanted to be happy, but the hook which held him would take months to extract, and its barbed point, up under the skin and against bone, pained him too much to feel blessed. He looked back over the last few years at the decisions he thought had been good. But if they had brought him here to this forsaken stretch of Gascon coast and this ramshackle village of bone and fin, then he knew, they must have been bad. Gregory so fashioned himself as unique, but at this very moment he wanted to be normal, to be an upstanding and obscure merchant seated in the bosom of his household. One day, but I will have to wait.

Not yet ready for words, he watched the gulls, calling and laughing as they dove and plucked for food. Immense green waves broke on a distant shelf, curling toward the shore and exploding in a spray of surf and roar, over and over again, as the day tilted to the west, and a blazing orange crevice opened up and devoured the sky. Gregory folded the letter back into its original creases and tucked it under his belt. He looked at Warren and squinted his eyes to show his displeasure.

"Why didn't you give the letter to me in Bayonne?" he asked. "Why did you hide it?"

From the look on Warren's face, he knew this was coming. For a long bout of silence, he absorbed Gregory's wrath, took his punishment, and submitted to his ire, but eventually he stiffened and gave his reply.

"For some reason, I knew there would be trouble in Bayonne," Warren said. "And I knew this letter would affect you. I needed all of you, Master Gregory, not half of you with the other half thinking of home. Please forgive me, for I meant no harm—but in retrospect, it was the right thing to do. Your quick wit kept us out of the gaol."

"What, I cannot think of two things at once?" he asked. "Surely you know me better than that."

"I do not doubt your faculties, Master Gregory, but I trust in your focus," he said. "Each day you are in Gascony, you are a fugitive and your life is at stake. It is already a difficult situation, so in Bayonne, I chose to make it as simple as possible. You may be angry with me, but you are too smart not to understand."

Gregory begrudgingly nodded his head.

"You are right, Warren." Eager to change the subject, he rallied into a new conversation. "So, you are still a bachelor, I hear?"

"Yes, but if this journey goes the way I want it to, then I will be declared suitable for marriage into the nobility."

"And are there any candidates for your hand?"

"Not that I have been told. All I know is it will not be my decision to make. The Earl of Southampton will choose for me, and he will choose whoever will make the best fit for his affinity."

"Ah, the price of your lordship, eh?"

"Yes, and a price I don't want to pay, but pay it I must, for I will never go back to ploughing wheat fields."

"And the earl likes you, so I am sure he will choose well," Gregory said.

"A proper lass with a pile of silver, rosy cheeks, satin hair and a talent for giving love."

Warren grinned. "That is the best I can hope for."

"Then get us back to England alive, and you will have what you want."

A gang of whalers pulled at the oars as the rowboat rose and dipped over the choppy swells of the bay. Ocean spray splashed over the bow, gulls circled above the stern, and on board, the whalers sang in time with the repetition of their labor. Out on the horizon, flashed the sails of many ships—a merchant fleet heading south to the riches of Spain. Tightly massed and of all sizes, they were bound together against the many dangers of commerce. Their holds fat with cargo, their sails filled with promise, just the sight of them charged Gregory's heart with cheerful notions of prosperity. One of the cogs broke from the others, and as Gregory hoped, a green and gold flag, Southampton's standard, unfurled from the top of the mast. When the rowboat arrived, a rope ladder was lowered, but before boarding, Gregory searched the faces of the crew and its captain to make sure these were his people. Recognizing the same grim lot that had taken him to Bordeaux in the fall, Gregory scaled the rungs and stepped onto the deck. Warren soon followed, and without a word, they joined the captain inside the private cabin beneath the after castle.

Gregory dug into his bag and pulled out the book, *De Mirabilibus Mundi*, and handed it to the captain. "The cover has been spoiled, but the contents are what counts, and they are in abundance."

The captain nodded his head, took possession of the book, and promptly stored it in a chest under lock and key. An enormous sense of relief overcame Gregory, for of the many tasks he was to undertake while in Gascony, retrieval of Marco Polo's book was one of the most important. By right, the manuscript, its pages illuminated with silver and gold and masterworks of painting, belonged to a powerful merchant in Siena, Mariano Taccola, and, in time, it would be returned to him. But the terms of the deal would be dictated by Southampton, who would take custody of *De Mirabilibus Mundi* upon its arrival in England. It would take time, but the earl would have a priceless item with which to gain direct entrée into the Mediterranean, and for an English nobleman looking to outdo his peers, a boon indeed.

The captain noticed the look of satisfaction on Gregory's face, and with a smile of his own, said, "A handsome finder's fee, I suppose?"

"And a delivery fee as well, so steer clear of the rocks and outrun the pirates, and you too will be in good stead."

The captain handed the ship's documents to Gregory. He thumbed through them. St. Mathieu, Blavet, the Ille de Oléron, and La Rochelle. The usual stops, fees and fines paid at each call, and inspectors extracting their cuts. He unrolled the bill of lading, and as he leaned against the after castle, studied its inscriptions. He went below deck to inspect the cargo. With Warren standing next to him with a torch, he counted the sacks of Cotswold wool, the sheets of lead and tin, the barrels of wheat and rye, and the planks of oaken lumber. The *Jonette* sailed for Seville, where this shipment would be traded for horses, wine, olive oil, and silk. By way of Southampton, all of it already under contract with the king's wardrobe. A fine piece of commerce, begetting of silver and goodwill in the royal chambers.

But as he went through the bill, twice and then three times, he noticed a package, an item not listed, snugged up tight between two barrels. He gave Warren a curious glance and then pulled it free, a leather bag, and heavy enough Gregory had to use both hands. He set it down, looked over his shoulder at the captain, and frowned.

"This is not on the bill of lading, and judging by the way it is half hidden, I hardly think it is a crewman's gear," he said. "Everyone smuggles, but with your experience, I should think you would be better at concealing your improprieties. As master of this ship, I must ask you, what is in that bag?"

"Perhaps you should take it up to the deck and see for yourself," the captain said, and ran a hand down his long, drooping mustache. "But before you do, is everything else in order?"

"Yes, notwithstanding the contents of this bag."

Warren hefted it over his shoulder and climbed up to the deck. Gregory and the captain shared a final look before leaving the hold. Gregory grew curious as he scaled the ladder. The captain did not seem concerned that contraband had been found on his ship, and if that were the case, then he had something in mind.

When Gregory reached the deck, he looked at the leather sack, sitting there at Warren's feet, then glanced at the captain. "So, what is it I have found?"

"Open it and see for yourself, for it is not an illegal good, but a gift from an important friend."

Gregory knelt down, untied the cord and pulled back the folds. He looked inside and saw a rolled coat of mail, a supple coat of polished, riveted steel, its expert workmanship immediately apparent. He pulled it out, stood up and held the coat at each shoulder so it dangled in front of him. A luxurious garment of martial vanity, a masterpiece, this coat, with its long sleeves, coif and ventail.

It spurred within him a quick daydream of valor.

"What do you think, Master Gregory?" the captain asked. "From the workshops in Cologne. The finest that can be bought."

"It is splendid," he said, still marveling at the piece. "But if it is a gift for me, then it is misplaced. I am not a fighting man, but a wine merchant. Though tell me, who has presented me with such a precious item."

Gregory folded the coat over his arm, and with a contrived expression of impatience, waited for the captain's reply.

"Your associate, Geoffrey Wool," he said, referring to the great wool merchant, Gregory's friend, in Boston.

Gregory turned to Warren, knowing he and Geoffrey had remained close over the years.

"What do you think?" Gregory asked.

"Master Gregory, Geoffrey is a great gift giver, and he is also keen on your circumstance," Warren said. "He knows you are in Gascony, and for as long as you are here, you are a fighting man."

The whalers rowed back to shore. Gregory jumped out of the boat, trudged through the surf, and felt glad to be back on land. He looked out to sea. The *Jonette* had already rejoined the fleet, as if its brief pause had never happened. Gregory dug into his pouch and handed the boatman a few deniers.

He and Warren made their way back to the hovel they had called home for the last four days. A dingy place with threadbare comforts in a town with little hospitality left, but the task had been completed. By way of Seville, *De Mirabilibus Mundi* sailed on its way back to England, meaning there was no reason to remain here.

"The fleet arrived earlier than I thought," Gregory said. "We have more daylight than I expected."

"I thought the same thing," Warren said. "Let's load the horses and leave this wretched place. We can make Dax before the gates close."

They sent word to the groom, and as they awaited his return, they made a light meal of dried pork and hard cheese. They packed their belongings in their bags and satchels, tightened their belts and straps, and cinched their brooches. When they were done, Gregory felt taut and together and ready for the road. Just about to put on his beaver and peacock hat when he noticed Warren giving him an outsized, deadpan look.

"What?" Gregory asked.

"You have forgotten something."

"And what is that?"

"Your mail."

"Whatever do you mean? It is here in this bag."

"I know, but you are supposed to wear it."

"In due time," Gregory said.

"Due time is now. The roads are dangerous, and we are about to leave."

"Are you serious?" he asked. "And if you are, why did you wait until I was in my gear?"

Warren laughed. "Because I wanted to see the look that is on your face right now."

Gregory shook his head and sighed, but soon enough he loosened the knots, ties and buckles binding him, and shimmied out of his cloak, mantle and robe. Down to his undergarments, he dug into the bag for the coat of mail and the gambeson—a padded shirt—that went with it. He donned the gambeson, and with Warren holding the sleeves up above his head, pulled his way into the mail coat. It sat heavy on his shoulders, but balanced and comfortable, too. Warren rolled the coif and ventail into a thick collar over the back of his neck, and Gregory returned to his kit of wool and leather. He pulled on his hat, and as he often did, pushed it low down over his brow. He looked down and saw that the mail coif shone from beneath the folds of his cloak and robe, which, he knew, would be seen as a badge of authority as he made his way deeper into Gascony.

"*Now* you look like a royal messenger."

The groom arrived, leading Black Saddle and Lady Tatenhill by tethers. Gregory gave him a denier, and then he and Warren mounted their steeds. Without looking back, they thundered out of Hossegor, leaving the locals to wonder who exactly it was who had camped in their town and who had filled its inhabitants with such holy terror.

Breaking onto the main road to Dax, the two of them opened up their horses and let them run with as much zeal as they wanted to summon. Black Saddle settled into his swift and practiced pace, the one that did not tax his powers yet was beyond the reach of a normal horse. Young Lady Tatenhill, bright with spirit but not yet mature in her abilities, ran three lengths behind.

Gregory looked into the sky at a bank of brooding clouds hanging over the moors, the vast wasteland stretching north to the Gironde. A shard of sun shone on a brackish stream, birds called from the brush, and beyond a sedge row, smoke lifted from a village of timber and thatch. He thought of his wife and said a quick prayer on her behalf. He wished Joan could see him in his fine coat of mail, and he allowed himself the conceit that if she could, then she would find him gallant and dashing as he drove his great courser down the road to whatever awaited him.

They feasted on Goursac and left it in flames. Not God's work, the priest knew, but once Alphonse had been seduced by his appetites, he had no place for pieties. The raid had invigorated him, bringing color to his bleached face, a snap to his step, and a moist luster to his eyes. Arrayed in his mail and gear, cracking the horse's reins, and pushing impossible demands deep in a dangerous land—Alphonse at his best when at his worst.

The cavalcade returned to Castlenaud with the loot, the retinue chattering and merry. Three hogsheads of country red, loaves of white bread, a cow and two pigs, and a box of silver and jewelry from the parish church added to Alphonse's larder—the old days made new again, and the uplifting promise of a long night of revelry in the lord's hall. The horses stabled, the fires lit, and the hogsheads tapped, the men convened at the hall as one of them worked his bagpipes, and as another beat on a drum.

"Priest," Alphonse said, "this Gregory does not know it, but he has furnished us with a fine day."

"Yes, but he had already taken much in return."

"Let me have this time for leisure. Do not spoil it with your usual quibbles."

One of his men filled his cup, and Alphonse took a hearty drink.

"I will let you have today." The priest gave a wry smile. "But I will also let you have tomorrow and the next, when your spirits are not so high."

Alphonse shrugged him off, launching into a spirited retelling of the raid, riding through the center of town, striking down the few who opposed him, and taking a maiden from behind as her parents watched. This was the real Alphonse, the cruel and narcissistic one who thought himself better than the king. Watching him regale his men, and seeing the obnoxious preen come over him, the priest took dark delight when one of the servant boys approached and gave him a rolled parchment. It had to be from Gregory, thought the priest, and if it was, it would surely sour Alphonse's stolen moment of happiness. As Alphonse shouted and laughed, and as his men sang his praises, the priest discretely unrolled the parchment and read the first line. He smiled.

"Lord Alphonse, another letter from Gregory," he said, bringing a halt to the festivities.

Alphonse knocked back a gulp of wine and slammed the cup on the table. "Tell us what the whoreson says!"

The priest climbed up on the table and cleared his throat.

Wearing a coat of mail does strange things to one's esteem. It makes him feel like more of a man, even when he knows it is not true. As a knight, albeit a sullied one, I am sure you know the charms of arms and armor. But it is new to me as I am now aged thirty-four, and for the first time find myself draped in riveted steel. They say this makes me a fighting man, which surely is hyperbole. But what I cannot deny is that a crude side has awoken in me. A supple coif is coiled about my neck. A long and sharp knife hangs from my belt. My steed will split a man's skull if it is my wish. Perhaps it is misguided, but I also say beware, for I grow more dangerous by the day.

Alphonse and his men split with laughter. Alphonse reached for the scabbard hanging by a belt from the knob of his throne. He unsheathed his terrible blade and held it over his head.

"It is I, not he, who is the man of danger."

His men raised their cups and concurred.

A
DIRTY DEBT
AT SAUGNAC

Gregory always considered himself lucky when he made curfew. A hot summer day, a sunbaked road with no obstructions, and a riding partner on an indefatigable steed, it had all come together at the open gates of Dax. Its Roman ramparts were patched and repaired, but still an imposing, towered loop of stone. The cities were dangerous, but much safer than the highway, so Gregory didn't mind as the town clerk took his time inspecting his writs of trade, and fleecing him for a denier. They entered the city, and as the gates shut behind them, and they trotted their horses to the stables, a bubbling sense of excitement overcame Gregory. Dax was famous for its hot springs and healing waters, and before leaving town, Warren had assured Gregory they would partake.

The next morning, they broke their fast with white bread, soft cheese, and watered wine. The city, perched just south of the bogs and moors, awoke with the peal of church bells, the ringing of smithy hammers, and the harangues of fishmongers, butchers, and spicers. Its quay was swollen with barges, its tight streets lined with prosperous shops, and a shadow of piety cast over it by the cathedral, Dax had long since recovered from the war. Smug behind its ancient walls and wise with the counsel of its jurats, the city flew its flag with no fear. Enlivened by the energy of the place, Gregory strolled through the market and bought a keepsake for Joan: a silver necklace adorned with a tiny dove carved out of amber. He put it on and tucked it deep beneath the folds of his robe. He thought of how nice it would be when he took it from around his neck and placed it around hers. Warren purchased a filigreed silver ring, a blue chaperon, and gave a puppet master a half penny at the conclusion of his show. So, he and Warren spent the morning, in good spirits and at leisure, browsing their way through the big and boisterous market.

Dax owed its prosperity to its healing waters, which bubbled up from a spring and into a masonry cistern in the center of town. The water then ran through submerged lead pipes to a vaulted conduit house, where it collected in great stone fountains carved with angels and saints and the scenes of miracles. It dripped from the spouts and into a catch basin, where servants dipped their vessels, only to fill the stone tubs where the wealthy and influential reclined in bliss. A tradition in Dax since the time of the Romans, and one repeated by a constant parade of visitors, the hot spring generated enough taxes, fees, and rights to make the town corpulent with coin and assured of its place in the uncertain world of post-war Gascony. And it was to this place of luxury and privilege that Warren took Gregory, and here where they shed their clothes and took to the eternal waters.

Gregory entered slowly, and with only one leg in, he waited. It was as if a thousand hands massaged his foot, calf, and thigh, and sirens begged him to enter in full. He climbed in, sat down, and without hesitation, slid beneath the surface. He remained submerged until out of breath, letting the water fill every crack and crevice of his naked body. He returned to the surface, leaned against the back of the tub, and ran both hands through his plastered hair. He looked into the candlelit reaches of the vaulted roof, inhaled the aroma of sandalwood and frankincense, and listened to the hypnotic drip of the fountain. The last year of his life flashed before him. The pain and doubt vanished as does a morning mist, while hope and optimism shone like autumn sun. As his lanky bones strengthened, the nicks and scrapes healed over, and the bruise on his arm disappeared, he drifted into a dreamscape of pleasing thoughts. He envisioned himself and son Gregory, daughter Herleve, and wife Joan, sitting prim and proper in his hall, receiving guests, humble in achievement. With luck and God's grace, he would make it home, he knew, and good tidings awaited his return. He clasped his hands behind his head, closed his eyes, and smiled as a new ewer of warm water poured into his tub. He remained that way, suspended in paradise, until all the demons had seeped out of him and drowned.

He rubbed his eyes, and from the stand sitting next to his tub, grabbed the cup and took a sip of Nérac. The wine went straight to his head, a luscious jolt of forgivable sin. He took another sip, and set the cup down. He turned toward Warren, who hadn't said a word since arriving, and saw on his face the trappings of bliss. Good Warren, he thought, too in need of rest and respite, and heavy with the weight of his lordship, fighting for the status not his by birthright, making of it a good chance. Wales, Ireland, Scotland, and now Gascony, he was forging for himself a record beyond reproach. Gregory was sure a few of his tribulations had washed away in this gurgling spring, and it heartened him that his friend would emerge renewed.

Yet, despite his agreeable thoughts, doubt nagged at Gregory. Taking the waters had been Warren's idea, one upon which he had insisted. And it had been a good idea, too, Gregory had to admit. But from what he had known of Warren in the days of the chronicle, and what he knew about him since that time, an idle day in a hot spring was not his way. Warren was of the horse and the sword, the gatehouse and the barbican. Much work needed to be done in Gascony, and Warren was not the kind to slog through his chores. Though he did not want to do it, and though difficult, Gregory shrugged off the sweet lethargy of the bath and set his mind to business.

"So, why are we here?" Gregory asked.

Warren stirred from his half slumber.

"To take the healing waters, of course," Warren said, but a false note in his voice told Gregory that was only part of the story.

Gregory propped his forearm on the rim of his tub and gave a weary smile.

"Warren, I know you are not here merely for such pleasantries," he said. "Your reason is particular, and it is time you tell me."

Warren cupped his hands, filled them with water, and drizzled it over his head. He rubbed his eyes, blew his nose one nostril at a time, and doused himself with another handful of water. Anything, Gregory thought, to delay the start of what he had to say.

"There is a feud between two families," he said. "It started during the war. One of the families is back in England, and they are content to let the feud die. But the family here, they demand satisfaction."

"What is the genesis of this feud?"

"What we always hear. Unpaid debts. Stolen horses. Looting. An old vineyard destroyed. And a young daughter—a beautiful girl ripe for the marriage market at Westminster—raped and ruined."

Gregory held out his right hand, and with his left thumb, massaged his palm. The healing waters worked into the waterlogged skin, unwinding the grip of the reins, loosening the hold on the quill. An old anxiety floated away on a curling waft of frankincense, and for a moment of content, as he gazed into the flickering flame of a candle, Gregory did not want to have this conversation. But talk he must, knowing this was the beginning of his next adventure.

"Who was the culprit in these crimes?"

"Lord Ingram de Ros," Warren said. "Do you know him?"

"No, but if he has done what you say he has, it is good I don't."

"His rival in Gascony, Lord Saugnac, has begged King Edward for compensation, but the king refused to honor the request. Lord Saugnac has since demanded the king send de Ros back here so he can pay for his transgressions—in combat to the utmost—but the king has yet to yield. De Ros and his family have been loyal to the king throughout his reign, and he will not sacrifice him to a minor Gascon noble. Instead he has sent someone in de Ros' place. Is it all clear to you now, Master Gregory?"

Still mesmerized by the tranquil comfort of the bath, it took Gregory a moment to comprehend what Warren had said. But when it came to him, he put a hand on each side of the tub and hoisted himself into a sitting position. So violent was his effort that water sloshed over the side of the tub and extinguished a tray of candles. He wiped dripping water from his brow, swallowed hard, and said, "They have sent you instead of de Ros?"

"Southampton suggested it, and I willingly agreed," he said.

"But de Ros is a pot of shit, and if you do his bidding, then you do the bidding of a criminal."

"When one is a lord, Master Gregory, one must accept duty he would not otherwise assign to himself," he said. "Saugnac has become a nuisance for the king, and if I end it, then it will be good for me—and for you."

"How for me?" Gregory said.

"You will be the witness. A supporter."

"And am I right to assume I have no choice in the matter?"

"Indeed," he said. "As your tasks are mine, so mine are yours."

"So, is this why we are here?" Gregory asked. "You treat me to this splendid bath, knowing it would dull the edge of my complaints?"

"Yes. This is your reward for the work you are about to do," he said, and took a quaff of Nérac.

Gregory slumped back down in the tub and watched the water roll over his chest. Soothing it was, this healing spring. Warm and eternal, kind to his aching bones and his pining heart. If only he could remain here, ensconced beneath the bath's squat vaulted roof, his body and soul drinking from the dripping depths of this shimmering pool. But solace was not the way in Gascony, so he took a sip of water and savored its metallic sweetness.

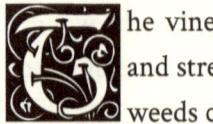he vineyard had yet to be replanted. The roads were potholed and strewn with debris. A burned-out village lay abandoned, and weeds choked the plum orchard. The watermill had fallen to rot. The door to the parish church, battered down years ago, lay in splinters near the steps, where lounged a pack of spotted feral dogs. From the church's

open portal, a dark and toothless maw, came the stale breath of decline. Just beyond the village, tucked inside a bend in the river, sat the manor house of Saugnac. The roof sagged, its pitched gables infested with pigeons and encrusted with their droppings. Its gatehouse a heap of rubble, its yard a blackened wasteland, this sprawling, timbered estate bore the pock marks of war, the pits and pustules of greed, the human disease with no known cure. But on this damp and leaden day, smoke belched from the chimney, light showed from a window, and high atop a leaning guard tower, a red and blue banner curled in the wind. It was to this dreary place that Gregory rode, Black Saddle picking his way through the detritus and decay, to deliver what he knew would be an unpopular message.

He trotted Black Saddle right up to the front door, and without dismounting, leaned forward, grabbed the iron knocker, giving it four good raps. He circled back and halted his horse, so he did not crowd the door. Before it was answered, he pulled his beaver and peacock hat down low over his brow, pushed back his cloak to reveal the hilt of his knife and the coif of his mail, and fixed on his face a long and baleful glare. Regardless of who greeted him, Gregory wanted them to see a menacing stranger in black, appearing unannounced in the gloom, staring back at them.

He heard the rusty scrape of an old latch, and the grated wicket within the door swung open. A sad face, pale and pasty with deep purple bags under the eyes, peered out. A spider of fear, dangling from a silky strand of doubt, dropped through his countenance, and his lips, swollen and chapped, pursed in a silent plea for pity.

"Your name and your business?"

"I am Gregory of London, and I must meet with Lord Saugnac," he said. "I am on the king's time, so do not keep me waiting."

The wicket window closed. Gregory could not understand what was being said, but from inside the manor he heard the back and forth of several voices, an argument, he guessed, ending on a shrill shout of rebuke. At last, the huge oaken door creaked open. Standing at the threshold was a balding, potbellied man in the tattered remains of what was once an opulent, fur-lined robe of silk and wool. He put one foot forward and cocked out his double chin in a dubious show of confidence. Looking out from behind him were his household servants, including the man who had answered the door, and a teenage girl in a grimy blue gown and veil. They appeared as a herd of frightened deer, mice on the brink of flight, or squirrels looking hither and thither before racing up the trees.

"Greetings, Lord Saugnac," Gregory said, his voice sharp and frosty.

The old lord bowed, held out his arms, and looking up from his stance of subservience, said, "It is an honor to receive a messenger from our blessed King Edward. Please, come into my hall for refreshment and respite."

Gregory dismounted, tied Black Saddle to a hitching post, and followed Lord Saugnac and his household into the shadowy depths of the hall. Lord Saugnac was different from most lords, Gregory noticed, in that his house-holders were not just his servants, but his confidants. Like one big family, they all sat at the table, and Gregory would have to speak to them as a group rather than speaking to the lord alone. With this complication in mind, he unshouldered his satchel, set it on the table, and as he opened the flap and reached for the documents inside, he looked around the table and made eye contact with each of them, Lord Saugnac, the bulbous butler who'd answered the door, the maiden, the cook, the laundress, the groom, and the vintner. All seven of them were expectant, and based on the shouting Gregory had heard not long ago, each of them capable of speaking their mind.

Gregory thumbed through the documents and arrived at the one he wanted. He pulled it from the pile, held it high so all could see, and as he looked at Lord Saugnac, said, "Five years ago, you demanded of the king five hundred livres, ten sous, and eight deniers, did you not?"

"An amount that has never been paid," the lord said.

Still holding the document high, Gregory continued. "You made the same request each year for the next four years."

"Yes, but only as a reminder of what the king had promised me."

"And if you don't believe him, he has proof." The Butler rose from his seat, walked over to a large wooden trunk against the wall, and retrieved a leather folder. He slapped it on the table, opened it, and after thumbing through the documents, and mocking Gregory as he did, he pulled out a fine piece of parchment with the king's seal affixed to the bottom.

The butler slid the parchment across the table. "If you can read your letters, perhaps you can read ours, too."

Gregory leaned over, propped on his left forearm, and with his right index finger tracing beneath each line, read the original writ of enlistment from 1294, when King Edward and King Philip had gone to war. Indeed, Lord Saugnac was entitled to repayment for all the horses he had lost, wages for he and his men, and for any damage done to his domain. Gregory knew Lord Saugnac's losses had been substantial, and that his claim was legitimate, but as he looked up from the writ and across the table at the impoverished nobleman, and as much as it pained him to do so, he feigned indifference.

"No, no, no, no," yelled the groom, who slammed his fist against the table. "Do not act as if it doesn't matter! Our lord was master of the horse before the war, and now he has nothing!"

"And his wine fetched a good price in Bordeaux, but the vineyard was torn from the ground, so his contracts are void!" the vintner said.

"Hogs fattened on this manor, and the cheeses aged in its cellars, once graced this very table," the cook said. "Yet now we eat salted fish and pottage!"

"His daughter was the most beautiful girl this side of the moors, until de Ros stole her virtue," the laundress said. "With tainted chastity, and no dowry, we cannot find her a suitable husband."

"And now you come here, telling us what we already know," Lord Saugnac said. "But tell me this, is your king going to pay me what is owed so I can put my manor back in order? Or has he sent you to tell us more lies?"

Gregory had expected an uncomfortable conversation with a broken man, not to be shouted at by a room full of servants. The grief and venom in their voices had taken him aback, and he felt for them. They had not been rewarded for their loyalty to the king. Instead, they had been punished. He wanted to arrive at a solution, to bring equity to this desperate household. But to do so would cloud his reputation and Warren's, something he would not do. So, he kept his composure, maintained the malevolent knit in his brow, and as he wrestled with his guilt, plucked the next document from the stack of authority.

"Just over one year ago, you sent another request to the king, only this time you did not ask for the repayment of debts." Gregory handed the letter to the cook, who then passed it to the vintner, who then handed it to Lord Saugnac. "No, instead of debts, you asked for a trial of arms, and to the utmost, at that."

Holding the letter at the top and bottom, reading his words—the words that could condemn him—Lord Saugnac trembled.

Gregory pushed the advantage. "Indeed, my lord, we have come with the intent to do battle," he said. "If you win, the king will honor your debt, but if you lose...."

The nobleman tossed the letter out to the middle of the table, and turned up his face in defiance. "It was written and sent in a moment of anger. The king would never agree to such a preposterous request."

"Oh, but he has." Gregory produced yet another document. "And he has reserved the right to send a designee of his own choosing."

The butler bolted up from his seat, and as his neck and face flushed red and ropy with veins, he shook his fist. "The king has agreed to such a foolish gambit, yet does not even send Ingram de Ros to face his transgressions?"

"De Ros is infirm and eaten through with the gout," Gregory said.

"Then who, might I ask, has been sent in his place?"

Gregory looked around the table, and as he did, he made sure to convey a frigid sense of inevitable doom. He locked into Lord Saugnac, and waited until an eerie brown shadow crept over his face. "Lord Warren of Lichfield, and he comes calling at dawn."

"But I am not ready!" Lord Saugnac protested. "You have come unannounced and you have given me no time."

"Perhaps so, my lord, but this is what you asked for. Though we may have inconvenienced you, it is your will that is being done. Ready your horse and your weapons, for the time of doing is at hand."

"It is easier to best an old man than it is to pay debts that are owed!" the Butler said.

"Indeed, you are right, but the circumstances do not change," Gregory said.

He collected his letters, tucked them in his satchel, and headed for the door. As he did, the laundress tossed a cup of wine in his face, the cook pelted him with a heel of stale bread, and the others damned him to the dank cavern of undying hell. He did not begrudge them their hate, nor did he question their fury. Instead, he admired them for their tenacity, even if it had gotten the better of them. He mounted Black Saddle, trotted him back to the forsaken village, and stopped in the open space in front of the gutted parish church. This used to be a bustling little market, he thought, where happy bumpkins lived out their lives. He made the sign of the cross, then rode out to the bivouac near the River Luy, where Lord Warren and his hired men-at-arms awaited.

Arrayed in a splendid suit of plate and chain, and crowned with a beribboned great helm, Lord Saugnac rode out to the field on a mighty roan charger. The giant steed whipped its tail and snorted, and as he pranced in a wide circle, his master saluting the crowd with a gauntleted fist, the horse paraded his virile girth. So nimble was this team in red and blue, and so game that, for a moment, Gregory thought someone else might be inside that armor and helm, someone much younger and more skilled than old Lord Saugnac. But once in place at the far end of the tilt yard, he opened his visor, and indeed it was he.

"He who has come to dispossess me himself shall be vanquished!" he said. "By the rules of this engagement, I offer no mercy and expect none in return."

The droves that had come out from seemingly nowhere to witness the spectacle responded with lusty shouts of support, and the ring of humanity tightened around the tiltyard. Amid the crescendo of the moment sat Warren, silent and stoic in the saddle atop Lady Tatenhill. Caparisoned in the earl's green and gold livery, and snug in his kit of leather and polished mail, he glared from beneath the rim of his conical helm. So square and solid he was, blond and bright, unmoved by the invective spat at him by the village teens and the toothless crones. A roundel of sunlight shone in his panoply, and the plume of greased crow feathers twitched in the breeze. A blooded English lord, his experience obvious, he came to court death on a backroad in Gascony.

The butler walked to the middle of the yard and pulled a red ell of cloth from his belt. He held it high above his head, and as he did, the combatants took hold of their shields and lances, and fidgeted in their saddles. Gregory, standing near a cluster of country nobles, made the sign of the cross. Dear God, give Warren the strength to win, and give him the wisdom to make the right decision. The butler yanked the cloth downward, and with a thunder of hooves and the savage bellow of three hundred voices, Lord Saugnac and Warren charged headlong over the yard.

Speeding toward the collision, they lowered their steel tipped lances, and then the unthinkable happened. Just as she reached full gallop, Lady Tatenhill planted her hooves in the turf and stopped. As she sounded a shrill whinny, she lurched backward and reared. Warren, unhinged by the calamity, struggled to gain control of her. He raised his shield and crouched behind it just as Lord Saugnac's lance cracked home. With the full weight of the charger behind it, the lance flexed, split, and lifted Warren up out of his saddle and knocked him arcing backward. He landed in a heap, face down and arms outspread. Saugnac's partisans, crude in their approval of his feat, urged him to gut and finish the boy. Dumbstruck, Gregory put a hand over his mouth and felt ill. He saw Lord Saugnac's eyes flash from deep within the great helm, and it was then he knew what was supposed to be easy would be nothing but.

As Saugnac made his pass, he dropped his spent lance and unsheathed his sword. He banked his charger into a tight turn, and with a violent slap of the reins and a prodding of his spurs, sent him toward Warren. Still shattered by the jar and crunch of the lance, Warren climbed to one knee and huddled behind his shield. The great charger drove at him with all his hooves stomping and mashing, trampling over Warren and his cover. With the fine blade cocked over his head, Saugnac turned his horse once again. Warren, shaking his head and gasping, got to his hands and knees. Saugnac chopped down for the kill. Keeping himself propped on his right hand, Warren reached into his belt with his left and pulled his knife. He held it up and parried Saugnac's assault just a breath before the sword took his life. The charger kicked out with a hoof, knocking Warren's helm clean from his head. Saugnac raised his sword and made ready for another strike. But by the time he swung downward, Warren had gained his feet. He weaved to the side and out of Saugnac's reach. Finding his balance for the first time in this duel, he sheathed his knife and drew his sword, *Fionnaghal*.

The collective encouragement from the crowd got caught in its collective throat, and only one person, Gregory, cared to cheer. He leaned forward, pumped out his fist and yelled, "Do not yield, Lord Warren!" Warren whistled three times through his teeth, and Lady Tatenhill, cantering across the yard, circled in behind him. Lord Saugnac, heaving for breath, unlatched the visor of his great helm and pulled it open. In an instant Gregory saw it on his face—disappointment and flagging belief. He'd had his chance and let it slip away, and now with Warren back on his horse and in command of his sword, the fight to begin anew. And so it did, the two lords thrusting and swinging, swords ringing, steeds closing and biting as a cloud of dust rose over this match of young and old. As Saugnac's strength gave way, Warren's remained. With every nuance of his talent, he bludgeoned his opponent, until finally, he unhorsed Saugnac with a punishing roundhouse from his armored elbow. Warren dismounted, sheathed his sword and yanked out his knife. He pounced on Saugnac, pried up his arm, and placed the tip of his blade up deep into his pit, where he could drive it into the old man's heart. The men-at-arms who Warren had hired in Dax rushed out to the yard, and with their spears and bills at the ready, formed a cordon around Warren and his opponent.

"Submit and renounce," Warren said, "and I will spare your life!"

"Jamais!" Saugnac said.

"Submit and renounce," Warren said again, "and I will spare your life!"

"Never!" he said, and spit in Warren's face.

Warren looked up and over at the butler, the maiden, the cook, the laundress, the groom, and the vintner. "Speak reason to this man, or you will soon be digging his grave."

They ran out to the yard, to within a few paces of the cordon, and as they did, so too, did Gregory. The blue-robed maiden, Saugnac's daughter, knelt down, held out her hand and, as tears rolled down her cheeks, said, "Father, please submit. You say you will have nothing, but you will have all of us. The war is finally over."

For a long while he just laid there and said nothing. At last he sighed, and when he did, the final gasp of defiance fluttered away. He looked into Warren's eyes, and with the faintest trace of relief in his voice, said, "I, Lord Heliland of Saugnac, do submit and renounce all my claims on our beloved and just Edward, King of England and Duke of Aquitaine."

Warren got up and sheathed his knife. He looked around in a circle at all the people who had come out to watch the battle. He pushed out his chest and set his jaw.

"You came here today and urged him to kill, but now it's time to stay and help him rebuild," he said. "Lord Saugnac defended his honor today, and his title still runs with this land."

Gregory had not wanted to come here. A dirty deed, dispossessing a man of his rightful credit. Expecting to leave here with a foul taste in his mouth, he was pleased when that was not the case. Indeed, a metallic sweetness played on his lips, and that, he knew, was from the healing waters of Dax. Warren's idea—and Gregory was proud to call him a friend.

The priest knew King Edward was old. Six decades or more, and weary of the Scots. Unpopular at home for his taxes, father to a rogue, and indebted to enemies and allies, the king's useful life was spent. Or so hoped the priest.

Tainted by his association with Alphonse, the priest had been excommunicated, and would remain so until his name, if ever, was cleared. The only way that could happen was if the king died, his inept son ascended to the throne, and by some act of court magic, Alphonse was pardoned. A tall circumstance if the king were young, but with Edward teetering ever closer to his dotage, and with angry Scots teeming on his northern border, and the French plotting in Paris, not implausible. And so, the longing for freedom teased him as he reached into the old wooden box and fished out the latest letter to arrive at Castlenaud. He returned to the upper hall where Alphonse sat, morose and brooding, over an empty bowl of gruel.

The priest knew this letter was not from the king. No seal, an inferior piece of parchment, and not accompanied by a royal messenger. Just a lonely little scroll, like all the rest, tied off with a simple piece of gut. But present it he must, even if its tidings did not bode well. He sat at the long end of the table, opposite Alphonse, and gave his lord a probing look of gloom.

"I grow weary of these letters," Alphonse said. He leaned back in his throne. "If I were to cut out your tongue, I would not have to hear them anymore."

"True," the priest said. "Or you could just as easily toss them in the fire."

"Too easy and not enough fun."

"Do not let the words of a stranger turn old friends against one another," the priest said. "I could have abandoned you long ago, but here I am, safeguarding your soul."

"You are here because you have nowhere else to go. Lies befit you, priest, but do not tell them to me."

The priest grinned as he untied the scroll. "I will keep my tongue, my lord, as you must keep your ears."

Curious as to what Gregory would say, he held the parchment close to a candle, its light washing across the neat lines of Latin.

If one travels in Gascony long enough, he meets all manner of people. Perhaps the best man I have met during my journey is Lord Saugnac. I think you know him. At least for a while, he fought on the same side of the war as did you. Until, as we all know, you decided to betray your allegiances and side with the French. This Saugnac, a good man and loyal to the end. But men stood ahead of him, way ahead of him, so when it came time to collect on his legal debts, there was not enough to go around. The solution? I dispossessed him, even if not the outcome I desired. His account void, his poverty assured. A gilded life dimmed to ignominy. You, Lord Alphonse, have already been pauperized by our dear king. And I am the one to enforce his will. If I can bring lasting destitution to an honorable man like Saugnac, then I will gladly do the same to a profligate such as yourself.

The priest looked up from the parchment and into Alphonse's eyes. "Do you still want my tongue?"

"No, but I will have Gregory's hand, the one with which he writes."

SISTER
GERTRUDE
OF POOR CLARES

Warren groaned and fell from his horse. He got to his hands and knees and tried to stand, but he buckled and then collapsed. Gregory made the sign of the cross, dismounted, and knelt at his friend's side.

"What is it, Warren?"

He rolled over on his back, his face contorted with anguish, clutching at his left calf. "It is my leg, Master Gregory."

Gregory grabbed his pack and used it to prop up Warren's leg. With *La Bonne Vie,* he cut off the boot, and when he peeled back a pant leg of breeches, discovered a ghastly wound. He stymied both the urge to vomit and to shout out in panic, because this trauma plunged down to the bone, soiled and about to fester. Collecting himself, he noticed the injury resembled the shape of a hoof. Memories of the duel earlier in the day came to mind, of Saugnac's roan charger trampling Warren. He had shown no ill effects. The rush of combat, Gregory guessed, and its tendency to mask pain. Fumbling through the list of things he needed to do, he felt overwhelmed.

"Can you make it to Dax?" He hoped the younger man would say yes.

"I cannot. I must rest, Master Gregory, or I shall soon perish."

Gregory dug through a saddlebag, fetched his tonic of chamomile and pomegranate, and gave Warren a sip. He knew it would not hold, but, he reasoned, a start. He stood up as straight as he could, peered eagle-eyed in all directions, and saw a reflection in the afternoon sun. He ran to it, thinking it a miracle when he realized what it was. A hillside spring, and its waters bubbled up from a source so unaltered and pure Gregory had no doubt the water was potable.

But many people, thinking the same such thing, sickened themselves with a hasty drink. So, Gregory took a few deep breathes, walked back to his horse, and from his bag of sundries pulled a white linen cloth. He returned to the spring and moistened it in the babbling water. He folded it and tied it off with a string. He tied it to a low hanging limb and waited for it to dry. He untied the cloth, unfolded it, and inspected the linen for even the slightest stain. When he did not see one, he concluded the water was right. Gregory held a cup down in the spring. He gave the brimming cup to Warren, and when he was done drinking, Gregory filled another cup and another, and bathed the wound as best he could. When it appeared as if Warren would at least survive the day, Gregory pitched the high-peaked tent. He dug his hands down beneath Warren's arms and dragged him inside. He propped up his head and leg, and plied him with a few more cups of spring water.

"I am going to Dax and will return with a medicus," Gregory said. "Say your prayers, but if you hear a calming voice, do not concede to its temptation."

Black Saddle needed no encouragement. The great stallion careered down the road, pushing back time, confronting the distance, barging through fatigue until he and his master arrived at their destination. Easy it would be if all he had to do was fill a skin and return. But Dax's healing springs lost their magic not far beyond the city walls. So, Gregory would have to find someone, a rare person skilled in the arts of medicine, and bring them back to his ailing friend. He wasted no time, and before the locals could even point at him and whisper, he asked this person and that, and went here and there, and soon found himself at the door of the apothecary. A full fisted knock he gave, and before an answer came, he peeled off his beaver and peacock hat, ran a hand through his hair, and otherwise tried to make himself presentable. The door creaked open. A stooped man in a black robe and feathered chaperon looked up at him with wise and watery eyes. A tart odor wafted out, and over the man's shoulders, Gregory spied all manner of pots and pans, many of them hanging over both merry and sullen fires.

"Your business?" the apothecary asked.

"A friend sits wounded," Gregory said. "If he does not receive attention soon, I fear he will go ill with the rot."

"And is your friend here?"

"No, near Saugnac. Four miles."

"Other than a simple tonic of fennel and nutmeg, I am afraid I cannot help you," he said. "I have appointments later today. Jacques de Pontours must have a boil lanced, and Lord Piers Donzac must be treated for scabies."

Gregory reached for his pouch. "Perhaps my silver shines brighter than theirs. Even just for a while."

The old man gave a smile of accommodation. "I assure you, it does not. But if your need is urgent, I know of a nun at the convent of Poor Clares who is said to be a physician of rare talent. Her name is Gertrude, and perhaps she can help you."

Gregory made haste to the convent, a jumble of vaults and arches built up against the city wall. The Poor Clares, Gregory thought. Humble adherents to the order of St. Francis, whose job, Gregory guessed, was to wash the clothes and linens of the town's bourgeoisie. Not a promising place to find a qualified physician, he thought, but under the weight of the present circumstances, he had no choice. He grabbed the piece of rope hanging from the clapper and rang the doorbell. As he'd done at the apothecary's shop, he removed his hat, assumed a posture of deference, and awaited the reply.

The wicket opened, and a dour nun looked out at him.

"I seek the services of Sister Gertrude," Gregory said, and bowed. "My friend has been gravely injured and is in need of healing."

The wicket closed, and moments later, the door opened. The nun, an imperious noble, unsmiling and staid, commanded the entrance to the convent. By the way she looked at him, severely and from a high pulpit of probity, he knew she weighed the veracity of his character, the authenticity of his plight. Gregory gave into her perusal, and for the first time in years, as Warren lay dying, he allowed himself to be seen as vulnerable. The nun searched all of him, too, peering not only into the recent past, but well into the depths of his life. Gregory felt it, the weight of her judgement, the pain of the inspection, indeed, her review charged him with self-doubt. She must have found something tenable, because her face softened, her arms outstretched in a heartened show of magnanimity, and she said, "Sister Gertrude will help you. Please, sit in the anteroom and await my return."

She disappeared behind a second door. Gregory sat on a wobbly little stool beneath a soaring arch, its pillars crowned with curling flora of stone. Perhaps it was his impatience, but it seemed a long tortuous while before the nun, accompanied by another nun, returned to the chamber. Gregory stood, expectant, willing, and showing his urgency.

"Je vous présente soeur Gertrude." She kept her head down, and due to the out-sweeping coif and veil, Gregory did not get a good look at her face. But her manner suggested earnestness and duty, and in her presence he felt comfort. She asked him about Warren's wound, and he told her only what she needed to know to treat it, wasting no time on the backstory. The consultation ended with Gertrude giving him a green pill and an unknown tonic in a sealed cup. "Give this to him immediately, and it should keep him until I arrive."

Gregory donated a full livre to the convent, gave them directions to the site, and rode out of Dax, peeling over the road back to Warren's sick bed. The tent stunk with the puss and bile of the wound and was hot with the pulse of Warren's fever. But he lived, and Gregory felt a spasm of relief when he placed the pill on Warren's tongue, cradled his head in his hand, and administered the tonic.

At the end of the day, Sister Gertrude arrived in a covered wagon, driven by a burly man-at-arms, and accompanied by a servant girl. She hitched up her habit and hopped out of the wagon. She put her hands on her hips, and though she appeared young and bashful, mustered an iron voice, saying, "Take me to him."

She lit frankincense and myrrh, and lavender and rose, and made of the tent a house of relaxing aroma. She pinned up her habit, front and back, and rolled up her sleeves. Into the ground she stabbed an iron pole affixed with a hook, and to that hook she attached an empty cow bladder. She filled it with vinegar. Once the bladder was plump with liquid, she peeled back a tiny adhesive plug at the bottom. The vinegar leaked from the orifice in slow drops, and thus formed a drip splashing into Warren's wound.

"I have never seen that before," Gregory said.

"It is peculiar to this region," she said. "Many years ago, a physician from Dax traveled to the Holy Land on crusade, and learned this technique from the Saracens. When he returned home, he shared his knowledge, and it has been handed down from generation to generation."

"What happens if the wound does not heal?"

"I will amputate his leg just below the knee, and if he survives, he will live the rest of his life as a cripple." She shook her head and frowned. But she did not remain somber for long. A gush of confidence reddened her cheeks, and her eyes lit bright with certitude. "I do not intend to fail. The moon is nearly full, your man is yet strong, and my plea for God's grace has been heard."

"How many times have you done this?" he asked.

She gave a quick smile.

"You are in luck, for this is my specialty. Here, and I'm sure nearly everywhere, hoof wounds are common. It seems every day someone is kicked by a horse or stomped by a cow. Indeed, I have seen this wound, or versions of it, many times."

Even as she spoke, she continued to work, and with Gregory quizzing her, she unpacked a vented iron box, tonged out a burning ember, and stuffed it beneath the pile of kindling she and Gregory had earlier assembled.

"Fire, our best friend in times of trouble." She squatted down and blew a jet of air deep into the knot of brush.

A flame licked upward, swept over the kindling, and stick by stick, Gregory did his part by feeding the conflagration. Sister Gertrude opened the lid of a battered wooden box, and inside a master's collection of pharmacy jars, some plain, some ornate, some tall, some short, yet all of them imbued with the wear and patina of heavy use. She plucked a dozen of them from the case and set them on a small table next to the box. She put a finger on her lip and thought for a while. Having found the answer, she pulled one last jar. Over the fire she placed an iron tripod, and from the chain hanging at its center, cinched a kettle. She set smooth stones around the fire, and upon these stones placed an assortment of pots, pans, and long handled skillets.

"You should not waste this opportunity, so watch and listen," she said.

Gregory, manning the fire with a long iron poker, nodded his assent.

"Bean flour." She put two heaping scoops of it into a pot with four cups of spring water. "Powdered fennel seed." She dumped one part into the mixture. "Finally, wheat flour." She poured half a cup into the brew. She brought it to a soft boil, and with her hand in a thick mitt, pulled it from the fire, and stirred the concoction with a wooden spoon before leaving it to cool.

"Galingale." She held up a dirty root. With pestle and mortar, she pulverized a thumb of it and mixed it into an elixir of two parts spring water and one-part red wine. Heating it over the fire, she poured it into a pewter goblet and let it steep.

"Ginger." She poured a measure of it into a cloth and tied it off. Dunking the cloth in a bowl of simmering white wine, she let it rest. "When the wine goes brown, it is ready."

She then held up a jar, removed the lid and said, "Sanicle." She poured a dash of powder into one of the heated pans, and topped it off with a mixture of water, white wine, a cone of hops, and heavy dashes of other powders, Gregory noticed, she had failed to mention. "Look at the moon, and walk around the fire, slowly, four times, and when you are done, pull it from the flame."

To keep the moon in sight the entire time, he circled backward and then forward, over and over and over again. When he finished the fourth rotation, he knelt down, wrapped his hand in the folds of his cloak, pulled the nectar from the fire and left it to cool. For a terrible heartbeat he felt a wet and foggy chill race down his arms, as if he'd just performed a forbidden incantation. As surety for his Christian soul, he made the sign of the cross, and, in silence, recited the *Paternoster.*

"We are ready," she said, and Gregory joined her in the tent.

She propped Warren's left leg on a roll of wool, and under the light of the flickering torches, inspected the injury. As she had cooked her brews, the vinegar from the bladder had splattered into the gash, loosening the dirt and debris. She turned his leg ever so slightly, and the pool of remaining liquid, as well as the dregs, drained out. Sister Gertrude tucked a piece of white silk deep into the crescent wound, snapped her fingers three times, and then pulled it back out.

She held the silk open in her palm and showed it to Gregory. Just as clean now as it had been before. "We are on our way."

She opened a foldout leather satchel filled with scalpels and knives, and pulled one with a blunt, rounded blade. From the pot of bean and fennel paste, she scooped out a dollop, working it into the crevices of the wound, and did so again and again until filled and smoothed over. She wrapped the leg in a piece of soft linen and looked up at Gregory, who watched over her shoulder. "Fetch me the ginger balm, the galingale, and the pan of Sanicle."

Gregory soon returned with all of it and set them at her feet. She dabbed the ball of ginger around Warren's right eye, swollen shut and blue, and for good measure, gave the ginger a firm squeeze so a few drops collected in the contusion. Straight from the pan, she gave the young man a quenching quaff of the galingale.

Setting the pan down, she made the sign of the cross, and from the movement of her lips, Gregory saw she prayed. She rose from her seat, stretched out her arms and shoulders, and she and the servant girl went about tidying her things and repacking.

"What is next?" Gregory asked.

"We wait for the poultice to dry," she said. "It needs time to pull out the injurious humors."

"Will he survive?"

"Yes," she said. "But there are a few more steps to make him whole."

Fastidious in her chores, she soon finished and returned to the stool next to Warren. Gregory sat across from her, on Warren's other side, and marveled at the woman looking back at him. Dressed in her coif, habit, and coarse wooden clogs, stinking as she did of sweat and toil, and with her crooked teeth and pitted cheeks, Gregory did not find in her the means of desire. Yet she radiated from within, and though no hatchling, she had the naïve sincerity of the teen, the apprentice's want of approval, and the fragile esteem of a broken heart. It all came out of her, showing in her eyes, as blue as spring hyacinths. When that slanted and jutting smile opened in her face, she flushed with an unforetold beauty, and for a blink of crackling intoxication, Gregory found himself lost in her.

He returned a sheepish smile, found the courage to speak of something other than medicine, and said, "You are not like the other nuns I have met in my time."

She responded with a bird of a laugh, regrouped with a stern look, and said, "I had hoped I was like all the rest."

"You are a holy sister, I can tell, but I detect there is a bit of the world in you," he said. "If I am wrong, and if I have pried, do forgive me. But if I am right, entertain me with your story as we sit vigil."

"You are perceptive, for I have not always been a nun," she said. "I am from Paris, from the family of Chatagnier."

"Paris?" Gregory asked, with the same high note of excitement that rang in his voice whenever he said the word.

"Have you been?"

"A few times," he said. "It is my favorite city."

"Then you have never lived there." She grinned and held up an index finger for emphasis. "It is a filthy pile of corruption, and what does not die there, surely leaves burdened with a malady."

"Paris never made me sick." He was embarrassed she had chided him. "But as you maintain, I have never lived there."

"I was married when I was sixteen," she said. "I had this splendid dowry and a wedding with all you would expect from a father who wanted to flaunt his wealth. Bells rang, rose petals fell from the sky, and the Bishop of Paris himself presided over mass. A choir filled the feast hall with its singing, and the wine of Cluny flowed. But I can tell you this—none of it made me happy."

"Indeed, ostentation is a poor substitute for love."

"My husband, Bertrand de Soissons, was a lout and a boor. I was conjugal with him but once, and with God's grace, he did not beget me with child," she said. "He died of the cough just a year after we wed. I sold everything and gave the proceeds to an orphanage. I moved here, to Dax, to live a life of chastity, poverty, and service as a Poor Clare."

"And what did your family say?"

"I was disowned, and even as I left through Porte Saint-Jacques, they hounded me with curses and harangues."

"You are far from home."

"Yes, but when one has no family, there is no need to remain, no?"

"But you are happy at the convent," he said. "I can see it in you."

"My uncle was an apothecary, and from the time I can remember, I was at his workshop, mixing and pouring and crushing this or that," she said. "It is all I have known and all I have loved. That is why they sent me here. The convent needed a medicus."

And so, the conversation gushed through the depths and channels of memory, back to Paris and to London, through the cities and backwaters of Gascony, and out into the unknown future they hoped to one day see. From the serious to the comical they veered, and from the philosophical to the mundane. At each juncture where they met, either Gregory led, or did Gertrude. Circling back to a topic they'd discussed before, or digging into another anew. It mattered not that strange night in the wilderness, when their banter was the bread of life, broken and served for the nourishment of all.

Just as Gregory began another story, Gertrude held up her hand and halted him. Back to the work in front of her she went, unwrapping the gauze and inspecting the wound. Gregory leaned in and watched as she traced a finger across the smooth surface of the dried poultice. He saw the knit of concentration form in her brow as she worked a scalpel around the edges of the trauma, deftly prying downward until she lifted out the plaster in one piece, like a wedge of cake. She turned it over in her palm and showed it to Gregory. The side that was down in the wound black and slimy. He looked at the injury, bright pink, and a smile came to his face.

"God bless you, Sister Gertrude," he said.

She handed him the foul loaf. "Throw it in the fire and recite the *Ave Maria*. When you are done, bring me the clay pot with the blue stripe on it, and the pan with the lid."

The soiled poultice sizzled in the fire as Gregory said the prayer. "Hail, Mary, full of grace, the Lord is with thee. Blessed art thou amongst women and blessed is the fruit of thy womb." He returned to Sister Gertrude's side with the pot and the pan, its hot handle warming through the mitt.

"How much do you think he weighs?" she said.

"Eleven stones?"

She looked Warren up and down, and put a hand to her chin as she appeared to sink deep into thought. She opened a jar, peering at Gregory as she did. "Opium."

Gregory gasped. Opium could kill a man if administered improperly.

Up until this point, he thought the procedure was all but done, that Sister Gertrude had succeeded. But all the optimism drained out of him at the mention of the word, for opium meant much work lay yet ahead. She took a linen from the pot of spring water, and wrung it out twice, and then dusted it with the opium powder. She tied the linen in a knot, stuffed it up under Warren's nose, and held it there until his chest heaved with a violent inhale. A moment later, his head drifted to the side, as if under a spell of sleep.

Gertrude took the lid off the pan, and up came a puff of steam. With a pair of brass finger tongs, she lifted out a fine needle with a long, hairline strand of gut attached to it. With her thumb and index finger on either side of the wound, she pinched the skin slightly upward, drove the needle through from one side to the other, and pulled the gut into a loop to form a knot. Over and over again, her fingers moving in a flurry, the needle flashing down the length of the injury, until stitched tight beneath a neat hatching of gut.

She dropped the needle in the pot, prayed for St. Raphael's help, and made the sign of the cross. "It is in God's hands now."

"But you have surely made God's task much easier," Gregory said. "In all my days, I have never seen such excellent work as yours."

They left Warren at rest and gathered at the fire, Gertrude sitting on her stool, and Gregory reclining with his head propped against his pack. He so wanted to ask more questions, to answer more about himself, and continue their earlier conversation. But he looked into the moon, seized by its hypnotic power, and before he could summon the will to resist, fell to sleep. When he awoke the next morning, he did not remember his dream, but he knew the demons that sometimes taunted him had been banished for the night. He stretched, wiped the sleep from his eyes, and felt blessed by the gorgeous day breaking all around him.

Gertrude sat near the fire, plucking feathers from the pheasant she had brought with her from Dax. It had been in a wooden cage the entire time, and Gregory had never known, nor had he asked, why it was in her possession. But now he knew. From the aroma rising from the kettle—a succulent waft of garlic and onion and fennel and black pepper, and perhaps even plums and pears and a glob of pork lard—it was evident a sauce was in the works.

Gregory went to the tent and peered in. To his relief, Warren appeared to be comfortably on the mend. Gregory found a private place for his morning business and returned to the fire. Gertrude butchered the pheasant into all its best cuts, and piece by piece, rolled them in egg and dusted them in flour. She laid the meat into the kettle, and before closing the lid, tied the giblets in a canvas cloth and tossed them in.

"Did you sleep?"

"Yes, just not as long as you." She worked the coals beneath the kettle. "Warren's fever is gone, and soon he will wake, famished and confused."

"And then he will eat pheasant," Gregory said. "A fitting way to break one's fast."

"The pheasant is for you," she said. "The broth and the offal are for Warren."

"So, going back to last night," he said, his voice almost boyish in its cheer.

But Gertrude's face went sour, she shook her head, and put a finger to her mouth in a request for silence. This gesture hurt Gregory, who found himself pouting when just a moment before he had shone bright with a smile. So, he sat there, glum and confused, staring into the fire as Gertrude, her servant girl, and her man-at-arms gathered her many things and assembled them for the trip back to Dax. He thought about last night, and in the many words they had spoken, did not find anything untoward. And then it came to him. The smile, authentic in its innocence, a fleeting glimpse of the secluded virginal girl. Nothing of note in the great hall or in the city stews, but forbidden within the cloister of the convent. Somehow this realization heartened Gregory, for if already in some phase of penance, he reasoned, it was because he had brought her enough pleasure to feel the guilt of sin.

In silence, she served him the sauced and breaded pheasant hot in a bowl. He devoured the breast and thigh, sopped up the juice with a heel of white bread, stuffing his gullet, licking his lips and fingers, feasting until he could feast no more. She watched him eat, as if it were her duty, and when he finished the first portion, she served him a second. When done, she took the bowl, washed it out, and packed it away. So delicious and filling was the fowl that Gregory felt a satisfaction beyond the mere taste and nourishment of the meal. Gertrude had put extras in it, and whether right or wrong, Gregory told himself it was her love. Not her love of him, he knew, but her love of life. Her love of kindness and charity. A wash of sadness overcame him, for he knew she would soon be leaving. Indeed, her man-at-arms had already attached the covered wagon to the mule, and her servant girl had climbed in.

"When Warren awakes, have him drink the broth, and when he is done, have him eat the heart and the liver," she said. "Throw the neck away, as far as you can, and if a spotted dog comes to scavenge, then you will know Warren will heal."

"And if the dog does not come?"

A flinty assurance showed in her eyes, and her lip curled with heart-wrenching faith. "He will come."

She turned and walked away, leaving Gregory to watch as she hitched her habit, hoisted herself up into the wagon, and pulled the curtain closed. He felt foolish raising his hand to wave, knowing she could not see him, but he did it anyway, just in case she watched him through a squint. Soon enough the wagon disappeared from view, and Gregory, nursing his loneliness, went and sat at Warren's side. Late in the morning, Warren awoke with a violent cough and bolted upright. With one hand he propped himself up, and with the other he rubbed his eyes.

"Where am I?"

"In a tent in the wilderness," he said. "You are recovering from surgery."

As Sister Gertrude had said, Warren was confused. Before he started asking questions, Gregory waved him off. "There will be time for talk later. For now, it is time to mend."

He handed Warren a cup of pheasant broth. Ravenous, drinking so hard his Adam's apple flexed, brown liquid spilled down the sides of his chin. Gregory filled the cup again and gave him another drink. He untied the linen cloth and fed him the heart and liver.

"Now sleep again, my boy, and let this meal give you good blood."

Once outside the tent, Gregory took hold of the pheasant neck and threw it as far as he could. Not pleased with the distance he had achieved, he walked over to it and tossed it yet again. He returned to the fire and fed it with a few pieces of fuel. He worked the coals until a roiling flame gave him warmth on this chilly morn. He had a skin of stale Jurançon and drank it in plenty. Tending the fire, sipping on wine, staring into the distance, thus went this empty day, when questions remained unanswered, and when a brooding calm was his only companion. As the wine asserted itself, and as he feared he would slip into doldrums, a gold and ruby sunset burst across the horizon. Inspired by the soothing bath of light, he stood, cupped his hand over his eyes, and gazed long into the western sky. Elation filled his heart, his smile a river of jubilance.

He looked across his shoulder, out into the field past the tent. A lanky pie-bald hound came skulking from the woods. When he saw Gregory, he stopped, pricked his ears and tail, and made as if to run, but then he lifted his nose, re-captured the scent, and bounded over to the pheasant neck. He snatched the treat, shot Gregory a mischievous gander, and scampered away. Incredulous but thankful, Gregory put a hand over his heart and shook his head.

"Sister Gertrude of Poor Clares. Oh, how I am glad I met you."

The priest awoke at dawn. Another empty stomach. Another day without pork or wine. Another day inside the walls of this wretch-ed place. He said his morning prayers, pulled water from the well, and pilfered a few eggs from the henhouse. Boil them he did, devouring the yolk along with a crust of mouse-nibbled bread and a heel of cheese. Every-one else slept. The priest, alone in the kitchen, looked out the window but finding little solace in the blazing day breaking across the valley.

He did his daily routine. A walk through the bailey, past the herb gar-den he no longer tended, up through a tower to the top of the wall, glanc-ing north to Beynac, and strolling all along the battlements. Out there, the world. In here, the end. The stench from the cesspit wafted his way. Turning up his nose, he propped both forearms on a smooth cut of stone and stared into the green and honey horizon. He knew every little water-way, every little village from here to Bordeaux. His land, his people, and he, estranged from both. The doldrums almost overtook him, but out in the distance he saw the glint of mail, a trail of dust. A single rider raced through the morn.

When the rider came within earshot, he called out. "Who goes there?"

The rider wheeled to a stop halfway up the climb to Castlenaud, peering up from beneath the brim of his helm.

"I bring tidings from Dax." He pulled a letter from his bag.

"And who are these tidings from?"

"From the same person as before—Gregory of London." The messenger rode up the remaining stretch of road and put the letter in the old wooden box. Before leaving he cut a black smile. "You have never seen such a man as he."

After the rider disappeared into the distance, the priest rang the bell and waked the garrison. He ordered the men to lower the drawbridge, fetch the letter, and bring it to him. He marched to the south tower, climbed the stairs to the uppermost room, and banged on the door.

"You woke me once, now you wake me again?" Alphonse said.

"Gregory has written you another letter." He leaned close to the door.

The door flew open, and there Alphonse stood, clothed in an open robe. "Read to me what this bastard says this time!"

The priest unrolled the parchment.

If I have learned anything in Gascony, it is that duels are never easily won. When death is the price, no man is eager to pay. And so, it was in Saugnac, when an elder outside his prime nearly bested the whelp who opposed him. A ghastly injury, an abscess that nearly took my friend's life. I paid out all my silver for a healer, drove my horse to the brink of collapse, and prayed as I never have before. I even performed a dark incantation, and besmirched the honor of a nun, in pursuit of my ends. My efforts proved fruitful. My friend is well, he rides with me, and if ever we should meet, you will have to deal with him. Such is his story. Now, it is time for yours. If you were sick with the fever, or if your wound bubbled with puss and bile, I would do nothing to ease your suffering. I would watch you die, standing witness to your end. When they asked me how it happened, I would say the manner of your demise mattered not. He is gone, I would say, and I heard him take his last rancid breath.

"You woke me for this drivel?"

"Yes, Lord Alphonse, I did," the priest said, in a voice of high warning. "But even as you are half asleep, you know it is not as you say."

Rotten Oysters in Mont de Marsan

regory removed the last suture. He breathed a sigh of relief, looked up, and smiled at Warren, who lounged on his saddle, his leg propped on his pack. It had been a fortnight since Sister Gertrude had worked her magic, and this, the pulling of the stitches, was the final act in Warren's recovery. A slow road they had taken, finding themselves at the village of Tartas on their way to Mont de Marsan, a sleepy place of peasants and fields, a church and an arched bridge over the Midouze. It seemed an easy place to stop and rest and bring an end to Warren's wound.

This should have been a happy day, but a burden weighed on Gregory's mind. He worried about the horse, Lady Tatenhill. She was silver like her mother, with a white whorl on her rump. But from her father she had chestnut points at her hooves and ears, and a chestnut blaze from forehead to muzzle. Long in places and robust in others, she offered a pleasing unity of grace and power. She was indeed, a rare horse of rare blood, the sun shining on her every day. By birth a racer and a fighter, her place was in the highest echelon of the breed, so young and green, but with the bold promise of glory.

And she had nearly gotten Warren killed.

Balking at the duel in Saugnac. Backing out instead of charging home. For all her beauty, and the potential stored in her regal physique, Gregory thought of only one thing—she was unreliable. She might do back in England, maybe, but not in Gascony. So, Gregory had waited until the right moment, Warren completely healed, to break bad tidings.

"The letter from my wife?" he asked.

Warren gave him a puzzled look. "What about it?"

"You made me wait, did you not?"

"Yes, but for a good reason."

"This time around, I am afraid it is I who have made you wait, and also, for a good reason."

"What have I waited for?"

"Your horse. She is no good."

He pushed himself up with one arm. "Whatever do you mean?"

"She betrayed you at Saugnac," Gregory said. "She is of fine lineage, but she is no Black Saddle, and is certainly no Moonbeam."

Warren stood, and so too did Gregory.

The two of them stared at one another.

"As I said in Bayonne, in time she will be the equal of both of them," Warren said.

"But we do not have time. We can sell her—for perhaps one hundred livres in Mont de Marsan—and buy another horse more suitable for what lies ahead."

"You would sell her, Master Gregory? Is that all you have learned in London, profits and deals?"

"I know much more than that," Gregory said. "You were recently on your death bed. Would you like to sleep in it again?"

"I will not sell Lady Tatenhill, not for all the silver in Gascony."

"Then pray she is equal to your hopes and let us not speak of it again."

regory rejoiced at the sight of the great belfry at Mont de Marsan, peeking up above the tree line, sharing its blessings with the town below. The priory, stained with time, sat astride the three rivers. Tired and hungry, done with the road, and eager to rest his nerves, Gregory quickened his horse. Warren followed suit, and despite their tiff at Tartas, they rode into town scowling, together unbreakable, and those who looked at them quickly turned away.

They arrived at the priory, its imposing façade towering over them. A novice led them around to the guest house next to the stables. And there they rested, ate fresh bread and bowls of hot pottage, and curled up for a good night's rest. The next morning, they broke their fast, visited the latrine, and made small talk with the other guests—pilgrims on their way to Santiago de Compostela in Spain.

Gregory took an interest in this because he knew the route, and if they did as he had done, they would eventually travel through Leschun, the little village up in the Pyrenees where Gregory had spent the winter transcribing Marco Polo's book. He sized up this gaggle of travelers. Most of them appeared to be of the simple sort, but among them a priest, a rugged man of the cloth who most probably knew his letters. Gregory gave him a kind look, sat next to him, and put a friendly hand on his shoulder.

"Dear brother, you are a long way from Santiago de Compostela."

"The more to test our faith and our love," he said.

"Will you head over the mountains?"

"Yes," he said. "We begin our assent from Eauze."

Gregory laughed. "I have been that way," he said. "You will come across a town called Leschun. There is a priest there by the name of Father Guillaume. He is a good man and a good friend. Hopefully by the time you arrive there you will be tired and will stay for a while."

"And his hospitality?"

"Oh, it is of the finest quality," he said. "When you have him in your confidence, ask him about a very important man named Marco Polo—write this down so you don't forget."

The priest dug into his pack, pulled out his Book of Hours, his quill and his ink. He opened the book, and in the bottom margin on one of the pages, wrote down the name.

"Who is this Marco Polo and why is he so important?"

"I will not spoil the surprise," Gregory said. "You will have to wait until Leschun to find out."

"And should I tell him who you are?"

"No, just say you met a man along the way. He will know who it is."

regory came to Mont de Marsan for news, if there was any, to be delivered to him by his distant cousin, Maynart, the infermerer here at the priory. This meeting had been set months ago, soon after Gregory left La Réole. Much had happened since then, too much, and Gregory was sure Maynart had a story to tell. He knew the telling would probably not be good, but he needed to hear it, and grew cranky and impatient as Maynart kept him waiting. He knew Warren felt the same way, but sitting here in the priory's guest house, road weary and surrounded by strangers, there was nothing they could do but be patient.

"You look defeated, Master Gregory, and I do not like it," Warren said.

"I want it to be over, but more is yet to come," he said. "I am too old for the dangers of Gascony. I need to be home with my wife and my children, my friends, and my business."

His companion frowned. "And that is your fate, and your fate will be done, but for now it must be deferred."

"I know, and that is what pains me," he said. "The decisions I make are only because someone else has made bigger decisions for me. If I look defeated it is because such is the case. I am a little man, when once I thought otherwise."

"But think about what happens when you are back home," Warren said. "Your adventures, your triumphs. Your wife and your heir. You will be more powerful than ever, and once again, your decisions will truly be yours."

"Will they?"

"I have no doubt, Master Gregory. You pay the price now, but when you are back in London, all of it will be to your benefit."

"You had better be right, Lord Warren, or I will come to your manor and denounce you as a liar." He managed a smile.

And so, they talked, hewing down beneath the frustrations of their predicament, moving into the easy conversation of friends, the simple banter when everything, yet nothing, is said all at once. Their comfort was interrupted by a stirring in the room. Lounging on the floor propped on one elbow, Gregory rose to a sitting position, looking in the same direction as everyone else. A dour monk, a tail of novices behind him, entered the room. Maynart, and he did not look pleased to be there. Gregory rose to his feet and tried to be upbeat, and when he bowed and introduced Warren, he made sure to tell Maynart he was a young and rising lord in the service of the powerful Earl of Southampton. But Maynart did not seem impressed. To the contrary, he greeted them with an empty smile and a tepid gesture, and in that moment, Gregory knew this reunion would not go well.

"Dear cousin, they said you would come," Maynart said. "Sorry to have kept you waiting, but a cough has broken out amongst the lay brothers, and as usual, the older monks suffer from the piles. I have treated their rotten oysters all day, so excuse me if I am glum."

"We all must cleave to our work, cousin Maynart." Gregory kissed him on both cheeks.

They sat at a table in the corner of the guest house, and soon thereafter, a novice appeared with a bucket of wine and cups. He poured a drink for all three of them. Gregory took a sip and just about spit it out, but he gave no clue as to his displeasure, and instead took another sip.

Maynart looked at Gregory long and hard. An accusing squint settled into his eyes. "Your uncle Helias has died. Not long before the Feast of St. Mark."

Gregory made the sign of the cross. "I feared he was not long for this world, but he made for himself a good life."

"Hugo still lives, but from what I hear, he is mad with grief." Maynart shook his head. "It is hard to imagine one without the other."

"Indeed, but Hugo is a strong lot, so it would not surprise me if he remains with us for many years to come."

"Let us hope," Maynart said, in a defeatist tone.

Though Maynart's manner was unenthusiastic, Gregory recognized it as intentional, that a lively emotion lurked just beneath the surface. Knowing it would eventually come out, he decided to force the issue. "I think there is something you wish to say, Cousin Maynart, so please, out with it."

Maynart took a fortifying drink of wine, set his cup down, and leaned in with a look so righteous and true, and so hot with virulence, that Gregory grew terrified of what he was about to hear. "I told you Helias has died, but I did not tell you how a retinue of riders went to La Réole, and they pressed him and Hugo with many questions. So aggressive were they in their enquiry that your uncles grew fearful for their lives. Indeed, so upset was Helias he stopped breathing right then and there, and fell to the ground, dead and undignified for all to see. Cousin Gregory, those riders asked about *you*. They asked about a manuscript. They said you had stolen it from them at Marmande. But that is not all. Just a month ago, they came here, banging on the priory door. They were convinced you were here, and it took Prior Symo quite some time to convince them you were not. These were not ordinary men, cousin Gregory. It was Bernard de Fumel, the lord of Bonaguil. If you tell me you do not know of this man, and if you tell me you do not know of what I speak, then I will have you turned out this very night—and the priory will keep your horses as recompense!"

Gregory did not have an immediate response. Helias, dead. Hugo, in mourning. Bernard de Fumel looking for his manuscript. This was too much for him to absorb, and for a long while he sat in silence, his elbow planted on the table, his head cradled in his hand, lost in the currents of doubt, tossed by the waves of grief. He looked into Maynart's eyes but saw no sympathy there. The monk had him, and before Gregory could recover, Maynart pressed his advantage.

"You say you have come here with a lord." He gestured toward Warren. "But all I see is a ruffian. Think about the pain you have caused, and think about the trouble you are in. Think of who you are, not who you think you are. I know Hugo and Helias gave you title to the franchise in La Réole, but had they taken the time to consider it, they would have found you unworthy."

When Gregory heard this, he collected himself, stood from the table, and gave Maynart a withering look of reprove. "Perhaps it would have been best if the franchise had been bequeathed to the priory here at Mont de Marsan. If that were the case, perhaps I would have gotten a better reception."

Maynart prepared to respond, but before another poisonous word came out of his mouth, Warren grabbed him around the collar of his habit, jerked him to his feet, and pulled him in until face to face. Gregory put his arm up in attempt to stop what was happening, but he knew it was futile, so he stood back and watched the encounter unfold.

"Monk, you have insulted Master Gregory, so you have insulted me," Warren said. "You may think you are safe here in your priory, but beware, for your tongue might get the better of you yet."

Maynart, sagging in the young lordling's grasp, looked to Gregory with pleading eyes.

Gregory gave an approving nod to Warren, who tossed Maynart to the floor. "We will turn ourselves out, cousin Maynart."

As the novices and pilgrims backed away in astonishment, and as Maynart climbed to his knees, Gregory and Warren grabbed their belongings and stormed out of the guest house. They made haste to the stables, but by the time they had rigged their steeds with tack and saddle, Maynart, Prior Symo, and a dozen others, had gathered there. Gregory and Warren tried to pass, but they formed a cordon.

"You have assaulted a man of God," Prior Symo said.

"And I will assault him again if he does not get out of my way." Warren spurred his horse and Lady Tatenhill lurched forward without hesitation. Rather than be trampled, the monks broke ranks, and Warren and Gregory rode on through the gap.

"Cousin Gregory, God will punish you for your insolence," Maynart called.

Gregory wheeled his horse around and pulled him to a halt.

"And God will remember your greed," he said. "This was not about Helias, Bernard de Fumel, or a manuscript. It was the wine, cousin Maynart. The franchise at La Réole. You know it, and so does your prior. Now, as I recall, the older monks have severe cases of the piles. You should concentrate on treating their rotten oysters, as you say. That is all you are good for."

They rode until they found a stand of oak, and once deep inside of it, made camp. Gregory had hoped to sleep in the warmth and safety of the priory, and to perhaps share a long night of wine with cousin Maynart, but he had no problem making due with the tent. As Warren built a small fire and prepared a meal of nuts and salted fish, and as his old friend hummed the lyrics to a tavern song from Lichfield, Gregory found comfort. They nibbled at their food and lounged near the fire, and for a long while the only sounds were the spit and crackle of the flames, the hoot of the owl, and the breeze in the boughs.

"So, Bernard de Fumel is looking for you," Warren said.

"Indeed, it appears he has won the tournament at Marmande, a feat I'd hoped he would not achieve," Gregory said. "He wants his book, but as you know, it is on its way to England."

"If he catches us and demands that you give it back, what will you tell him?"

"I will tell him it is not possible, for it is not."

"He will not like that answer, Master Gregory."

"It is the only answer I can give. Anything else would be a lie which he would easily detect."

"Then let us hope he does not track us down."

As he chewed his last morsel of salted fish, Gregory grabbed a stick and stoked the fire. He looked over and noticed how the orange light showed in Warren's face, and how it made him look much older than he was. But doubtless the lines of worry were there, the creeping vagrant of time, coming to spoil what it could. He remembered when he first met Warren and how young and innocent he had been, the good lad from Lichfield, the town trophy, the tears in his mother's eyes when he'd said goodbye. Those golden days were gone, perhaps never to be tarnished, but also never to return. The thought of it saddened him, for in Warren he saw the press of life, the unstoppable wheel rolling over any and all. How could it have happened to his friend?

How could it have happened to me?

"When I stole the manuscript, Fumel was a landless mercenary who had no real authority," Gregory said. "I thought it would remain that way. I thought he would lose, and in the process, lose his claim. But instead he has won, and now that he holds the estate at Bonaguil, his claim is quite valid. He wants what is his, and now he has the standing to try and find it."

"Should we fear him, or is he yet another fool, in over his head?"

"I am not sure, but we should likely find out soon."

"But you made a copy of this book, a copy you still have on your person."

"Yes, but I will not tell him."

"And why not?"

"If possible, I want to keep it for myself."

"But why didn't you send your copy back to England with the original?"

"Because, then the Earl of Southampton would have it, and in that case, I might not ever get it back. The earl has what he wanted. The copy is mine."

"It has been a long day, but I am not yet ready to sleep," Warren said.

He sat up, pulled a skin of ale from his bag, and took a drink. He held out the skin for Gregory to take, and he did. As the ale gushed through his mouth and down his throat, he felt an unexpected quickening of merriment.

"Read to me again, Master Gregory," Warren said. "Take me to the land of the Great Khan."

He dug into his pack and pulled out the cylindrical case of boiled leather, and from it he pulled a thick roll of parchments. He thumbed through them and found where he had left off the last time he'd read to Warren—Marco

Polo's visit to the City of Heaven, the city of Kinsay. So fair was it that the Great Khan spared it in that season of sword and fire. Its bridges and streets of stone, and its markets bulging with wares beyond count, the city boasted mansions and monasteries, its lake and hot baths. Boats and barges, banquets and weddings, and covered carriages rumbling here and there, it was a city of commerce and leisure, of gardens and gold, the sparkling capital of Manzi. Polo, a man like no other in a place like no other, and to think of him was to quash little thoughts, to abandon nagging doubts, and to choose light over darkness. Gregory soon lost himself in the reading and grew fluid with the occasional droughts of ale.

He took a break from his recitation and looked up from the parchments. Warren reclined on his bags, his hands crossed behind his head, his feet propped up on a saddle. Gregory started to laugh.

Warren glanced at him, perplexed. "What is so funny?"

"Not too long ago you looked old and used," Gregory said. "But now you look young again."

THE
SIEGE FIRES
OF LARRESSINGLE

There they were, Gregory and Warren, on the edge of the Valence family feud. It perpetuated an old gripe, a contest between sisters, both of them spoiled by their father's love, both of them rotten with ego and greed. Unable to agree, unwilling to compromise, they chose instead the cruel way of the feud, the shame and lust of fratricide. And so, one had usurped the other, the younger over the elder, stealing the patrimony. She barricaded herself within Larressingle, a fortified town surrounded by vineyards long since uprooted, burned to the ground, hacked to stubs, and otherwise destroyed by the warted, cackling fiends of war.

They rode in from the Church of Sainte-Marie in Montréal, once they had gotten word from the besieged. Gregory made the sign of the cross and shook his head as he looked out over the desolation. Corpses hung in trees, buzzards circling above, a charred siege engine overturned, the decaying remains of dogs and horses, and the crude stench of malignant desire. The walls remained standing, a guard tower jutting into the sunset, the central keep brooding over the town's shuttered windows, chained doors, and godless chapel.

Nightfall approached, and with it the growing hint of wind and drizzle. Torches flickered on the walls, where twilight gathered in the helms of the town's defenders. Below, behind a rampart bristling with spikes and spears, where timber beams covered a dank ditch, huddled the besiegers. Their trickery stymied, their bribes refused, their assault repelled, they sat and waited, perhaps not as famished as those inside the town, but doubtless in dire want of their usual comforts.

Hidden in a clutch of trees, Gregory and Warren waited past nightfall.

Gregory nodded toward the town. "You say they are waiting for us?"

"Yes, upon my signal they will lower the gate and let us in."

"And do you still believe that?"

"No." Warren graced his elder with a rogue's smile. "But it is our mission, so we will do as we have been asked. If the gate does not open, we will head on our way, but if asked later if we tried, we can say yes and have truth on our side."

"Yes," Gregory said, his voice lilting with sarcasm. "If the gate does not open, at least we will have the truth."

"I do not hear confidence in your voice, Master Gregory."

"Because there is none. Since you arrived in Gascony, we have nearly been thrown in the gaol in Bayonne. You nearly died at Saugnac. We were driven out of Mont de Marsan. Bernard de Fumel now hunts for us. And now this? When will our lives get easier?"

"One day they will, but not tonight. If we get in, I trust you will not give voice to your doubts."

"Oh, do not worry. They will be locked away."

Gregory thought about their situation, related to him in detail by Warren, and sighed. The two sisters, Clementia and Claudine, had competed for years. What began as spite had bloomed into irreconcilable hatred. Sideways glances and petty lies during childhood had given way to all manner of abuse as teens. When their father, Renaud, died during the war, the stakes of their animosity only redoubled, as they no longer fought for the treats of familial affection, but for assets and deeds. To Clementia, the eldest, went the town of Larressingle and its charter of sovereign rule. To Claudine, the youngest, went two country manors owing fee to the lords of Armagnac. In a world without flaw, and in a sisterhood without strife, this arrangement was fair enough. But in Gascony, what was good was worth fighting for. So young Claudine, in defiance of her father's will, outmaneuvered her older sister, stormed the town of Larressingle, and with her suite of hungry belligerents, squatted in the town's tower. Clementia, the rightful heir, on the outside looking in, with her own war band camped in the sick and squalor of siege.

Had it been up to Gregory, he would have let them play their game to the end—someone would win, and someone would lose, and in a generation no one would care. But the two sisters were not the only women here at Larressingle. A third one, Martha of Agen—a budding *Rosa Gallica* betrothed to one of Kind Edward's favorites back in England—was a hostage held by Claudine, who had demanded a royal writ legitimizing her claim to Larressingle. In exchange for the writ, she had promised to hand over the girl. It was a reckless request to be sure, as Claudine at best was of middling status, and at worst an upstart without right or recourse. But out in the wilds of Gascony, such gambits were known to reap rewards. So, Gregory stood on the edge of the Valence family feud, wishing he wasn't, and in his satchel, sitting atop the stack of dark letters, Claudine's precious writ.

"Are you ready, Master Gregory?"

"Lead the way, my lord, and do not falter."

Warren made a circle with his thumb and index finger, stuck them into his mouth and whistled three times. He waited a moment and did it again. Gregory peered across the wasteland, and to his distress, saw movement in Clementia's camp. Riders climbed onto their mounts, footmen grabbed their spears, and the hounds, their ears pricked and their tails pointing skyward, lifted their heads and bayed. But above the clamor, Gregory heard three whistles from the city walls, and a ball of flame rose from a brazier on the battlements. Warren slapped the reins and worked his spurs. Lady Tatenhill lurched out from the woods and dashed into the night. Barreling over the pocked and splintered terrain, cutting and veering through the wreckage, she found the path that wasn't really there, and sprinted through the danger.

Gregory and Black Saddle followed, but the great stallion proved fickle, as his love and skill were reserved for the open field. Though he galloped with urgency, and though he sought to serve his master, the obstacles impeded him. When the gate opened with a wash of light, Warren rode through, but Gregory and Black Saddle still trailed by ten lengths. Looking over his shoulder, he saw a short phalanx of riders pulling in behind him. Fiendish on their steeds, made thin and savage by the siege, they closed in on him with weapons drawn. Hounds coursing to his left and his right, and with barbed projectiles whizzing by, Gregory hunched over Black Saddle's withers and worked his spurs. A patch of trampled earth opened up, Black Saddle went full on the hoof, and as a hound leapt and snapped at his tail, and as a rider reached out to grab Gregory's cloak, they cut across the bridge. They skidded to a halt as the gate slammed and barred behind them.

Jittery with the rush of the chase, Gregory looked from beneath the brim of his beaver and peacock hat, and found himself surrounded by a company of miscreants. He had figured as much, but what bewildered him was that Warren and Lady Tatenhill were nowhere in sight. He swiveled his head from left to right, glared at the men who held him at spear point, and shouted, "I am a royal messenger with letters from the king! Do harm to me or my companion, and you will surely have a date with the gallows!"

"We will do you no harm," one of them said, "but the bargaining will be harder than you expected."

They forced him to dismount, took Black Saddle away, and led Gregory over the rubble-strewn ward and down a stone street to the tower. He looked at it, standing dark and sinister, and from a high window, saw the golden glow of a fire and heard the echo of voices. A face, enveloped in shadow, appeared in the window, and with a shudder, Gregory knew it was Claudine. His captors jostled him as they led him up the spiral stairwell to the fifth floor. The door creaked open, they pushed him through, cinched his arm behind his back until he winced, and held him upright as captured prey. Those in the room split with laughter and jeered, and a dwarf, clad in a garish kit of red and yellow, humped on Gregory's leg with vulgar delight. Claudine, leaning against the wall near the window, clapped her hands and motioned for silence. After the crass outburst died down, she took a few steps forward, stopped, crossed her arms over her chest, and looked Gregory up and down.

"*Vous êtes en retard.*" She pouted her lips in disapproval. "We expected you a week ago."

"But I am here, so tell your men to back away for I have brought what you asked for."

A simple nod and they released him from the arm lock. He rubbed his elbow, stretched his shoulder, and glanced at the dwarf with a dismissive frown. He removed his hat, tucking it under his arm. He mustered the flinty stare of truth, of three dozen deaths and the promise of more, his London look of black money, secret favors, and poisonous lies.

"I am not leaving here without Lord Warren."

"Perhaps you will, but as you may have guessed, I will ask for a new agreement," she said.

Indeed, the plucky smile of the upstart crept over Claudine's face. In her sly brown eyes, Gregory saw her ambition, detected the unhinged motives driving her, and that though she had delved deep into the dark caverns of her soul, she would delve deeper still. The worst was yet to come, and Gregory hoped it would not arrive at his expense. He sized her up once more, knowing he would have to find and exploit a weakness in order to win. The silky lines of youth had given way to the toil and worry of adulthood, had been despoiled by the indignities and guile of the feud. Her ginger hair was cut short, so she almost looked like a boy. But beneath her robes she wore mail, a large knife hung at her side, and as more of her essence came to light, Gregory knew her remorselessness was total. More than a boy, Claudine Valance resembled a cutthroat, and when she licked her top lip and rested her hand on the pommel of her knife, Gregory knew he was in for a long and difficult night.

They sat at the trestle table, Gregory at one end, Claudine at the other, and her men on either side between them.

"Do you know Clementia, my sister?" she asked, making a face of loathing.

"I have not had the privilege," Gregory said. "And until tonight, I had not had the honor of meeting you, either. I am only a messenger, and, I assure you, I have no interest in how your little private war turns out. But here I am, and I bring you victory. That should be enough."

"Clementia is a dirty whore." She propped her elbows on the table and rested her chin on her interlocked fingers. "I should know. I have seen her suck a man's root, and even watched her take it like a dog. And she surely drank a tonic of goat's beard, for she was never heavy with child. She is a whore, I tell you, a creature of sin, and being dispossessed is the least of her punishments."

Claudine's men grunted and nodded in approval, and the dwarf made a lewd gesture with his mouth and hand.

Gregory ignored them. He remained prim and superior, determined not to succumb to their depravity. "I am not interested in your sister's inclinations, nor in her penalties. I am here for Martha of Agen, and I need to see her soon. If she is injured or dead, or if she has been tainted in any way, then sooner or later you will have to answer to men much more powerful than I."

Claudine tilted her head, her eyes widened, and she held out her hands as if pleading for an audience. "There are many who think my sister is not even legitimate. They say she was whelped on a tanner's daughter, and that she was foisted on my mother while she was yet begotten with me. You see, when a woman is with child she has her season, but there are those who say I arrived two months early. And why? Because my bastard half-sister slipped from the loins of another women, not the loins of my mother. She could not have had two children in such a short amount of time. My father, and damn him for this, gave Clementia the claim to Larressingle in willful error."

"You know your family history well, but I did not come here to learn of your lineage," he said. "I am here for Martha of Agen, and when we are done with that, we will negotiate the release of Lord Warren of Lichfield."

"But you must believe me," she said. "You must believe in my cause and know I am just."

"Here is my belief." He pulled the writ from his satchel, laid it on the table, and stabbed it with his index finger. "Look, the Seneschal of Gascony, a direct representative of the king, has affixed his seal to it. Now bring me Martha of Agen and honor the exchange you yourself have requested!"

Claudine stood from the table, paced over to the window and looked out. She jerked her head in an abrupt convulsion, and a crossbow bolt whizzed by her face. It slammed into the wall on the other side of the room and fell to the floor. She backed away from the window, turned to Gregory, and gestured toward the bolt as if to make her point, and said, "If ever I have the pleasure of capturing my sister, I will see to it she is raped, so she gets what she wants, and then I will cage her, starve her, and that will be my entertainment."

Gregory did not know how to respond to such a sentiment, so he didn't. He looked at her, held out the writ, and when she did not react the way he wanted her to, he shook the writ, as if to tell her to hurry and be done with it. He did his best to portray confidence, but he was anything but. Surrounded by armed men, held captive in a besieged tower, and with the whereabouts of Martha and Warren unknown, he saw no end to his predicament. Still, he hoped it was sinking in, that Claudine realized he was an important man with an important gift, and that reneging on the deal by asking for more could bring about her downfall.

She snatched the writ from his hand, opened it, and began reading. Her men watched, intent and impatient, because they knew, as did Gregory, that their fate, and not just Claudine's, was written on that fine piece of parchment. Done reading, she held the writ above her head and smiled. "We have done it! Larressingle is mine! By the king's word, Larressingle belongs to me!"

Her men, this collection of the gaunt and destitute, those who had risked it all to help Claudine commit her crime, rose from their seats and rejoiced. The dwarf climbed on the table and skipped across it, kicking out his feet and clicking his heels, stoking merriment with his buffoonery. Gregory had no reason to celebrate, his work far from done. In the din of the commotion, he and Claudine glared at one another, and from the placid look in her jaded eyes, he knew the standoff between them had just begun.

As he considered his next step, his next words, and as he absorbed a new stab of apprehension, there came a calamity so immense and dumbfounding that for a long moment of confusion, Gregory stood and stared as the world around him exploded.

A fireball, twice the size of a man's head, of solid stone and with a long sizzling tail, had smashed through the tower's timber roof, demolished the table where Gregory had recently sat, careened off the floor and slammed against the door, splitting it down the middle and torqueing it out of its hinges. The crack and thunder of it all had left him momentarily deaf, but when his hearing returned, he heard the shouts of life and the groans of creeping death.

The dwarf, so recently coarse and jovial, lay a flat and leaking mess on the floor, as did two others. But Claudine yet lived, and as the pitch and flame gathered throughout the room, she collected herself, yelled at what remained of her men, and led them through the door and down the stairs.

Gregory found himself alone, in danger of being consumed by the fire. But rather than panic, he surveyed the room. He saw Warren's gear in the corner, a sword and shield on one of the slain, and a handsome gold and emerald ring on the dwarf's right thumb. As the flames licked at his feet and hissed in his face, Gregory grabbed all of it, allowing himself a wink of relish as he plucked off the ring, and so burdened, slunk from the room.

The tumult outside the tower, a terrible crescendo leading up to the end. A battering ram crunched against the gate, the defiance of the defense and the threats of the attack, the crackle of fire and the smashing of stones, the whisper of bow strings and the catcall of steel. There, too, rang the anguish of those not long for the night, and the harangues from those who sent them to hell.

When Gregory arrived at the second-floor landing, he stopped in front of the door. He cupped his ear and leaned against it hearing many agitated voices. He tried the handle, but as he expected, it was locked. He breathed a sigh of despair, but his spirits suddenly soared as a recent memory flittered through his mind. As he'd knelt down and twisted the ring off the dwarf's thumb, he had seen a hoop of keys fastened to the belt of the dead man beside him. Gregory dropped everything, cursing himself as he raced back up the stairs. The room was engulfed in flame, and Gregory knew he would be roasted if he dared enter. Yet as the corpses burned and as the juices bubbled out of them, he saw the keys winking in the belly of the inferno.

He scratched the back of his neck, taking account of his surroundings. He saw the spiral stairwell, a narrow landing on the second floor and the fifth, a room burning out of control, and another room where Warren—and presumably Martha of Agen—were imprisoned. Even as he despaired, an idea dawned. He darted back down the stairs and fetched Warren's sword, *Fionnaghal*. He pulled it from its leather and gem encrusted sheath, and for the first time, held the great blade. It shimmered with a haunting greenish-blue, emoting the glory and peril of lordship, loud with the murmurs of the slain, and equally so with the plaudits of the rescued. Despite the urgency consuming him, Gregory held the sword upright and found himself lost in its spell of power, beckoned by its promise of clout.

He shook loose from the delusion and ran up the stairs.

There, at the threshold to the burning room, the door, split down the middle, wrenched from its hinges, and leaning diagonally across the entryway. He leaned in with his shoulder. The hulking piece of oak didn't budge. Nor did Gregory quit, and as it seemed his strength would fade, the door tilted forward. He gave it one final heave and stood back. The door teetered for a moment, and in that instant when it could have fallen back, Gregory made the sign of the cross, praying it wouldn't. The door creaked and fell forward, sending ash and flame rising in a hellish gust.

Gregory pulled the hood up over his hat, wrapped the cloak tightly about him, and inched his way across the door. When he reached the end, he knelt down, cocked *Fionnaghal* high above his head, and hacked down at the dead key holder. The blade cut through the man's belt, and from there Gregory used the tip of the sword to pluck the keyring free. He tilted the sword upward, and the bundle of keys, fastened to a big iron hoop, slid clinking down the length of the blade, catching against its crossguard. As the flames tried to claim him, the smoke tried to choke him, and as a rafter fell and tried to crush him, he turned and fled the room.

He looked back and did not know how he had gotten in and out alive, but when he saw a peculiar green flame lick through the doorway before flickering out, he knew he had cheated fate.

He burst down the stairs. When he reached the landing, he turned the sword down so the keys slid off and clanked against the floor. Knowing they were too hot to touch, he lifted his robe, pulled down his breeches and urinated on them. He aimed well, too, pissing on each key until all of them hissed and steamed.

Putting himself back together, he tilted his head to better hear what happened outside. He heard the jarring thump of the battering ram on the weakening gate, the grunts and growls of those trying to keep it closed. Gregory wrapped his hand in a fold of his cloak, and so protected, picked up the keys. One. Two. Three. Four. Five. And then six. The key slid into the hole, and when he cranked it leftward, he felt the latch lift. He pushed the door open and stepped inside.

A stench fouler than the wet shit of Satan made him double over and wretch. On his knees and wiping vomit from his chin, he peered into the room. To his relief he saw Warren, alive and chained to the wall. Next to him sat a girl in a soiled red robe and a veil. Gregory guessed this was Martha of Agen, and she, too, was chained to the wall. She appeared pale and weary, a black eye and a swollen lip, but very much alive.

The sight sickening him was of many more people, some of them already dead and decomposing, rank piles of hair and flesh, while others, brittle and emaciated, wallowed in their own effluviums. Still others, appeared not yet broken, but clearly the victims of fiendish neglect. In the center of the room sat a large oaken chair, its seat padded with a thick cushion, its back draped with a wolf skin, and accompanied by a matching foot stool. Strewn at the base of the chair were empty wine goblets and the bones from past meals of beef, fish and fowl.

It all came to him, and Gregory recalled the disturbing words Claudine had uttered not so long ago, when speaking of her sister, Clementia.

I will cage her, starve her, and that will be my entertainment.

Transfixed as he absorbed the horror, Gregory barely heard the shouts and pleas from those who begged him to set them free.

"Warren!"

"Get us out of here, Master Gregory, and upon our return to England, you can name your price," he said.

"I will hold you to it." Gregory sorted through ring of keys with shaking hands. He found the right one, and when the lock fell free, Warren pulled the chain through the series of iron beckets lining the wall. In one powerful tug, eight men were set loose. Soon on their feet, they were relieved by the turn of events but angry and ready for reprisal.

"We came to give Larressingle to Claudine, but now we are going to take it from her," Warren said.

Gregory handed him his sword and showed him to his gear, where Warren retrieved his shield and his helm. The men destroyed the chair, breaking it into heavy pieces so all of them were suddenly armed with clubs. They rallied around Warren, who gave Gregory a reassuring nod before leading them down the stairs, out of the tower and into battle.

Gregory remained with Martha of Agen and the infirm. He herded them out of the chamber, closed the door behind them, and there on the landing they huddled in silence, devouring the half-loaf of bread and cured meats Gregory pulled from his pack. With the cloak held tight over his nose, he returned to the room and went to the window. The shutters bolted shut, but squinting through a crevice, he watched Warren and his troop of hungry fellows charge across the yard, sounding the bloody howl of war, and plunging headlong into the rear of Claudine's retinue.

They threw themselves against the foe, hacking and cleaving without pity, until Claudine's line buckled under the weight of their onslaught. The gate split open, a mighty yawn of destruction, and the nose of the battering ram poked through. A flood of mailed men, their wild eyes and weapons bright in the moonlight, poured through the breach. Gregory winced at the slaughter, as the intruders butchered Claudine's men into hideous stumps and pieces.

Finally, only Claudine remained, and there she stood, armed with a knife, clad in her rigged suit of armor, clutching the writ, as her enemies encircled her. Warren and his men, the few remaining, backed away, giving the field to Clementia, who arrived astride an elegant bay palfrey. Her supporters parted, giving her a narrow lane through which to ride into the center and greet her defeated sister. Both of them remained silent, glaring at one another, seeming to savor the dire moments before the final confrontation.

Gregory's mouth fell agape, he put a hand to his chin, and swallowed a lump of anxiety. He burst out of the room and grabbed Martha of Agen by the hand. "Come, girl, it is time to leave!"

The two of them circled down the stairs, out from the tower and down the timber landing to the yard. They hastened to the gathering and joined Warren, who stood outside the ring of men surrounding the sisters.

Before the next act in this drama commenced, Gregory held up his hand, cleared his throat, and spoke in a dark, threatening tenor. "Lady Clementia, before claiming your patrimony, you should know Lady Claudine is the rightful holder of the Larressingle estate."

As a gasp arose from many, Clementia turned in her saddle, peering out from beneath the raised visor of her plumed, blackened helm. A toxic grin danced in her eyes, and she gave Gregory a suspicious glare. For a half beat of a pounding heart, Gregory saw in her the bedevilment of surprise. But as quickly as the doubt had come, it went, and with her shoulders squared, her head held high, and with the siege fires bathing her armor in a haunting orange wash, she said, "I am the rightful heir, by my father's will."

"You *were* the rightful heir, but Lady Claudine has a royal writ superseding your father's word," Gregory said. "You see, no man in Gascony has more authority than King Edward."

"He speaks the truth," Claudine said. She held the writ high over her head, making sure the royal seal could be seen by all.

"There is a copy back in Bordeaux, and I assure you, the seneschal knows exactly where it is," Gregory said. "If you destroy this one, they will come with yet another. Larressingle is no longer yours, and that is now the law of the land."

It pained Gregory to watch the shadow of doom creep over Clementia's handsome face, to see the light die in her eyes, and to witness her shrinkage from warlord to fool. It angered him that Claudine, a criminal in another time and place, began to gloat.

Above all, it hurt him to know this happened because he and Warren had come here, because they did not have the power to defy the men who made the rules, who set the standards, and indeed who shaped the universe according to their wants and needs. Martha, a young and innocent bride, had a lout of a lord back in England ready to claim her hand, and all of it for status and riches.

But Gregory had to get out of here with what he came with and what he came for, and the price for his interests was Clementia. Though he did not want that price to be paid, he knew it must. "My Lady Clementia, I am afraid you are trespassing."

Claudine looked at him, gave a demented smile, and then turned her attention to the men all around her. She brandished the writ anew. "You are on my land, and if you are on my land, then you are loyal to me! Come over to me, and do it now, and let us be rid of this whore, Clementia, lest she start more trouble."

Clementia turned her horse and slapped the reins in a bid to escape, but before the steed could get going, one of her men drug her down from the saddle and pinned her to the ground. At Claudine's command he stood her up.

Claudine leaned in and kissed her on both cheeks. "Sister, that is my last act of kindness."

She drove the knife handle-deep into Clementia's neck.

A lifetime of hatred spit and spewed from the wound, and Clementia, the father's favorite who had been cheated by the world, fell pale and limp. Claudine climbed up on the bay palfrey, trotted it around in a wide circle, and then wheeled it to a halt.

"Kneel down, you rotten dogs, and submit to your new master!" she said, and to a man, they did.

Looking across the lowered shoulders of her new host, she locked eyes with Gregory.

He took a bold step forward. "You are not my master. I have given you your reward, now it is time to give me mine. Martha of Agen, Lord Warren, and both of my horses."

Her sneering lips curled in warning. "And if I say no?"

"Oh, but you shouldn't."

"And why is that?"

"Because, there is no second writ in Bordeaux. And besides, you never would have been able to serve the first one."

The two of them adjudged one another, and in those tense moments of scrutiny, Gregory still wasn't sure he had bested her. But finally, she nodded assent, saying, "You are a clever man."

She snapped her fingers and pointed toward the stable against the town wall. One of her original followers—a man Gregory recognized from the tower—ran off and soon returned leading Black Saddle and Lady Tatenhill by tethers. Gregory and Warren mounted their horses, with Martha of Agen snugging up in the saddle with Warren.

"Treasure your lordship, Lady Claudine—and don't forget to bury your beloved sister in consecrated ground," Gregory said.

They rode out through the shattered gate, through the debris and across the charred vineyard, past the broken wagon, the dead dog and the hanging tree, and up the hill to where it was green again. Gregory reached up and pulled out not one, but two crossbow bolts lodged in the rolled mail coif around his neck. He and Warren exchanged knowing glances as he tossed them to the ground.

"As I told you at Hossegor, you are a fighting man," Warren said.

"And now, I believe you."

Gregory knew he would never forget Larressingle and its feuding sisters, Claudine and Clementia, but he wished he could. They headed northeast, to Agen, the siege fires glowing in the distance.

Another day and another letter brought another mystery to be revealed. Wrapped around an arrow and shot over the wall, the projectile landed on the roof of the stables and was fetched by the groom. Taking it in hand, the priest shook his head and frowned. Nothing good would come of this, he knew, but here it was, beckoning him with the promise of ridicule and scorn.

"Lord Alphonse, another letter," he called, and as he headed up the turning steps to the hall, a gaggle of householders filed in behind him.

He found Alphonse in a familiar place, sitting in his old throne, crouched over the corner of the table playing chess with one of his men.

Alphonse looked up from the board, his intelligence set in his face, and opened up with a sardonic smile that charged the room with energy. "Read to me the words from this piss-pot of a man."

The priest, ever mindful of theatrics, bent into a deep bow, opened the note with a ceremonial flourish, and as the householders gathered around, began a formal recitation.

I have recently come from Larressingle, where two sisters, Claudine and Clementia, feuded over their father's fiefdom. It was a foul affair, full of venom and lies, tarnished love and polished hate. I stepped into the middle of the feud and took a side. When I left, one sister held the deed, while the other lay dead and bleeding on the ground. A sordid moment stinking with greed, but such is the case in the absence of scruples. All of it made me think of you and me. If siblings, and you were the heir, Lord Alphonse, I would do everything in my power to usurp your lands and titles. If in reverse and I were the designee, I would do my utmost to deny your ambitions, to bequeath to you nothing. Either way you would not be worthy of an inheritance. You are a mistake from conception, an abomination from the womb, a wretch through pubescence, and a reprobate of a man. The thought of us being kin made me sick, but I became well when I remembered it was only a thought, that it could never be, you and I as brothers.

The priest did not want to look up from this letter because he knew the backstory. Indeed, Alphonse had a younger brother, Andreas, his closest friend and fellow in arms. Captured by the English just a year ago and hung from a tree in the village below. Alphonse had watched from the battlements, remaining stern and defiant, but nonetheless wiping a tear from his eye. No doubt thinking of him now, recalling the rotting corpse that dangled for days until Alphonse snuck into the village and cut it down.

"He cleaves deep, my lord," the priest said. "Perhaps he mocks you by chance, or maybe he knows more about you than you think."

Alphonse leaned back in his throne and gazed into the raftered reaches of the hall. Lost in thought, the past caving in on him, he watched a blackbird flitter from its nest and bank through an open window. The priest nearly laughed—the sour laugh that always courted trouble, but he remained silent, appreciating that, at last, Gregory had gotten to Alphonse. The stranger with the pestilent quill had plunged it into the outlaw's heart, stabbing down into the echoing chasm of regret. A promising life gone astray, talents wasted on conceit, Alphonse was revealed a victim by his own hand.

He did not mope for long. Sitting up straight, he gnashed his teeth, and asked the priest to give him the letter. He looked at what he could not read, and glared at the priest. "My brother, Andreas, do you really think he knows of him?"

"He must, my lord," the priest said, knowing it would only stoke Alphonse's ire.

"And do you remember the promise I made on the very day my brother was murdered?"

"Yes, my lord, that he who mentions him would die a terrible death."

"He has been to Larressingle." His voice was ripe and vengeful.

"And before that, Saugnac, and before *that,* Bayonne."

"Which means he comes closer."

"Yes, Lord Alphonse. Perhaps you will make good on your promise."

THE
PEASANT PAUL
OF BAJAMONT

Agen—the city appeared on the horizon as a jewel, a suspended moment from a delightful dream, a hidden treasure sprouting up from the ground, so Gregory could find it. Clustered on the right bank of the River Garonne, a high shelf of stone rising on the left, Agen—a beautiful little burr that had worked its way into the flowing garment of Gascony.

His neck sore from looking over his shoulder, his stomach empty, his mind wounded by what he had seen and done at Larressingle, Gregory needed Agen and any succor it could offer.

"I crave spiced duck seared in garlic and olive oil, and a wine sauce thick with bone marrow," he said. "What do you think?"

"I have never heard a finer idea," Warren replied, and with a slight jostle of the reins, Lady Tatenhill trotted ahead.

Gregory remained behind, and for a moment he allowed himself the pleasure of watching the gallant lord and lady. Martha of Agen rode tucked in the saddle with Warren, her back resting against his chest and her head on his shoulder, his arms enveloping her as he clutched the reins. Were it not for the circumstances, it would have been unseemly. To those who did not know the backstory, that she had been rescued from captivity, it was. But Gregory chose not to spoil this little romantic moment, so he rode from behind, silent and smiling, as Warren and Martha, quite comfortable on top of Lady Tatenhill, ambled into the town.

They had been on the road for four days out of Larressingle, and in that time, Martha, betrothed to an influential noble back in England, had grown close to Warren. Almost apoplectic in the immediate aftermath of their escape from the siege, chicken broth and cabbage pottage had revived her. By the next morning, after bathing in a creek and putting flowers in her hair, the sixteen-year-old princess bubbled with energy, showering Warren with seductive laughs and coquettish looks, and doing her best to charm him. By the looks of it she had succeeded, as Warren bantered with her in his broken French, and a soft expression graced his otherwise rugged face. Gregory understood. Both of them enjoyed simply being alive, and the road from Larressingle a beautiful stretch lined with vineyards and orchards, church steeples, and watermills. Let them have this golden time, even though in England, years from now, it might perhaps cause problems.

They arrived at Martha's house, one in a short row of gabled, half-timbered houses with three stories, a chimney, and an arcaded storefront of stone. Gregory judged it a splendid house, a burgess' house, a house of love and money. Warren helped her down from Lady Tatenhill, and as her feet touched the ground, out from the arcade ran her parents, younger siblings, and a gaggle of household servants. They hugged and kissed her, shouting and laughing. Overcome with the weight of the moment, Martha fell to her knees and cried, and as her mother fell to the ground with her, the father collected himself.

He spoke to Warren. "And who has brought my daughter home?"

Before he could reply, Martha rushed to Warren's side. "This, papa, is Warren of Lichfield—and I no longer want to marry Hugh Walsingham!"

The cream of elation suddenly curdled, and after he and Warren exchanged a glance of alarm, Gregory doffed his hat, assumed a look of placation, and addressed the father.

"She is young yet," Gregory said, "and knows not what she says. She has been through a lot, so please, forgive her this moment of indiscretion."

"Do not speak for me," Martha said.

Her father tried to put a hand on her shoulder, to corral her, but she shrugged him off. "If Hugh Walsingham really wanted my hand, it would have been *he*, not Warren, who rescued me from Larressingle."

"Dear girl," Gregory said, "Lord Walsingham is in England, and it was Warren's sworn duty, and mine, might I add, to pull you from Claudine's evil clutches. Do not confuse work with affection."

Martha turned to Warren, giving him a look of such distress and vulnerability that, to Gregory's dismay, he melted. She fell into his arms and he pulled her in hard and tight, cupping his hand behind her head, and locking his arm around her waist.

"This will not happen." The father stomped his foot, a vein bulging in his neck. "She is to marry Lord Walsingham during the feast of St. Peter! I appreciate what you have done, but now that you have done it, the rest of it must go as planned!"

Gregory felt for the father, and if he were in his place, he would probably do the same thing. The father had not asked for any of this. All he wanted was to marry his daughter into a powerful family, be done with it, and reap the rewards. But now this, his carefully laid plan, not to mention his luck, crumbling in front of him. Here in Gascony, the current situation did not amount to much, but back in England, if word spread, and Gregory knew it would, Warren would be in the unenviable spot of having insulted a lord of much higher station than his own. The price to pay for such an affront was bankruptcy, perhaps even death—or both in due time. In that scenario, Gregory saw his own outlook wane. Though beautiful, the song in her voice enchanting, and though it pleased him that she saw so much in Warren, she was not worth the trouble.

"Warren." He narrowed his eyes. "We are leaving Agen—now!"

Warren and Martha looked at him with wounded eyes, and in the tender agony they shared, Gregory saw that they might already love one another. It hurt him to be cruel, but he could not think about that now. He had to think about his home, and Warren's, and the benefits accruing to them if they returned in full compliance with the orders to which they had been assigned. Indeed, Martha appeared a red rose in the summer sun, but flowers also grew in England.

Gregory did not say another word. He expected Warren to do as he was told. And while it took him a while to summon the gumption to push her away, he did. He stiffened his shoulders, squared his jaw, and in his unflinching way, climbed back on his horse, and in a blink, was once again the fearless warlord looking out into the distance, searching for enemies. He worked Lady Tatenhill into a wide half circle and rode her back in the direction they had come. Martha, dumbstruck, wiped a tear from her eye as she watched him leave.

Gregory donned his hat, pushing it down deep over his brow. "Martha, you will like England."

He slapped the reins, and Black Saddle trotted out of town.

They rode in silence, and from Warren's manner, Gregory knew he was angry. Gregory didn't necessarily blame him. He had been rude, and he guessed he had not only embarrassed Warren, but had offended his status as a lord. Gregory was sure that he felt as if the decision to stay or leave should have been his, and if he were to whisk Martha away and claim her as his own, even if a mistake, that it still should have been his mistake to make. By intervening, Gregory asserted himself as Master Gregory, despite the fact Warren held three estates in Staffordshire and owed direct allegiance to the Earl of Southampton. A lot had changed since they had first met all those years ago, but one thing had remained the same—between the two of them, Gregory still held rank. Let him stew over this nagging little fact and at some point, he will see the wisdom of leaving Martha behind.

They rode into a village of which they did not know the name. Gregory still wanted spiced duck seared in garlic and olive oil, and a wine sauce thick with bone marrow, but in this village he was sure the offering, at best, would be a vegetable stew. He resigned himself to disappointment, pulled his horse to a stop, and scanned the surroundings. They consisted of a main road and a cluster of low slung houses, small gardens, wheat fields, and peasants finishing a long day of labor. Nothing out of the ordinary, but these days, trouble seemed to lurk everywhere. He dismounted, dusted himself off, and glanced up at Warren, who remained seated on his horse. From the look in his eye, Gregory knew the danger, or at least the conflict, wasn't somewhere out there, but right in front of him.

"Did it please you by making me look like a fool?" Warren asked.

"Trust me, you would have been more of a fool had you brought her back to England as your bride," he said. "But the answer to your question is no, I did not take pleasure in doing what I did."

"Do you ever get tired of being right?"

"Warren, Lord Walsingham can have you disinherited and jailed—or worse," he said. "Your hope is that Martha's father keeps his mouth shut, and that Martha forgets she ever met you."

"Do you think I am so low I can't manage my own life, that everything and everyone is bigger than I?"

"I think nothing of the sort, but I do think you are young enough in your career that you cannot afford to make a terrible blunder. Warren, Martha is betrothed to another man."

"An old man. They are not to be wed until the feast of St. Peter," he said. "We might be back by then. What if I go to the wedding?"

"If you stand in the back and say not a word, then no one can fault you."

"But what if I make a scene?"

"Then I will disown you—and so will Southampton—and the others will feed you to the wolves."

Rather than wearing him down, he saw that his answers had only heightened Warren's ire. Gregory had seen Warren give himself over to fury. Had seen him fight and had seen him kill—but he had never been the target of Warren's ferocity. Now that he was, he had a whole new understanding of why people feared him, and why he held three estates in Staffordshire. A lord, his status became his most valuable possession, even if it rested on the lowest tier of the hierarchy.

Looking at his reddened face and into his blazing blue eyes, Gregory felt a tremor of fear. And what terrified him most was that he did not know what would happen next.

"You would disown me?" Warren asked. "I can remember when you said you would always consider me among the best of your friends and family. I guess your status is now more important than your loyalty."

Gregory gave an acid laugh of disbelief. "I was loyal to you back in Agen when I kept you from stumbling on the root of young love."

"No, in Agen you asserted your dominion over me."

"Yes, I did! For all your achievements, you are not yet grown! I have the means to buy my way into the nobility right now if I so choose. And in so doing, my title would be higher than yours. You are a country squire who has yet to be invited to Westminster!"

"I knew I'd get you to say it," Warren said. "You have always been better than me and you always will."

"And if you took Martha's hand in matrimony, then suddenly we would be equals? What a foolish notion."

"That was never my thought, but if you say it, then it must be true."

As Gregory was about to reply, a commotion caught his attention. Black Saddle had wandered deep into the village, clattering this way and that, tossing his head in a show of violent agitation. A child wanted to approach him, but his father wouldn't allow it. When the child protested, the father struck him to the ground with a backhand. The child got back up, and when he did, the father yanked him by the hair. Gregory held his breath as the horse lowered his head and charged at the man. He grabbed his son and rolled out of the way, but Black Saddle turned and pressed the attack. The man huddled over his child, shielding the boy from danger, but he himself left exposed.

"No, Black Saddle!" Gregory ran toward the commotion.

But he knew that he was too late. Black Saddle reared, and when he came down, he planted a front hoof square across the man's head. A hideous crack, a shriek of pain, and then the man went limp. The boy, hysterical and crying, crawled out from beneath his father's corpse and fled. The courser didn't chase him. Rather, he kicked and trampled the dead peasant, quickly turning him to mush. By the time Gregory arrived and grabbed his tether, Black Saddle was again, as he usually was, placid and regal.

Gregory looked into the eyes he knew so well. "God, what have you done?"

He looked over his shoulder at Warren, silent and astonished. The argument over, only to be replaced by a new, much bigger problem—Black Saddle had killed an innocent man. As Gregory took stock of the new situation, a sense of dread bubbled up into every crevice of his person, a hot, virulent dread making him weak at the knees and sick to the stomach. He was overwhelmed by an enduring dread that, he knew, would linger in him for the rest of his days. He could mount and ride away, knowing he would never see this village again.

But gazing down at the mangled peasant at his feet, he knew he would be cheating. He knew God watched and waited to see what he would do, and that no matter how fast or far he rode, he could never out-distance his judgement. So, he waited as the villagers gathered and walked his way.

Armed with weapons and tools, their expressions eager and grim, the members of this mob rallied behind a cocksure teen, a sunbaked ploughman, and no doubt, the hard-bargainer in this corner of the world. A spear slung over his shoulder, a thick knife at his belt, his hands and bare feet stained with soil, this stout fellow burned with the yearning of his people. They wanted blood, Gregory knew, and they would have it this day. As Gregory and this peasant surveyed one another, several men levelled their crossbows, loaded with the sinister barbed-tip missiles.

"Your horse has made a mess," the peasant said, and spit.

"Indeed, he has," Gregory said. "My deepest apologies."

"Your regrets are not enough," he said. "Here in Bajamont, it is eye for an eye and tooth for a tooth. You have taken Bertran from us. What do you give in return?"

"Name your price," Gregory said. "I will pay the fee."

"It is you or the horse. You do not have long to decide, so which shall it be?" He positioned his spear, clutching it with both hands at the ready.

Gregory knew a bluff when he saw one, but nothing of the sort showed in this man. Honest down to his roots, Gregory knew the end of an era was at hand. Dear Black Saddle, the galloping hero of so many of Gregory's tales, at last had arrived at the finale. All he had ever done was run, and the day he had done different was the day he would die. But he had ended the argument between Gregory and Warren, and if that had been his last deed, then he had been loyal to the end.

"Take the horse, and live with regret in this world and the next." He let go of the tether and turned away. He looked into Warren's eyes as he heard the spear plunge, as the anguish of doom shattered the heavens, and as the earth shook when mighty Black Saddle fell.

"We are even now," the peasant said. "Collect what is yours and be gone, for if you stay long, then you and your friend will join this horse on his journey to hell."

Gregory turned, and though he did not want to bear the torment, he knew he must. He looked down upon his old friend, still breathing as eight years of life leaked out of him. Gregory knelt at his side, scratched his muzzle, and Black Saddle responded with the flick of an ear and a whisk of his tail. In an uncontrollable convulsion of grief, Gregory put his face in his hands and wept. In this dark moment of despair, when at first he had been blind, he somehow saw a burst of light, a warm beacon of eternal elation, a source of unrelenting joy.

He thought of the chronicle, that august era in his life when he had risen from obscurity to the highest echelon of his class. True, his wits and Warren's sword had much to do with it, and no doubt Moonbeam had played her part. But the fourth piece of the puzzle had been Black Saddle, his sweeping sprints and grinding runs, his fearsome entry into cities and towns, and the endless courage with which he served his master. He remembered the time he first saw the horse at Durham, young and not yet blooded, but already with an unquenchable thirst for victory. Gregory had no idea how Moonbeam was going to beat him in that fateful race, and to this day, did not truly know how she had. Perhaps it was love, for at the core of her soul, love had been Moonbeam's greatest gift, and one she furnished in full. But in little time, Black Saddle matched her propensity to give, and as the chronicle crept into the final stage, when the weapons came out and people started to die, Black Saddle made it known that his refusal to lose was complete. To try him was to fail. To finish second or third was easy, but to finish ahead of him, in first, was impossible.

Of all his moments, Gregory knew, the ride from Huntingdon to Stourbridge had been Black Saddle's finest. His supposed equals had raced in close pursuit, with thousands awaiting his arrival, and in between, a rutted road that had yet to feel the fury of his hooves. Stupendous that day, he had run, trees bending as he passed, clouds swirling up above, and a million birds flocking in his dusty wake. His effort did not emanate from his physique. It came from the mists of time, way down deep in the murky pit of his lineage. Working for all the horses that had come before him, those who had made him, and to say to all of them, *I am the fastest you have produced, and over the hill in another life, when I should meet you at last, we will race, and I will win. I will trample all your battles and wars, all your happiness and sorrow, your sunny springs and bleak winters, and I will tell you that if you have ever birthed a king, then it is I.*

And it was this horse that breathed its last breath, closing its eyes, never to open them again.

Gregory, drained by the gush of his remembrances, rose to his feet. Soon thereafter, Warren arrived at his side. He dismounted, and as he had done many times before, and took to the dirty work. He went to unhitching Black Saddle's magnificent tack, the network of straps and buckles and loops and hooks holding the riding apparatus in place. Bit, bridle, and reins, talismans and trinkets collected over time, the saddle and Persian rug padding, the spiked face mask, the red ankle boots, and the bags of gear. A big pile of leather and brass works, all of it crafted by the hands of masters. Even though it looked like looting, Black Saddle's kit was much too valuable to abandon. So, when Gregory looked at his horse for the last time, only to see him laying bare against the ground, he did not wince with guilt, nor did he ask why. Much riding and fighting still needed to be done, and soon, so it would be a waste to try and replace the priceless accoutrements. Warren hefted this burden over his back and across his shoulder, and before walking on down the road, looked to Gregory with a dutiful shine in his eye. "Take Lady Tatenhill. She is yours now."

Still standing within striking distance of the peasant's spear, Gregory dared not dally. He walked to the horse, whispered her name, ran a hand across her shoulder, and waited for her response. Lady Tatenhill gave a gentle neigh. He grabbed the pommel, pulled himself up into the saddle, and claimed his new steed. He had doubted her before, and for good reason, at Saugnac, when she had nearly cost Warren his life. Since then Gregory had not seen enough to convince him that she was a worthy successor. But with his feet planted in the stirrups, and with the reins tight in his hand, he knew she would do. She stood a bit taller than Black Saddle, and a bit longer, too. Still, not much more than a strap of a horse, broken but not broken in, smart but not wise. Gregory took heart in knowing her best days were ahead of her. The only offspring of Moonbeam and Black Saddle, after all, so she had plenty to prove and the bloodlines to try and outdo them. Gregory gave her a go, and Lady Tatenhill skipped into an effortless trot, turning in a wide, graceful circle as the mob of villagers looked on in awe at the strutting silvery dame. She came to a stop right in front of the onlookers, scratching her hoof and snorting, as if to say, I have seen you murder my father, but I yet live.

From beneath the brim of his beaver and peacock hat, Gregory peered out at the boy who this day had evened the score. Brown headed and brown eyed, his face a rusty spade, Gregory guessed his age at seventeen. He was a ploughman through and through, born, bred, and to die in these fields. This moment, this killing, would become the achievement of his lifetime.

"Please, tell me your name," Gregory said, "so that I might blacken it."

He planted the butt end of his spear in the ground, bowed out his chest and set his chin. "You may call me Peasant Paul of Bajamont, and I care not what you say."

THE
RUBY RUN
FROM GOURSAC

regory did not ride for long. Once he and Warren travelled a safe distance from Bajamont, he dismounted. They loaded the gear on Lady Tatenhill and continued the journey northward on foot. It seemed strange, walking, when he had done very little of it during these hard months of exile. But, at least for now, it seemed right, a certain form of penance for any conceits that may have otherwise tainted him. Losing Black Saddle would torment him for many years, he knew, but so humbled and sharing the road with Warren, plodding along in this world of meager returns, he somehow felt renewed.

He kicked at a stone. "Tell me, Warren, what did you take from this?"

"Only you loved Black Saddle more than I," Warren said. "He gave his life so that our friendship would endure. When we argued—it was vanity, while Black Saddle was nothing but selfless. He was a champion, and even a legend, but above all a servant."

Gregory bent down and picked up the stone he had kicked, and threw it skipping down the road. "My sentiments, too. So where are we now?"

"I am Warren of Lichfield and you are Master Gregory, and each of us craves a succulent side of duck."

Both of them laughed, clapped each other over the shoulder, and thus did they walk, side by side, Lady Tatenhill following on her tether, through the remainder of the scorching day.

They found a bend in the creek alongside the road and made camp for the night. A fire, fresh fish, and an onion stew served as their repast. They shared the last skin of wine, small talk and banter, everything but a serious discussion about what they had just witnessed at Bajamont. But as was their way, they could not keep their minds off the journey, the tasks, and the perils surely ahead. The conversation settled on the arrest warrant and Alphonse of Bayonne, the final trial, the last deed before the return home. Gregory sighed with fatigue just thinking about it, but in the gold and purple light of a creeping sunset, as the creek babbled and as the finches chirped, he figured he had the nerve to do what needed to be done.

"I know you have sent him many letters, but my guess is, Alphonse does not really know who you are, and will not be prepared for your talents," Warren said.

"That is my hope," he replied. "And that he won't be ready for you, either."

"Are you scared?"

From the bottom of the fire Gregory grabbed a stick, its tip charred. He tossed it on top and watched as it was consumed by the flames. "I am terrified. But I have been that way many times before and it has never stopped me."

Warren stoked the fire. He took a quaff of wine. "In the last few years I have been in plenty of battles. I have seen men lose and I have seen them win. But there is no one like you, Master Gregory. You are a merchant, no doubt, but when you are up on your horse, and when the danger is thick and heavy, you are your own man."

"I think it has a lot to do with the fact that I don't want to die," he said. "Not then, and not just yet."

"We all have our time, Master Gregory, but yours will not come soon."

"You do not know that."

"No, I don't, but I believe you will always fight for tomorrow."

A weary, wistful smile crossed Gregory's face. "And I have always trusted your instincts."

regory bolted up from his sleep, a soothing dream replaced by chaos and confusion. At first, enveloped in darkness, his eyes adjusted to the night. What he saw made him hot with alarm. Three men were wrestling Warren to the ground, the lot of them rolling through the glowing bed of coals, sparks spraying into the air and across the ground. A wrenching struggle in which Warren's great strength proved telling, but not enough. They pinned him on his back, holding him in place with their hands and their knees, pressing him without mercy, stretching him until his joints nearly popped. He clutched the hilt of *La Bonne Vie* and made ready to stand and attack, but as soon as he did, an arm cinched around his neck. Pushed face down in the dirt, gasping for air as he tried not to choke. Whoever it was behind him yanked him to his feet and locked his arm behind his back. He tried to squirm free, but the vice had already been tightened. Thus disabled, Gregory realized what had happened. They had been captured.

As Gregory spit dirt out of his mouth, and Warren, heaving with exertion and anger, remained subdued, more men appeared on the other side of the creek. They crossed and came up from the gulley, and when they entered the faint sphere of firelight, Gregory, to his chagrin, recognized them. The Page he had duped out of *De Mirabilibus Mundi*, and his lord, Bernard de Fumel.

Fumel thrust his face to within a nose of Gregory's. "Where is my book, you maggot?"

Along with his disappointment, Gregory swallowed a few grains of dust. He steeled himself, staring Fumel in the face. "You will never get your book back. It is already in England and in the possession of the Earl of Southampton. If it was so important to you, perhaps you should have kept it under the protection of a better man."

Gregory knew he would pay, and he did. Fumel stepped back and the Page stepped forward. First, he punched Gregory in the stomach, and then he walloped him across the chin with an overhand right. Gregory's captor let him drop to the ground, and the Page, his boots shod with iron, proceeded to kick and stomp him until bleeding and silly with pain. Crumpled and moaning, stripped of all dignity, Gregory looked up at the man of whom he had made a fool. As Fumel looked on, the Page stood over Gregory, debating, Gregory knew, whether or not to kill him right then and there. Beaten as he was, Gregory needed to act or he, as well as Warren, might not see the light of dawn.

He held his stomach and coughed. *"Nous sommes fonctionnaires royaux."*

The Page glared down at him, assured of his advantage. "If you are a royal official, then surely you have a possession valuable enough to compensate me for the embarrassment you caused."

With the back of his hand, Gregory wiped a drip of blood from his nose. Now was the moment, he told himself, to make a fool of the Page for a second time. "Take the horse. And consider it my apology."

The Page turned and looked longingly on Lady Tatenhill, a spoil of which he never could have dreamt. He walked over to her and reached out for her tether. A smug pout on his face, he looked back at Gregory. As he gloated, Lady Tatenhill lurched forward and kicked the Page plumb in the knee. He fell to the ground with a sickening pop and groan, clutching at the wound, writhing in pain. Fumel's men roared with laughter, and some of them even jeered the Page as he lay fetal and whimpering.

Though he struggled, Gregory rose to his feet, dusted himself off, and closed the door on this unexpected test of wills. "I know someone who can heal that for you, but she is far from here."

He felt sorry for the man. The hoof had opened up a ghastly slash of meat and bone, and left untreated, or treated improperly, he would waste away and die. But such were the dangers of the road, and, Gregory knew, the fate of a man who should not have crossed him. Get good with God, and do it soon, for you are about to meet him. Gregory turned his attention to the real challenge,

Fumel, and with a sharp look, gained the lord's audience. His men closed in around Gregory, but he stayed them with the raising of his index finger.

"I am a royal official," he said, staring at Fumel. "Rather than take me as a captive, it would perhaps be best to take me as a partner."

Fumel—the saffron sheen of the east baked into his stubbly face, his green eyes, drops of polished heliodor—took his turn matching wits with Gregory. A man of the rivers and the steppes, of the mountains and the vast ranges of Great Turkey and its cities of gold, Gregory knew Fumel had seen and done much more than himself. No hoax would be played on this man, no easy escape, and no feat of daring that would go unmatched. Looking into his face, he saw someone who still controlled the outcome, even if his Page lay broken on the ground. An unnerving calm surrounded him, the confidence that had brought him back to Christendom, laden with treasure, but landless and without title. Now he had all of it, Bonaguil and its rights over labor and trade, to do as he pleased, a lord in Gascony with but few from which to seek permission. Gregory never thought the day would come when Fumel would get the jump on him. But now that it had arrived, he sensed something that gave him hope. Somewhere inside the shell of leather and armor, beneath the lavish trappings and the glamor of the east, beat the heart of a reasonable man.

"A royal official?" Fumel said. "What did you have in mind?"

"For starters you can let go of my man," he said. "By the king's law, he outranks everyone here, even you, so in pursuit of your own ends, let him go."

Fumel gave his men a cautious cue. Warren gained his feet, straightened himself, and fell in next to Gregory. There they stood, face-to-face with Fumel and his dozen.

"You are still my captive," Fumel said. "We will only be partners if I like what you say. And since you don't have my book, your words had best be tall."

"Indeed, they are," he said. "But take us to your castle so we may negotiate, properly."

"Don't do it, my lord," the Page said, still sprawled on the ground, groaning and grabbing at his knee. "He yet has another trick to play."

Fumel turned this over in his mind, probing Gregory as he did, searching for a scheme. Rather than allow the Page's words to go unchecked, and to allow Fumel to come to an unsuitable conclusion, Gregory played his gambit.

"Take my horse, take our bags and weapons, and be off and on your way," he said. "But know that if you do, you would have left a much bigger treasure on the table."

"Why not negotiate here and now?" Fumel asked.

Food and wine, thought Gregory, and a fire and beds for him and Warren. Rest and oats for Lady Tatenhill, a stable and grooms to brush her coat. Let us go far, far away from Bajamont, where Black Saddle met his end. And offer the deal, a deal with irresistible terms, a deal so sweet, Fumel will forget all about his precious book and ride headlong into an uncertain future, where he will help claim the prize—Alphonse of Bayonne. But Gregory was careful not to reveal the stakes, and instead, gave a slight shrug of his shoulders, and said, "I should like to sit at a table in your hall when I make my offer."

"Deception will cost you your life," Fumel said.

"Oh, there will be none of that."

Fumel narrowed his eyes. He and Gregory shared a cunning smile.

"Mount up men, we are taking the prisoners to Bonaguil," Fumel said.

Two days later they arrived at castle Bonaguil, a polygonal pile of honeyed stone on a high, wooded crag. The chapel bells rang, a horn sounded from atop the tower, householders flooded the courtyard, and to Gregory's delight, the scent of roasting pork wafted through the air. They feasted on that pig, the scraps tossed to the dogs, and gulped from a hogshead of stout country red. A minstrel strummed on his lute, in a high voice singing of love lost and found. Candles flickered, the fire crackled, a hooded hawk perched on its podium. The men laughed and jested, repeating the stories and jibes they always told. A gaggle of prostitutes in the corner, murmured amongst themselves and occasionally batted a furtive eye. This was a lord's hall, full of the reckless cheer that accompanies the lord's return. Fumel, seated in his carved chair, draped in a lavish red robe, and with a bejeweled goblet in his hand, presided over the scene with a reserved content, joining the joviality, but maintaining his decorum.

Gregory and Warren sat at opposite ends of the table, making sure no man could mistakenly accuse them of collusion. Warren, meanwhile, made the most of this moment, boasting of this feat and that, blurting out jokes none of the men in this hall had heard before, and bellowing through one of the old English war songs he'd learned along the way. The big blue eyes, the gap-toothed grin, the shiny blond hair folded into a braid hanging at his shoulders, he reeled them in, winning them over, showing the crusty men at this table the strangers were cut from the right piece of wool. Thus, did Warren make his mark, clearing the way for Gregory to offer his barter.

He rose from the table. Reading his intent, Fumel motioned for silence. To formalize the proceedings, Gregory doffed his hat and bowed. A servant boy brought him his pack while another cleared a spot on the table. He pulled out the cylindrical case of boiled leather, the gold ring he had taken from the dwarf at Larressingle, and the royal arrest warrant. He laid them out on the table, and for a long moment said nothing, instead allowing the objects to speak for themselves. And indeed, Fumel and all his men gazed upon the display with aggressive curiosity. Once he was satisfied the spell had been cast, Gregory began. He opened the cylindrical case and pulled out the rolled parchments on which was inscribed *De Mirabilibus Mundi.*

Fumel clutched at the armrests and leaned out from his chair, a crease of expectancy opening in his brow. "Is that what I think it is?"

"Yes, and it is mine," Gregory said, a note of guilt in his voice. "But if I do not do as I say, then it will be yours."

He picked up the ring, holding it with his thumb and index finger. He positioned it so the light from a candle flickered in the bouquet of gemstones and glimmered down the curve of hatched gold. In the ancient past perhaps it was worn by a duke or a king, a splendid ornament Gregory valued at one hundred livres. "I will trade you this for a horse, and not just any horse, but one of your best. Do you have one worthy of this ring?"

"If this is what you give, then I will find one."

Gregory set the ring back down on the table and picked up the arrest warrant. The royal seal bespoke of unassailable authority, of terrible power, and with it in his hand, Gregory himself was a terrible man. He peered into Fumel's swirling fathoms, and in little time arrived at the bottom, finding there the fear and respect this noble had for his king.

"This is for Alphonse of Bayonne," he said. "Do you know of him?"

"Indeed. An outlaw with a bounty on his head."

"If you help me serve this, the bounty will be yours," he said. "Does that interest you?"

Fumel looked around the table at his men, a grim smile showing in the corner of his mouth. "I am interested. Tell me the terms."

"By right, Alphonse's keep at Castlenaud is mine and Warren's to loot, but it is also an asset over which we have discretion. *En échange de votre aide*, we will give you license to take what you can from there. If you were to have a fortnight at your disposal, I'm sure you could dig enough holes, pry back enough boards, and loosen enough stones to discover the treasure he hides. Surely this is worth more than a manuscript—and surely it would be enough to mend any rift between us."

Fumel, surprised and pleased by the offer, queried further. "But what assurances do I have this is not a trap?"

"What, me in cahoots with Alphonse of Bayonne?" He held out the arrest warrant. "This does not convince you beyond doubt?"

"It does, but for my complete comfort, I need more assurances."

"Well, you will have a hostage." He gestured to Warren. "He is worth a sack of silver back in England, and if anything were to happen to him, my heart would surely be broken. That should be assurance enough. A lord to hold for ransom?"

"Your terms are acceptable, *but...*" Fumel looked down the table at Warren. "Does he agree to be a hostage?"

Warren stood. "I will gladly submit if we renege, but we will not. Otherwise, I have much work to do, so do not hinder me."

Fumel leaned back in his throne, took a sip of wine, and motioned for the minstrel to resume. His men returned to their boasts, and the prostitutes cupped their hands and giggled anew. Fumel tilted his cup in Gregory's direction, a gesture of conciliation. "I am glad I caught you."

"So am I."

The next morning, Gregory and Warren met at the stables and took a long look at Fumel's considerable collection of horses. Like any good lord, he had one for each occasion—hunting, travel, and war—and an assortment of spares. The groom told them which ones were off-limits. The personal mounts of Fumel and his top men. But even with the reduction, Gregory and Warren had many from which to choose. They thought about what lay ahead of them and how they wanted to go about executing it. Once they reached consensus, it did not take them long to select Warren's steed. In a stall at the far end of the stables stood a rust red warhorse with black points. Not a lean courser like Gregory and Warren rode, but a genuine charger, a hulking equine monster bred for one thing and one thing only—a lust and talent for close combat, an uncontrollable urge to break the line, topple the banner, and trample the king.

Warren turned to the groom. "What is his name?"

The groom stopped and cocked his brow. "Devil's Work."

"Then tell Lord Fumel we have our horse," Warren replied.

To the priest it seemed as if a dark cloud hung over Castlenaud. All around it the summer had burst upward in a fetching swath of green, the blue skies filled with birds, bees foraging in the blooms, and the peasants working the fields of grain and grape. A Gascon June emitted the sweet breath of God, the blessing of life for any and all, but not at

Castlenaud. The packed earth around the well displayed the detritus of neglect strewn in piles against the wall, the same people, the same sullen faces, the same lingering feeling of desperation. Gray and black and brown, the stone walls bore down, crushing the souls within. The season has changed, the priest thought, but in Castlenaud it has not.

The priest stood on the battlements for a long while, silent as he stared into the magenta sunset creeping across the sky. The peasants in the village had just started their crude songs of love and longing, the annual rite fueled by their cups and flagons of reek wine. The priest envied them—poor and prideful, ignorant and plain, born in the place where they would remain, with friends and family, a certain beginning and a certain end.

Enraptured by his thoughts, the priest, at first, did not notice the approaching rider. But there he was, one hand holding a torch, the other on the reins, racing up through the valley. As he ascended the switchback, the priest studied him. He had never seen this man before. A real fighting man in a pig-snouted helm, plate and mail, girded with a sword and riding a fantastic black courser. He clattered up the cobbled road to the old wooden box, pulled a message from beneath his chest plate, and dropped it inside. He whipped his horse around and looked up to the top of the wall. When their eyes met—the rider glaring out through the narrow eyehole of his helm—the priest convulsed with a hot swallow of panic.

Gregory of London?

"Tell me your name?" the priest called.

But the rider ignored him. Coaxing his horse with voice and spur, he galloped away, his red cape, lined with a strange spotted hide, whipping from his shoulders.

The draw bridge lowered. The priest shambled out to the box, grabbed the letter, and went running—back over the bridge, across the courtyard, up the cobbled lane, through the door, climbing the spiral stairwell to the great hall. Somehow this was different, he knew, his movement so urgent he tripped and fell, gasping as he did. Collecting himself, he lurched into the hall, where Alphonse and his man drank from a purloined hogshead of short wine.

"My lord," he said, his chest heaving, "I have another letter."

Lord Alphonse's face changed sharply, his lip curled with loathing. Looking around the table at his men, he said, "I am just drunk enough to listen to whatever it is this dung heap has to say. Read it now, read it loud and damn this Gregory for yet another interruption."

The priest caught his breath, grabbed a cup, and took a deep drink of wine.

Greetings, Lord Alphonse.

I am in Goursac, the village you looted during the Feast of St. Margaret. I am looking down the road from whence you came, knowing it would not take much for us to share our fates. You, the enemy of our dear king, and I, his enforcer.

Both of us know your blacklist is substantial, but those sins were committed long ago. What concerns me is what you have done since I have come to make your acquaintance. Do you remember the little girl you raped in Goursac? She took her own life out of shame. Where once there was love, now her parents bicker, confused by the torment you introduced. If for nothing else, for that you should hang. But in the wake of calamity, there is life. The bell tower you toppled is being repaired. The barn you burned down has been rebuilt. The livestock you took? Replenished by the good people of Saint Cybranet. One thing you forgot to destroy was the pear orchard. And what a beautiful orchard it is. The trees in perfect lines, the limbs now heavy with fruit. I and my men have eaten these pears, and they are delicious. You should come to Goursac and try one. I will pick it myself and hand it to you.

The priest looked at Alphonse.

"Goursac," they said together, sharing a grim moment of glee.

Alphonse bolted from his throne, thrust his fist in the air and said, "We ride at dawn!"

regory thought about the Page. Lady Tatenhill's kick to the leg had killed him—an abscess, a fever, delirium, and death. Gregory had kneeled at his sickbed and prayed, and along with Fumel and the priest, remained in the room when the Page took his last breath. Gregory had not wanted this outcome. Embarrassment and pain, he certainly intended, but not the end of his time.

Gregory thought of all the people who had died because of him—Gilbert le Blanc, Helias, Marcus of Burwell, Walter of Helmsley, Lord Corby, Lord le Gaunter, Margery Alesworth, and all the nameless, faceless people who had cycled through Kings Court back in London. He heard all their voices at once, calling out to him, begging him to join them on the other side. And thus was he haunted as he sat high in the saddle, peering into the distance at a cloud of dust, the dust of many riders, billowing from the northern approach to Goursac. He sighed and made the sign of the cross. He took tight hold of the reins. His hand quivered, tears moistened his eyes, and the voices came again, whispering his name, barely audible over the rising thunder of the oncoming cavalcade.

Washed, combed, and shoed, her ankle boots buffed and fitted, rested, watered, and fed, Lady Tatenhill flinched at the sight of them, a dark horde piercing through the horizon, a gang of steel demons come to settle the account. Rather than fight her nerves, Gregory rode her around in a wide circle, bringing her to a halt where she had begun, giving her a piece of ground to hold as her own. Warren had crushed Gregory's second ruby into countless pieces, and with masterful beads of hot lead, had soldered the dust and shards at intervals all along the bridle and the reins, and down the middle of the spiked face guard. A crown, Gregory thought, that Lady Tatenhill had yet to earn.

He leaned inward and rubbed the neck of the horse he had once wanted to sell. "Run as your father did, and fight like your mother, and you will have no trouble this day."

Gregory straightened. He donned an under bonnet, pulled up the mail coif, and then pushed his beaver and peacock hat down over the top. He reached into his pouch and pulled out a brooch. Red with three gold lions—the royal arms of King Edward. He pinned it to his black cloak, fastidious in his effort to make sure it was level. Once fastened, he looked to his left. The pear orchard, its limbs heavy with ripening fruit, stretched out across the flatland. To his right, the village of Goursac, all its gates and doors bolted shut. And dashing in on the road in front of him came Alphonse of Bayonne and his band of brigands. Wilted by a molten gust of fear, Gregory felt himself go faint, and in an instant of panic, thought he would fall from his horse. But he held onto the reins, regained himself, and with a stoic confidence that was little more than show, watched as Alphonse and his retinue encircled him.

Alphonse, flanked by a sullen priest, trotted his horse into the center and halted within a length of Gregory.

As the dust settled, the two men weighed one another. Gregory, his gear oiled and polished, his face tanned from the sun, and Alphonse, pale and gaunt, his kit a patchwork of soiled glory. Yet he had the numbers, and he had lived in the shell of his former self for years now, and so appeared comfortable, even happy, with the dreg he had become.

Gregory knew Alphonse came to win, not to surrender. So, as the two of them eyed each other, he from beneath the brim of his hat, and Alphonse from behind the raised visor of his dented war helm, they shared this precarious moment as equals. Compared to what Gregory had seen in his lifetime, Alphonse was not much to behold. Armed with an assortment of blades and draped in mail, but no plume, no cape, and no splendid ornaments. Just the rugged will of a man who refuses to comply, the truculence of a criminal who gladly defied his king. He wore his outlawry with great panache, too, flaunting his decay, parading his despoilment, embracing his sin so he flickered like a dim midnight star.

His blue stallion fidgeted. He tightened the reins with one hand and gestured outward with the other. "Where are your men?"

"Scaling the walls of your castle." Gregory saw it in his eyes, a blink of disbelief, a hairline fissure in his granite bravado. Before he recovered, Gregory pressed his advantage. "If you don't believe me, let us go there and I will show you."

Gregory waited, and as he had hoped, the tiny crack in Alphonse's composure opened into a cavernous breach, and there he sat, on his beautiful blue courser, sideswiped by the discovery he had been duped. In that moment of plummeting, that haphazard circling to the damp bottom, and as a curl of confusion showed in his brow, Gregory worked a spur and snapped the reins. With a kick and a snort, Lady Tatenhill erupted out of her stance and bounded toward a gap between two riders. They pulled their weapons, but before they could strike, Lady Tatenhill raced past them, breaking free, claiming the head start on the potholed road to Castlenaud.

She wanted to stretch out and give it her all, but Gregory eased her into an even gallop, where she did fine work. Gregory looked over his shoulder, Alphonse and his men in angry pursuit. Ten lengths behind and yearning to gain, they had just stormed down this road, so try as they might, they did not have the kick to close Lady Tatenhill's lead. And so, it went, through a village and over a hill, across a bridge and past a vineyard—the swift filly out in front, and her pursuers, one by one, falling off the pace.

Except for Alphonse and his blue stallion, who remained within six lengths, and to Gregory's alarm, showed no signs of relenting. Nor did Lady Tatenhill, and as the chase neared the homestretch, she found her youth over and again, indefatigable in the quest to make her name. Gregory's eyes grew wide at the sight of what was up ahead. A parched washout across the entire width of the road. He knew what Black Saddle would have done, jump it and keep on running. But terrible thoughts of Saugnac, when Lady Tatenhill had balked, seized Gregory's imagination, and in that bleak moment, when the smallest mistake meant catastrophe, he did not know what to do. Reaching the point of no return, he guided her to the left, tearing through the weeds and rough, divots arcing in her wake. She veered out around the obstacle, nearly stumbling as she did, before pulling back toward the road. Gregory glanced over at Alphonse to see what he would do. His blue stallion leapt over the gap with ease, landing in stride. When Lady Tatenhill retook the road, she led by just a length. It took a while, but indeed, the race had finally begun.

From behind him he heard Alphonse urging his horse, a series of desperate exhortations and the cracking of his whip. Gregory responded in kind, slapping the reins and working the spurs.

"Ride, Lady, ride!" He did not know if it was his urgent coaxing or her own primal ardor, but Lady Tatenhill sounded a dank belly snort, reached for infinity, and found a terrific stride. All the work she had done in her life, became preamble to this wrinkle in time, when she discovered the full satisfaction of speed. Yearning for her spot in the story, she tore down the road, fields blooming, finches calling, a petal falling from the rose. The morning collected in her bejeweled bridle, and if the moon and the stars, and even those in heaven, were to look down on Gascony at that instant, they would see a ruby ray of light shooting across the land.

Yet she could not shake the blue stallion snugged up on her right hindquarter, and even in her spell of magnificence, he had gained on her.

Alphonse reached out, grabbed Gregory's cloak, and tugged. On the verge of being pulled from his horse, Gregory yanked *La Bonne Vie* from its sheath, turned in the saddle, and took a wild swipe at his adversary.

Dodging away from the blade, Alphonse let go of the cloak.

Both riders regrouped, exchanging rotten scowls, and the duel played back to the horses, now barrel to barrel, nose for nose, sprinting to the horizon, where up on a cliff overlooking the river loomed the towering silhouette of Castlenaud.

They reached the assent, a cobbled route, a switchback, and the final leg to the gatehouse. Alphonse pulled his knife. The fight between him and Gregory began as a vicious struggle of slash, parry, and thrust, both of them soon nicked and bleeding. Cutting across from the outside, Lady Tatenhill lunged for the inner turn, all heart in muscling past her opponent.

As she swept through the curve, Alphonse rose in his stirrups, hoisted his blade, and swung down for the kill.

The knife sliced through Gregory's beaver and peacock hat—and glanced off the mail coif beneath. Half dazed by the force of the assault, and for a thought seeing double, Gregory drove his steed without mercy. As Lady

Tatenhill climbed the final approach to the gatehouse, courting collapse, she opened a lead of three lengths.

Gregory glanced up at the battlements. One of Fumel's men, standing taut, raised a crimson square of silk. The signal given, the drawbridge descended. Lady Tatenhill dashed across it. Charging past in the opposite direction went Warren and his war beast, Devil's Work.

Armed with a sawed-off lance and tucked in behind his shield, Warren met Alphonse just as he crossed over the drawbridge, which closed behind him. The blue stallion, so valiant in his efforts, so spectacular throughout the ruby run from Goursac, buckled at the sight of the hulking destrier stomping his way. He planted his hooves, slid to a stop, and in one final attempt at heroism, tried to weave away.

But before he could, Warren arrived to deliver the finish of his choosing. He leveled the shortened lance and put it square on Alphonse's chest, driving him up and out of his saddle, tossing him to the ground. Any other man would have remained down, but Alphonse, panting and grunting in agony, gained a knee. Warren made another pass, again landing the lance, again putting Alphonse on the ground. Again he found a knee, and using his sword as a prop, managed to stand. Wobbling, looking about in confusion, groping for elusive answers, the outlaw at last confronted his demise. He tilted his head skyward and howled. Once the baleful sound had escaped to the heavens, Fumel's men swarmed him with thick leather thongs and oak truncheons, beating him into submission. They stripped him of everything, save his undergarments and stood him up, limp and near bare.

"To you, I present Alphonse of Bayonne," Fumel said.

Gregory fetched the warrant from his satchel, holding it high for all to see, in his possession for nearly a year, the loadstone binding him to his duty. He had never wanted to possess it, had never wanted to serve it, this folded and sealed square of royal parchment. He held it in both hands and made ready to open it, but before he did, a sinking thought overcame him. What if this wasn't an arrest warrant, and all of it had been a ruse to lure him here, where his enemies knew he would fail? Alphonse allowed to go free—Fumel without the promised loot—the two of them suddenly in alliance. It was enough to give Gregory pause, but not enough to make him stop. He broke the seal, opened the document, and before reading it aloud, scanned it in silence. He glanced up from the warrant, waited for Alphonse to look him in the eye, and allowed himself a cruel smile of relief. Gregory cleared his throat and sat tall in the saddle.

"By order of the blessed Edward, King of England, Lord of Ireland, and Duke of Aquitaine, you, Alphonse of Bayonne, are hereby sentenced to be hanged at Bordeaux for the crime of treason. You are also to be drawn and quartered for aiding and abetting King Edward's enemies in a time of war. Your parts will be taken and displayed in all four corners of Gascony as a warning to others not to do as you have done. Forthwith, your chattel is forfeit, and your title is void. You will receive the last rites, and if it is your wish, you can repent for your many sins. But the verdict of guilt and the penalty so imposed cannot be appealed."

Gregory refolded the warrant but kept it clutched in his hand. He now knew what it was to be a royal official, and even at the dawn of this knowledge, he sensed the corrupting lure of power. Alphonse, once mighty, made small in defeat—out-smarted, outrun, out-fought. He stood speechless and sagging between two of Fumel's men.

Dear God, it has not been easy, but it is *done*.

A lonely wind curled through the bailey, and a raincloud shrouded the sun. A crow perched atop the gatehouse reminded Gregory he could not fly away. So, there he remained, victory in front him, yet grappling with the vestiges of despair. Warren rode in beside him. He removed his great helm, shook out his braid, and put a gauntleted hand on Gregory's shoulder. His presence filled Gregory's heart with peace, even if all around him stood the icons of conflict and war.

For a long pause, Warren said nothing, but when at last he did, he voiced the treasured words of a friend. "Lady Tatenhill—she suits you."

The dust-covered filly twitched her ears and neighed.

"Indeed," Gregory said. "She is a fine horse."

EPILOGUE

RISING JONQUIL OVER THE SEA

They sailed with the Christmas wine fleet, a fortnight of hell across the cold waters. Gregory didn't mind. His ship, the *Jonette*, sat deep with the bounty of La Réole and the Bordelaise, and of all the freighters sailing up the coast of France that season, his contained the most precious cargo—Lady Tatenhill, Devil's Work, and the blue stallion, too. Her holds were packed with garlic, olive oil, and rolls of silk from Lucca, sheaths of Spanish leather, feathers from the Levant, and a big pot of saffron.

He and Warren had stayed in Bordeaux with Jean du Mont, to rest and to fete, and to witness the execution of Alphonse of Bayonne. Hanged to within a breath of his life, and then drawn and quartered, his head was planted on a long iron spike and left on display near the *Palais de L'Ombrière*. In exchange for early passage back to England, Gregory agreed to travel with—and be the crier for—Alphonse's gruesome quarters, packed in salt and wrapped in leather, which royal officials took to all four corners of Gascony to leave on display.

Gregory and Warren circled back to La Réole, where Gregory knelt and prayed at Uncle Helias' grave, feasted with Uncle Hugo, and had his last ruby set in the silver necklace for his wife. The farewells said, the business done, they returned to Bordeaux, boarded the *Jonette* and headed for home. On the thirteenth day of the journey, the River Thames opened in front of them. On the strength of the tide, they raced into the bowels of England, arriving beneath the smoggy heights of its ancient capital, dear London. The ships anchored in the pool, and from there they approached the waterfront in a rowboat. Gregory stood at the prow, one foot propped on the gunwale. He removed his hat, took a deep breath of air, and in it he tasted the juicy innards of the squalid city. After a year without it, a delicacy, so he breathed in again and rejoiced. From the waterfront, a boy pointed at him, jumped up and down, and in a high voice of reverence, said, *"It is Gregory! Gregory has returned!"*

Soon a crowd gathered on the pier. There rose a peal from the mighty bells of St. Martin's. Gregory looked back at Warren.

His young friend smiled. "You go. This is your moment."

Gregory leapt to the pier, and once on solid footing, ran down it to the throng awaiting him. There were plenty of strangers but familiar faces, too. Alan Spicer, the four Williams—William Purchase, William Pepper, William Stokes, and William Hawkins—and many others, all of them happy and laughing. Corralled in hugs, showered with kisses, they hoisted him up on their shoulders and carried him up Royal Street, setting him down in front of his stone-and-timber hall. At the door stood Joan, as radiant as the sun rising jonquil over the sea. Next to her stood a wet nurse, baby Herleve cradled in one arm, and baby Gregory in the other.

"Dear husband." Joan bowed. "It pleases me that you are home."

"Dear wife, I have fought many battles to have this day."

A native Texan, Richard Massey lived in New England, the Midwest, and the Deep South before settling in Northwest Arkansas in 2007. A career reporter with over a decade of experience, he has written everything from fluff features to hardcore crime stories. While he's been to just about every juke house on the Mississippi Delta, he also appreciates the Rembrandt collection at the Metropolitan Museum of Art in New York. Mr. Massey has a bachelor's degree in history from Ohio State University, and a master's degree in journalism from Ole Miss.